lso by Sharon Arms Doucet
ı Large Print:

ıddle Fever

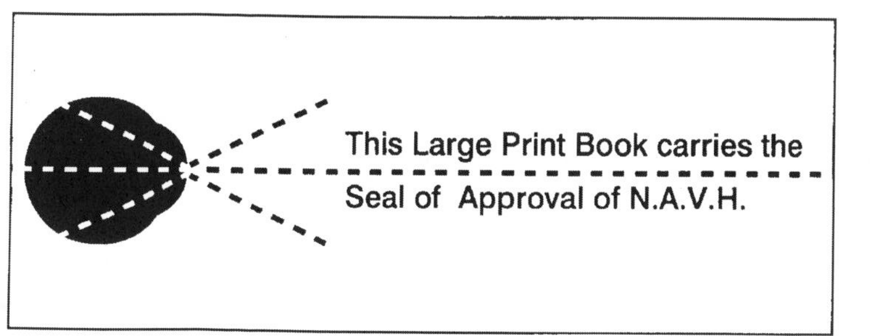

Back Before Da

Back Before Dark

Sharon Arms Doucet

Thorndike Press • Waterville, Maine

Published in 2005 by arrangement with NAL Signet,
a division of Penguin Group (USA) Inc.

Thorndike Press® Large Print Senior Lifestyles.

The tree indicium is a trademark of Thorndike Press.

The text of this Large Print edition is unabridged.
Other aspects of the book may vary from the original edition.

Set in 16 pt. Plantin by Elena Picard.

Printed in the United States on permanent paper.

ISBN 0-7862-7142-6 (lg. print : hc : alk. paper)

For Miriam and Windle

and all the Crow, Markland,
Sevier, and Arms tribes,
the ground from which I sprouted

National Association for Visually Handicapped
serving the partially seeing

As the Founder/CEO of NAVH, the only national health agency solely devoted to those who, although not totally blind, have an eye disease which could lead to serious visual impairment, I am pleased to recognize Thorndike Press* as one of the leading publishers in the large print field.

Founded in 1954 in San Francisco to prepare large print textbooks for partially seeing children, NAVH became the pioneer and standard setting agency in the preparation of large type.

Today, those publishers who meet our standards carry the prestigious "Seal of Approval" indicating high quality large print. We are delighted that Thorndike Press is one of the publishers whose titles meet these standards. We are also pleased to recognize the significant contribution Thorndike Press is making in this important and growing field.

Lorraine H. Marchi, L.H.D.
Founder/CEO
NAVH

* Thorndike Press encompasses the following imprints: Thorndike, Wheeler, Walker and Large Print Press.

Acknowledgments

Profound thanks to my editor, Ellen Edwards, for her gentle, patient, and perceptive guidance in making this a much better book. My gratitude to agent Frances Kuffel for her vision and confidence in the work, and to the good folks at Maria Carvainis Agency for doing the details. To Robert Olen Butler, under whose tutelage this work was begun, thanks for his guidance and insistence on that "white-hot place." Thanks also to Luis Urrea for his early enthusiasm and encouragement.

A huge *merci beaucoup* to Jan Rider Newman and Barbara Conner, who patiently read and reread various versions and gave me their invaluable feedback. To my dharma sister and dear friend, Carolyn Krusinski, my eternal gratitude for pointing the way to the Shambhala path of wisdom and for leading me on those early journeys back to myself.

The expedition into the Tennessee cave,

which I've never had the privilege of visiting, is loosely based on material gleaned from Charles Faulkner's book *The Prehistoric Native American Art of Mud Glyph Cave* (Knoxville: University of Tennessee Press, 1986). Halka Chronic's guidebook *Roadside Geology of Colorado* (Missoula, Pit: Mountain Press Publishing, 1980) was very useful in providing geological terms and specific site information. I learned a lot about the plight of the uranium miners from the interviews in Peter H. Eichstaedt's book *If You Poison Us: Uranium and Native Americans* (Santa Fe: Red Crane Books, 1994). The book *Metal of Dishonor: Depleted Uranium*, from the Depleted Uranium Education Project (New York: International Action Center, 1997), was useful in its presentation of works by many scholars and experts in the field. The shamanic journeying episode is very loosely based on methods described by Michael Harner in his book *The Way of the Shaman* (San Francisco: HarperSanFrancisco, 1990), and through my own experience.

To my family, thanks for your patience and fortitude. And to the Masters, Teachers and Loved Ones, thank you for your ever-generous guidance in keeping me connected and moving forward.

Part One

Sedimentary

Sedimentary rock, one of the three major types of rock, covers about three-fourths of the earth's land area and most of the ocean floor. Most sedimentary rock starts forming when grains of clay, silt, or sand settle in bodies of water. Year after year, these minerals collect and form broad, flat layers called *beds* or *strata.* After thousands of years, these beds are squeezed into compact rock layers by the weight of other layers above them.

Chapter One
Half-Lives

I step barefoot off the back step, into the cool damp of the Louisiana morning. The vibrant green of the grass soaks into the bottoms of my feet, between my toes, and works its way up into my chest. I am a kid again, on the first day of summer, with no school and no clocks, only open space lying before me like an endless recess.

It's the day I've been pushing ahead of me for aeons, when the last of my two children has flown the coop. The final faculty meeting is behind me at the arts high school where I pay my eternal dues, and I am poised to commune with me, myself, and I. Yikes.

Pistache, the black Lab, wags both ends at me before plopping himself in the grass to wait for duck season. I drop beside him, touching the thick green St. Augustine grass with both hands. While the rest of the country pampers and cajoles lawns into a season's growth, here in the Deep South we wage a nonstop battle to keep it from taking over. Each patch sends out runners that then send out others, forming a complex and inextricable mat, like the family relationships of my adopted Cajun homeland.

And now it's over half my life I've lived in south Louisiana. The half-life of Frances Marie Broussard, née Aldren. My father the uranium geologist would probably make a crack about the decay of radioactive material measured in half-lives.

My destination du jour is the sagging side porch, which my husband long ago transformed into an art studio for me. As the story goes, before I met him, I was en route from my native Colorado to art school in New York. All our married life, J.P. has been sure that one day I will come to regret my folly and fly away to regain the life he deprived me of. I've never been able to convince him that he probably saved me from myself.

Nor have I done the studio justice over the years, except to produce some local scenes and landscapes in a style somewhere between late Matisse and early kitsch. Thick, colorful strokes that my professors would have called derivative. And I would probably agree, except that that's how I see this place, thick and noisy and colorful. Definitely not the stuff for the world-weary postmodern art world.

For Mother's Day J.P. presented me with a bouquet of fresh tubes of oil paint to replace my old ones, which were gnarled and dusty from lack of use. The pressure's on, and I've run out of excuses.

I can't tell him about the trick I've lost, the one where your vision shifts into some sort of overdrive and you see into the essence of a thing. Like these blades of grass. Once I could have fathomed the variations in the life and looks of each and every one, and felt its personality as I captured it on canvas. But try as I might, I can no longer see like that, and I don't know why. I've misplaced the magic wand, a fact I've long since accepted as a sacrifice to the pedestrian demands of "real" life.

And now that I have the time to find it again, I have no clue where to look.

But hey, it's my life. Today I think I'll play hooky, catch up on the soaps, lie around all day and read a good book. Tomorrow I'll tackle this work of getting back beneath the surface.

Today is my father's sixty-ninth birthday.

Maybe next year I'll throw him a big party, invite everybody he knows and really cheer him up.

I dial his Denver number.

His *hello* is subdued, meaning he's off as usual on a brooding streak. I launch into my off-key rendition of "Happy Birthday to You," one of the few traditions that have survived the splitting of our once-nuclear family.

His chuckle sounds forced. "Hi, Frannie. How's my girl?"

"Good. What's happening in the Rockies?"

"Not too much." Beat. "It's a nice day."

"It's got to be cooler than here." OK, so the weather's not going to be the topic of the day. "Get out there and go fishing or something. I'd give anything to be up in those mountains."

"I don't do much of that anymore."

"You ought to, Daddy — that's what you always wanted to do when you retired. Or are you too busy with the contract work for Aloco?"

"Busy enough. I guess there's a lot of things I used to want to do."

I search for a topic that won't elicit a depressing comment, feeling as if I'm reaching through murky water. "You'll have to come down for a visit when the weather cools off. The house is so empty with both Maggie and Neville gone." Impatience rises in my chest. "I wish I could be there with you today."

"But you're not here. Nobody's here."

No, Dad, just a few hundred thousand Denverites. I make small talk about J.P.'s business, the kids, the price of rice in China. It isn't long before the topics peter out.

"Well, I'll let you go, Frannie." His voice picks up a bit. "Take care of yourself and J.P. And tell your mother hello for me."

Tell my mother hello for him? The woman who ruined his life by ditching him for another man? A blow from which he never recovered, despite a second failed marriage? Tell my mother hello?

"OK, Dad. Happy birthday."

"Bye, punkin'." Is he crying? "I love you."

"I love you, too."

Defeated, I put the receiver back into its cradle.

"J.P.?" His cell phone can find him on any construction job.

"Yeah, babe, what's up? You working?"

"I'm working at not working. Will you take me out dancing tonight?"

"Aw, Frannie, I'm supposed to go fishing with T-Will in the morning. And this heat is getting to me — I'm beat."

"Oh, but it's been so long. Let's go to La Poussière." I picture the old dance hall in its low frame building, the sweet darkness and the French music pounding at the walls.

J.P. sighs, then chuckles. "If that's what you want, that's what we'll do. I'll see if T-Will and Vera want to go. Maybe we'll go eat some crawfish on the way."

Chapter Two
La Poussière

The waitress at the Crawfish Shak sets a round tray heaped with bright red crustaceans in front of each of us. J.P. and his younger brother, T-Will, have ordered theirs extra-spicy in their age-old rivalry to see who can blister his mouth the most. I cross myself like a good Catholic and set about peeling the tails and chomping down on the sweet white flesh laced with red pepper, garlic and lemon.

T-Will and J.P. inevitably turn the talk to the construction company they co-own and the new minimall they're subcontracting. Meanwhile my sister-in-law Vera leans over and grins. "Guess who I saw at Mass this afternoon," she says. "Wanda Cormier! Can you believe she had the nerve to show up, and with her kids, too? She even received communion." Wanda was recently caught in flagrante delicto with her husband's best friend and is now the subject of universal cold shoulders, even though her husband's a bum and the friend's very good-looking.

"I guess that means she's confessed and been forgiven," I answer. "The scarlet letter has been removed from her breast."

"Hey, Vera," says J.P., exaggerating his Cajun accent, "you heard the one about Boudreaux on his deathbed?"

"No," says Vera, "but I have the feeling I'm about to."

"Yeah, he was this close to dying," says J.P., holding up his thumb and index finger, "but he thought he smelled crawfish boiling. 'Oh,' he says, 'if I could just have me some crawfish one last time, I could die happy.' So he crawls to the back door, gets it open, and sure enough, there's his wife, Marie, boiling a big sack of crawfish. He grabs himself one, manages to peel it and is just about to put it to his lips when Marie slaps his hand away. 'What you think you're doin'?' she says. 'I'm eating my last crawfish,' says Boudreaux. 'Oh, no, you don't,' she says. 'I'm fixing these to serve at your funeral.' "

Vera cracks up, and T-Will leans over to say, "Is that what you're gonna do for my wake, honey?"

I smile demurely and bite into a cob of

corn, washing the kernels down with a slug of cold beer.

It was a fateful day when I met my husband at a mid-seventies Jazz Fest in New Orleans. I had skipped out on the last week of classes at the University of Colorado, and hopped a bus with my crazy cousin, Hannah. We headed south, looking for Easy Rider or Blanche DuBois or Marie Laveau. The bus deposited us on the edge of the French Quarter, where the gardenias were blooming and the early May breezes blew off the Mississippi River as if they were looking just for me.

As Hannah and I got closer to the festival, I swear you could have felt the drumbeats through the sidewalks. People from all over the country were shedding their winter skin along with as much clothing as they could get away with. You went from tent to tent and from stage to stage, the music swaying and throbbing inside you and making your juices flow as if for the first time. And the food was so exotic your soul could barely stand it.

It was Dr. John, or Professor Longhair, or one of those crazy New Orleans piano players singing about walking on gilded splinters, when I noticed J.P. doing some free-form two-step on the blanket next to ours. He was dark-skinned and handsome, his hair long and his black eyes glistening.

I'd never heard of a Cajun before — this was pre–blackened redfish — but the sound of his rich voice was like wiggling my toes in the green grass. He took us out that night to all the local haunts to hear music so sexy and soulful I thought I was on another planet.

What can I say? That was it. I nixed my plans for art school, ditched my boyfriend, Neil, and moved south. J.P. — short for Jean-Paul, so romantic — and I lived in blissful sin for a time. But his family soon proved an immutable force. That's how I found myself miraculously transformed into a Catholic so I would be good enough to marry him, even if I was an *Américaine*. I agreed never to get a divorce, which I haven't, and to raise my children as good little Catholics, at which I did my dutiful best in order to stay in the good graces of the culture.

As a bonus I gained a whole extended family — J.P. is one of five children — just as my own was fracturing. My mother had met Walter and, after a few surreptitious months, had run off with him to Florida. Daddy was crushed flat and never really got back up. Brother Mitch had followed his bliss and the drug culture to California by then, and I was left with the impossible and unreasonable task of trying to cheer up my own cuckolded father. So I was glad for an excuse to escape.

After the nosebleed dryness of the West, Louisiana was a foreign land, verdant and wet and barely tamed. And J.P. seemed so solid and real, especially compared to the height of the hippie culture I'd left behind in Boulder. It was as if he were made out of Delta soil, as if he'd risen up out of the earth and might just sink back into it on some dark night. I wanted a piece of that groundedness, that sense of belonging to something besides the whims of pop culture.

Besides, he made me laugh.

La Poussière, "the dust," is one of a handful of old-time dance halls left in rural Acadiana. Walter Mouton and the Scott Playboys have played here every weekend for years, and the tables surrounding the dance floor are crowded with regulars. We choose a table against the wall, next to an elderly foursome sitting squarely around a bottle of Old Times and setups of Sprite. The dour waitress almost smiles at J.P. when he tells her how good she's looking tonight.

At the first pickup notes of the fiddle, the tables empty and J.P. pulls me to my feet. We follow the crowd and hit the dance floor like fish in a current. J.P. presses me into his solid warmth, holding my right hand jauntily in the air and imbuing me with grace.

The music arrives more through the subtle moves and pressures of his hipbones than through my own ears. The accordion notes blare straight into my gut, the wailing fiddle hits me between the eyes, and the sad French lyrics break my heart right in two.

A fast two-step follows, and we alternate between the old-fashioned clutch, with our upper bodies nearly immobile over fancy footwork, and variations on the jitterbug.

My feet keep gliding until the last accordion squeeze of the night.

As J.P. unlocks the back door, I take a good look at him under the porch light. Still trim, with a head of wavy black hair, which he helps a little with the tube of Grecian Formula I found in his drawer a few years back. His olive skin is darkened by years in the sun, his step light, and his smile big and contagious. His forearms below his rolled-up sleeves are hairy and muscular, his body compact, and his earthiness still turns me on.

Remembering how alone we are, I pull him by the belt buckle into the bedroom and begin to slowly unbutton his shirt, which always drives him crazy. Soon we're moving together in the last dance of the night, making all the noise we want.

My eyes jerk open before dawn. Daddy's face has been looming in my dreams.

Something's wrong.

J.P.'s snoring softly, having put off the fishing expedition until late afternoon. It's an hour earlier in Denver, too early to call, but I pull on shorts and a shirt and go to the kitchen phone, my head swimming from last night's beer. Eight, nine, ten, eleven rings. Dad's the only person left on earth without an answering machine.

I fumble through my tattered address book for the number of his next-door neighbors, the Stewarts, who've kept a sympathetic eye on Daddy through all his ups and downs. But I'll wait an hour.

I start some coffee in the old French-drip pot, whose stained rings mark the mornings of my life. Today I find comfort in the descending order of white enamel pieces nesting together, each with its own place and each knowing exactly what's expected of it.

I know it's hard for my father to live alone, especially since his seven-year marriage to Edith fell apart a decade ago, for reasons I've never really been let in on. But isn't it up to each of us to find happiness within ourselves instead of depending on other people for it?

I wander down the hall to Neville's room, still just as he left it. The painting I gave him for his tenth birthday, of our old red barn flanked by the battle-scarred pecan tree, hangs on the wall over his bed. I remember how, when he unwrapped it, he gave me a spontaneous hug worth more than gold.

From the moment Neville emerged from the blinding pain of my labor, I loved him so fiercely I could have eaten him alive. That thick black hair, the little crease between his eyebrows, the tiny fingers clutching mine. But from the get-go he was so stubborn, so contrary. He always knew what he wanted and saw no reason to compromise.

For a long time he lived for football, even played in college; then one day last year, he quit school and joined the damned Marines. That made me cry, proof that I'd failed dismally to pass on any of the pacifist ideals I'd once held so dear back in the seventies. Thankfully he's still mopping up the mess in the Balkans at the moment, having so far avoided the Middle East, much to his father's dismay and my uneasy relief.

I move on to Maggie's room, my sweet Magnolia, named after the J. J. Cale song. The oil painting I did for her, an abstract blossom of her name, is barely visible on the wall under its shrouds of Mardi Gras beads, scarves, and discarded rally ribbons. She's the opposite of Neville, hasn't got a clue what she wants out of life, but will have a darned good time figuring it out. I'm in love with her, too, as if she's an image I got right for once in my life.

For some reason I flash on the first time Daddy held her. He had come to visit not long after she was born, and when he reached out to take her from me, his hands trembled and I swear he broke out in a sweat. Then he handed her back as soon as he could to go off with the boys.

Lately that tiny baby has taken to calling herself Mag to go with her pierced nostril and the lizard she got tattooed on her left shoulder. After her first year in college, she's taken off for the summer to find herself in the big, wide world.

Our house, which last belonged to J.P.'s great-aunt, was built around the turn of the last century. Down the road live his mother, two of his brothers, and one sister, on family land that's been parceled into strips. Will and Vera built a big brick house on a concrete slab like J.P. wanted to do. But I held out for the charm of the old farmhouse that nobody else wanted, with its mimosa trees and flower beds and big red barn. It would be back to the Garden of Eden for this old girl.

What I ought to do is spend the summer working on the house. There's not a room that couldn't use a makeover, and if I got up early before it gets too hot, I could even scrape and paint the outside.

At least I'd know what I was painting.

When I dial the Stewarts' number, a groggy Adelaide answers. My throat tightens, my pulse jumping in my neck. "Adelaide, it's Frannie Aldren, calling from Louisiana. I just wondered if you'd go check on my dad. I know it's early, but . . ."

"No problem, honey," she says in the voice that used to soothe me when I skinned my knee. "I'll send Don over and call you right back. Give me your number."

I hang up and can't decide what to do with my hands. The minutes tick by, glowing squarely on my digital watch. Whatever happened to the days when time was circular, fluid, not a series of bright red numbers clicking off in exact measure?

The better to track your half-life, I guess.

They've had plenty of time to get next door and back. I nibble a piece of dry bread.

At last the phone shrills and my heart flops over. "Yes?"

"Frannie? Don Stewart." Something's wrong. "There's a policeman here needs to talk to you."

"Miss, ah, Aldren?"

"It's Broussard, but yes?"

"Your father is John Franklin Aldren?"

"Yes. What is it?"

"I'm afraid there's been some kind of, er, accident. We've found him in his car in the garage, with the engine running. Mrs. Broussard, I'm afraid your father's dead."

My knees unlatch and I aim for a chair. My mouth moves but nothing comes out.

J.P. materializes behind me as the phone clatters to the floor. He picks it up and says a few *yeses* and *I understands,* then writes down a number and hangs up. His hands grab my shoulders as my head begins to shake back and forth, back and forth, a pit of molten lead spreading through my gut.

As we pull up to the Lafayette airport early that afternoon, I am loath to leave the comfort of the car with its vents blowing cold air straight into my face. J.P. has booked my flight, coordinated plans with Mitch in California, and helped me pack. His mother called to say she would have a bazillion Masses said for Daddy, and Vera showed up with fig cake to help, but her voice came to me from far away.

Now J.P. checks my luggage and hands me my boarding pass, hovering, solicitous. "You sure you'll be OK? I hate to send you on alone. If we just weren't already behind schedule on this job . . ."

I answer with a numb shrug.

"Mitch's plane comes in half an hour before yours, so he should be there to meet you," he says, as if in comfort. "Let me know when and where you decide to bury your daddy, and I'll book the next flight."

"He belongs back in Tennessee with his family." I'm saying this to the Powers That Be as much as to J.P. Of course, there's never been any question where a Broussard would be buried, right on top of the rest of them in the family plot next to the church.

"Do what you gotta do, babe."

He'll try to get hold of Neville and Maggie, he says as we reach the security area. I lean into the hollow of his shoulder. He holds me tight and mutters into my hair. And then he's gone.

As we leave the ground, I stare at the sheer green carpet that is south Louisiana. From above it looks as if civilization has barely chopped a foothold into its swamps and forests. But we soon veer off to the west, over the flat prairies full of patches of development and trailer parks and rice fields. And then Louisiana is behind me and I'm on my way back to the first half of my life.

Chapter Three
Skin and Bones

This cannot be possible. There's been a mistake: my father is not gone. He did not snuff out his own life, and I am not flying through the air in order to put him in the ground.

Gnawing away at my belly is the fact that I haven't seen him for the last three years, since he came down for Neville's high school graduation. He arrived with my grandfather's Marine bayonet, which he ceremoniously presented as a graduation present and which I suspect may have had something to do with my son's decision to become a Marine.

I see my father's tall, broad-shouldered form, the little paunch of his stomach, the age spots on his tanned forearm. Deep blue eyes, sad smile, chestnut beard gone to white.

It wasn't my fault that he got so hard to talk to, especially after Edith dumped him. The thing that really bugged me was that he had no trouble talking to J.P., or Neville either. Every time they were together, the three of them took off as soon as decency allowed and hit the swamps or the mountains, to fish or hunt or camp. In the early years, he even invited them up to hunt elk and deer with him. While I appreciated the fact that J.P. so easily filled up the silences, it left me with the feeling I'd had since girlhood, that Daddy was somewhere else instead of there for me.

So I admit, I gradually stopped inviting him to visit so often. When he went anywhere, he'd go back to see his sister, Aunt Lena, who never left Tennessee.

I always thought that someday, somehow, he would come closer, that the gap between us would close, and we'd get comfortable with each other. But now that will never happen. It feels that something fundamental has gone, as if the earth I had thought so solid has shifted under my feet.

Yesterday's phone call. *"Are you OK, Dad? You sound so down."*

"Nobody's here. . . . Take care of yourself. . . . Tell your mother hello for me. . . . I love you."

My hand flies to my mouth. What was I supposed to say? How was I supposed to know?

* * *

The Denver International Airport shines on the plains east of the city, its white canvas spires leaning into the sky like a village of drunken tepees. DOA, the locals call it, for all the disasters that befell it during its construction, some say because it was built on an Indian burial ground. Beyond it on the horizon gleam the sparkling peaks of the Rockies, the craggy backbone of the continent, every morsel of which used to hold for my geologist father the secrets of all Creation.

Deplaning, I scan the expectant faces assembled around the security gate for Mitch, fellow child of woe. But he's not there. Surprise, surprise.

Suicide. The word hisses through my brain. *Suicide*. The killing of oneself, of one's self. The trading in of the great gift of life, the throwing in of the cosmic towel. The word inexorably linked with my father from here to eternity.

At last in the main terminal, I'm about to veer into a bathroom when I see the tall, familiar form of my little brother, shoulders hunched with carry-on bags. "Mitch!" I call out, waving.

As the distance between us diminishes, I'm taken aback by how gaunt he looks, and also by the resemblance to Daddy that dances around the edges of his face. His hair is sprinkled with gray and cropped close to his head, and his skin has begun to lose its tone. Those early years of heavy substance abuse, and the bitter breakup that cost him his wife and two kids, haven't helped, I'm sure. We've kept in only polite touch over the years, and I have to remind myself that even my little brother is now approaching middle age.

"My plane from L.A. was late," he says. "Where's the car rental in this god-awful place?" Not hello, not hail, fellow orphan. He does lean over to peck me on the cheek. My eyes meet his for just a flash before he turns away.

He goes to rent a car while I wait to collect the luggage. I'm wheeling my suitcase out the door toward the shuttle bus stop when I hear the blare of a horn. An arm is waving frantically from a car window, topped by an unmistakable head of short red curls. "Hannah! Hannah, my God, you're here!" Maybe I'm not abandoned after all.

Our cousin bursts out of the car to give me the huge hug I was waiting for. "J.P. called to let me know when you'd arrive," she says. "Mitch!" At his appearance, she throws her arms around his neck without hesitation, then holds us both in the sweep of her arms. "You guys, I'm so sorry about Uncle Frank. It's just awful." She pulls back and peers into our faces. "Are you OK?"

Now there's a question.

"Come, my carriage awaits," Hannah says.

"I've already rented a car," says Mitch.

"Good for you. Then I'll take you around to pick it up. You've got to cross half of Kansas to get to the rental car places." We cram ourselves and luggage into her small, mileage-conscious car.

"If you want, a friend of mine offered you his house here in Denver. He's just left for Peru. It's much closer than my place in Boulder."

"That's nice," I say numbly. Mitch shrugs.

An attendant meets us with our rental car. "Mitch, follow us," says Hannah. "Come on, Frannie, you ride with me."

"Jawohl, mein commandant," he says, folding his height into the compact's driver's seat.

"Ah, Mitch," says Hannah under her breath, and we giggle as she pulls onto the wide highway that crosses the open plain to Denver. She looks over at me. "How you doing?"

I take a look at the mountains, then rub my sore eyelids. "It's just too gruesome. It keeps hitting me all over again. Have you heard any more details?"

"It sounds like a pretty clear-cut case."

We chat idly on the way into town, as the heavy metal weight inside pins me to the seat. Hannah turns down a street lined with elms reaching for each other across the pavement, pulls into the driveway of a redbrick two-story, and lets us in the back door. The place is all white plaster walls and mission oak furniture, with tapestry upholstery and Oriental rugs in wines and russets. In the living room, what look to be pre-Columbian figures squat on the shelves, totem poles leer from the corners, and one wall is covered with masks.

"Cool," says Mitch. My laugh is tinged with nerves as the hollow eyes stare from the wall. Some of the masks are friendly, brightly painted or hung with fantastic feathers, while others glare with contorted, menacing expressions. Quite a peanut gallery for our own little drama.

"My friend Bernie's an anthropologist," says Hannah. "His specialty is shamanic cultures. Come on upstairs and choose yourselves a bedroom."

"You know your way around here pretty well," I say.

"Yes, I do," she says and throws me a smile.

I choose a west bedroom where I can see the mountains. There they sit, as always, placid and unperturbed by the endless bustle that goes on at their feet.

In a way these mountains are the gods of my childhood, the great stony bulk you could always count on to be there. Life with Daddy was a series of impromptu geology lessons that resulted in my own private creation scenario, a saga of upheaval and erosion, of earth giving in to its internal pressures, cracking, splitting, buckling and warping. The arching and smoothing that filled in the rest of the continent with its sedimentary debris. And that in the process put Louisiana, some of the youngest land in the world, on the map.

In the high-ceilinged kitchen, Hannah pours us cups of coffee. It's like the old days, the three cousins, except that now we're the grown-ups ready to bury one of the old guard.

"When you called this morning," says

Hannah, "Mr. Stewart went over and knocked on Uncle Frank's door. No one answered, and he thought he heard an engine running in the garage. It was locked from the inside, so he called the police, who broke in and found him." She drops her gaze to the floor. "There were rags stuffed under the garage door and a garden hose running from the exhaust pipe through the driver's window. They said he'd been there at least twelve hours."

So damn deliberate, so tidy. Twelve hours — I talked to him late in the afternoon. And they found him early the next morning. That means he must've done it soon after our conversation. The lead in my stomach hisses.

"If it helps any," says Hannah, "he probably just went to sleep."

I spring to my feet. "Come on, Hannah, your body knows when it's being poisoned. You have to force yourself to keep breathing that stuff in."

Hannah shakes her head. I look out the window over the sink, the mountains barely visible between neighboring roofs. "What's next? Does anybody know?"

"You have to go identify him. Then they'll release him to the funeral home wherever you want him to be buried."

"I want to take him back to Tennessee," I say without turning.

"Back to Tennessee?" Mitch's voice is strident. "What's the point of that?"

"Because he told me once that was where he wanted to be buried." I can feel my heels digging into the floorboards.

Mitch huffs. "That Aldren cemetery's out in the middle of the boonies, and when Aunt Lena's gone, it'll be forgotten. He'd be better off here. Besides, I've got a job to get back to — you're talking a good week to get all this together."

"Don't let us inconvenience you," I spit out, surprised by my own vehemence. I take a breath. Mitch doesn't like to be bullied. "Tennessee was always home to him, and I know that's where he would want to be, beside his mother and father and his grandparents and great-grandparents."

"It would cost a fortune to ship him there."

"He's got money in the bank."

"There's cremation," says Hannah. I shake my head, the thought of reducing my father to cinders beyond my capacity to handle right now.

"A Louisiana jazz funeral?" she counters. The corners of my mouth turn up despite myself.

"Let's go get the police thing over with," says Mitch.

"Hannah, did he leave a-a note or anything?"

She shrugs. "Not that I know of."

Nobody should have to do this. They want to show us a video, but I insist on seeing him in person. Just like in the movies, they pull him out of a cold-storage drawer and draw back the sheet.

This is my father, puffed and gray and turned to stone. The image swiftly supplants every other picture in my memory.

As I crumble into sleep, the back of my neck feeling like a loaded slingshot, I try to find another image. Eighteen years' worth of individual days of my childhood, thousands of hours when I shared the same house with him. I carry the imprint of him in every cell and molecule and atom in my body. He is half of what I am, another of my half-lives.

And yet I can't see his living face. And if I can't, who will? Will he just vanish from this world without a trace, a name on a headstone in a forgotten graveyard?

I hear heavy footsteps in the living room.

The Russians — they're here! I scoot under my bed, pulling the bedspread down to cover the gap, but it falls to the floor. I back up, pressing my spine against the wall and hugging my knees to my chest. The door to my room opens, and three pairs of tall black boots on uniformed legs stride into the room. One rummages in the closet, one knocks over my desk chair, and one walks slowly toward the bed. He knows I'm here. He starts to lean down. Any second now his face will appear, and I will be caught.

I wake up, crying, "Daddy!"

My old Cold War nightmare has left me drenched in clammy sweat. I get up and stumble to the window, gulping in fresh, cool air. What on earth brought back that dream now? The Communists were the bogeymen of a generation's children, the threat of nuclear annihilation that we swallowed daily along with our sugary breakfast cereal. A threat that somehow vanished through the vagaries of history, along with our nightmares.

And then, when our generation got old enough to gripe about it, we were all going to change the world and end war forever. Ha! After Vietnam petered out, after our baby-booming necks were no longer at stake, our idealism dissipated before our very eyes, and we bought into the whole greedy system without a whimper.

And now my own son is wearing a uniform and a gun and risking the life I gave him. I couldn't even pass on my ideals to my own flesh and blood.

I could do with a drink. I tiptoe down the stairs, past the wall of masks, and find an open bottle of red wine in the refrigerator. Pouring myself a hefty glassful, I walk out into Bernie's backyard and sink my toes into the soft, cool grass.

So if my father's lying there in the refrigerator with a tag on his toe, where is he really?

Emptying my glass, I sprawl on the warm flagstone patio, spreading arms and legs like a human sacrifice. The stars dazzle overhead, crisp and clean and too myriad to begin to count. They're never like this in Louisiana, where it's too damn humid.

The stone soaks into my spine as if, cicada-like, I could crack open my shell, and a new me, fresh and wise, would step out. And maybe that old husk of myself would get washed downstream, down the Platte, the Missouri, the Mississippi, wending its way across the continent and into the

Atchafalaya River. And J.P. would snag it with his fishhook in wonder.

A star streaks slowly westward across the sky and goes out.

Chapter Four
Oxygen

Daddy is ahead of me on the mountain trail as the earth buckles and opens. I see him fall into the crack; then the ground settles down again, the path falling back into place. There's no one in front of me now, no one to catch me if I fall.

Hannah's shaking me awake. "Frannie, it's your mother on the phone." I rouse and steel myself.

"I'm sorry for not calling, Mom. Yesterday was . . ." There are no words.

"Never mind. I've just made my reservations to arrive in Denver this afternoon. I know you'll be busy, so I'll take a cab. I'm staying at the Brown Palace."

"You're coming?" I feel a flood of relief, but don't want to admit it.

"He was my husband and the father of my children. What are your plans so far?" she asks.

I take a breath of courage. "Take him

home to Tennessee."

She sniffles. "All right. But you'll have to have a memorial service there in Denver."

"We will? Why?"

"You can't just whisk him off forever without giving people a chance to pay their respects. Besides, that would look like you're ashamed of him."

But I am. "I'll see what I can do. I'll call you at the hotel. And, Mom? When I called him for his birthday, I guess right before he . . . he told me to tell you hello."

A gasp and a choking sob, then my mother hangs up.

Hannah, dressed in orange linen, hands me a mug of coffee. "I've got to get back to Boulder for a while," she says.

"You're leaving me to the wolves?"

She touches my cheek. "You can handle them. Just don't be afraid to admit you're scared."

Mitch is in the kitchen eating cereal. The sunlight from the big window sinks into the creases in his cheeks. I give him a peck like I used to do to gross him out.

"Good morning, brother dear."

He feigns disgust, but asks, "Sweet dreams?"

"If that's what you call the Communist invasion. You?"

"The sleep of death."

A small smile passes between us. "We go to the funeral home at eleven," he goes on. "We need to get him some clothes."

The bottom drops out of my stomach. "At home?"

"That's where his clothes are," says Mitch.

Another cloud rolls over the morning sun.

"Mitch, can we agree on the Tennessee thing?" I venture as he drives us through the Denver streets. "It's not a question of what *I* want, but what Daddy would want."

"Spare me the sermon, Frannie," he answers without taking his eyes off the road. "Dad couldn't be pleased in life, so don't think you're going to make him happy for all eternity. You're going to do what you want no matter what, just like you always have."

This isn't how I want it to be — scratching the scar tissue off old wounds and going at each other just as we did throughout our childhood. I touch his arm. "Can't we try to pull together on this? We need each other now."

"Oh come on, Frannie, you never needed me in all your life."

"Of course I do. You're my little brother."

To my astonishment, I see Mitch wipe a tear from his cheek.

On Arapaho Circle, named for the buffalo hunters who once roamed this land, my childhood home hunches down around its nasty secret, ready to defend its territory. A group of boys playing street hockey stops to stare.

We follow the sidewalk to the Stewarts' house next door to get the key. A morning talk show blares in the background as Adelaide hugs us, looking like a chubby ad for senior citizens' vitamins in her walking shorts and earphones.

"I'm so sorry for you kids," she says matter-of-factly. "But you know, he hasn't been well for a long time — sort of withdrawn into himself, hardly aware of the outside world. I'd see his lights on at all hours of the night. I've wanted to call you, but Don thought it was none of my business."

"It's OK, Ms. S. It's not your fault," I offer.

"Here's the key. Do you want me to go with you?"

"No, thanks. Was there anything else — maybe a note?"

"I don't know, honey. The police didn't want us touching anything." She's on her way out, so we take the key and our leave.

"So much for the baroness of the bomb shelter," says Mitch, at which I burst out laughing. The Stewarts were the proud and only possessors in our acquaintance of a bomb shelter, which they built at the height of the 1950s fearmongering. It gave them a strange and haunting position in the neighborhood hierarchy, because we couldn't help wondering if they would take us in if the worst happened. We were all extra nice to their two boys just in case.

Of course, Daddy always said the shelter would do absolutely no good if the real thing came along. "You should know," Mom had said icily, "since you're the one giving them the goods to make the infernal bombs." This was a recurring theme: Mom's fear that the uranium Daddy earned his living seeking was going to be the death of us all, Daddy maintaining that it was for our own protection.

The present descends as we trudge next door to our old homeland. The place feels hostile now, our red rental car ludicrously cheerful in the driveway. After the key clicks, the door swings open.

The living room is the same as it always was: the green couch I lay on through adolescence, the TV a silent eye in the corner. In the kitchen beyond I can see a few breakfast dishes in the drain and a glass beside the sink. As I step inside, my nostrils balk and my hand clamps over my mouth. There's a smell like heavy smog laced with an edge of something sweet.

"I can't do this." I turn to get out, running into Mitch's chest. "Shit! Shit!" I'm hammering on his chest and he puts his arms around me and we weep together.

After a few minutes I pull myself together and march into the kitchen to find Kleenex. We wipe our eyes and blow our noses and we're in, over our heads but there's nothing for it.

The house is clean, too clean. I'm sure he left everything in order, down to the last bill written in his neat, even script.

"This is giving me the creeps," says Mitch. "Let's just get his suit and get out of here."

"What'll we do with the house?"

"Sell it," he answers quickly.

"Who would buy a house where somebody's killed himself?"

"Who says they have to know?"

We tiptoe down the hall, past our old rooms to Daddy's. The bed is made, the room neat except for his old leather Samsonite suitcase, the one he soaped and polished and kept like new all through my childhood. It lies open in the middle of the floor like a gaping mouth. In it are some short-sleeved shirts, neatly folded, some khaki pants, underwear, and socks. I stare at the suitcase, stunned.

"Where the hell do you think he'd been?" says Mitch.

"He hadn't left yet, the clothes are all clean." What had stopped him from going? Where?

My eyeballs are heavy as I drag my gaze to the dresser. In a small frame is a picture of Mom and Dad from before they were married, all gangly legs and vintage hair and sheepish smiles. Next to that are two pictures each of Mitch and me, our high school graduation photos and our wedding pictures. I look at the girl I was, young, thin, my head tilted toward J.P. And my groom with thick black hair and dark eyes, taking the camera head-on. We were just kids, little older than Neville is now.

And there's Mitch at his big church wedding to Cindy. In his tux, he had more heft to him than the scarecrow he is now. He's grinning openly in the picture, something he's obviously forgotten how to do since the divorce, the bitter custody fight over the kids he never sees, the years behind the desk of a big insurance company, tallying up the damage to cars and homes and bodies and lives.

Quickly we choose a navy suit, white shirt, plain tie, then shoes and socks. Pieces of clothing that last held living flesh and blood.

Back down the hall, Mitch makes a right turn for the front door, but I keep going straight. My hand is on the doorknob before he says, "Where are you going?" I open the kitchen door to the garage.

The smell, which I'd gotten used to, hits me again. Sweet, like gardenias past their prime, edged with metal like the taste in my mouth. Daddy's white Pontiac stares at me with bulgy headlight eyes, its chrome grille grinning like a character in some old movie where the cars come alive.

I clench my fists and move down the two steps. Sure enough, a bright green garden hose snakes along the floor to the back of the car, a pile of towels and old sheets beside it. I force my feet forward until I am standing at the driver's window. The air seems to be charged with electricity, almost visible in jagged waves.

Carbon monoxide. The same stuff that pours out of our exhaust pipes every time we turn on our engines. Just one atom of oxygen away from what we give out with every exhalation from cradle to grave.

I let out a breath but can't make myself breathe back in. What am I looking for? Some scrap of paper, the corner of an envelope the police missed — there must be something to explain this, something more than just the end.

As my own lungs run out of oxygen, I bolt back into the kitchen and fill them. Mitch is leaning against the wall just inside the kitchen, his hands braced behind him as if facing a firing squad.

The undertaker's voice rises and falls in soft, sympathetic tones as he helps us choose a casket and write the obituary. The memorial service is set for the following evening in the chapel of the funeral home, since Daddy didn't have a church.

Mom has checked herself into a suite at the Brown Palace downtown, so as not to be a bother, she says. Sitting at a big desk in her little living room, she looks out over the smoggy distance to the Rockies and makes a list of people to call. Her face-lift is holding up well, her hair an ash blond this time. Her white trousers skim health club–slim hips, and her lavender silk blouse drapes nicely over still-high breasts.

Leaving Daddy a quarter of a century ago was the best thing that ever happened to my mother — she lost twenty pounds, landed a job in sales with a big cosmetics company, and quickly worked her way up the corporate ladder. She married Walter, a good-looking stockbroker who's retired now and keeps her busy on the golf course.

"What was the name of that family that lived across from us?" She taps her teeth with a pencil. "Wilson? Wilcox?"

"Oh, Mom, let's keep it simple. Close friends, the people at work. There's no need to make a big show out of this, especially under the circumstances."

"Whatever you say, Frances." She pats my cheek.

As Mitch sprawls in an armchair, I realize it's been years since the three of us have been in the same room together. If it weren't for the circumstances, this old-home scenario would feel kind of good.

"Shall we just order supper from room service?" I offer.

"Supper?" says Mitch. "Where you from,

Daisy Mae? Here in God's country we eat dinner."

"Frannie really has been down in those swamps too long," my mother offers. "Whatever you two want, you're the bosses. But I much prefer to go downstairs to the restaurant."

Mitch and I exchange surreptitious grins.

The posh restaurant is all deep greens and dim lights. Mom orders a good bottle of French chardonnay and the grilled salmon. Unable to concentrate on the list of fancy entrées, I order a Caesar salad.

No one has to work at conversation when my mother's around. Following a brief inquiry after her grandchildren, she launches into the details of a hostile takeover bid for her company, Walter's plans to buy into a time-share in the Grand Cayman, and her golf game. You can barely tell she's working at keeping it light.

Her words weave in and out of my concentration, and I find myself eavesdropping on a couple at the next table discussing estate planning. Their vowels are clipped, Western, like pebbles rolling around in the mouth, their edges polished off as they come out. It's the accent I grew up with, but tonight it sounds harsh and cold. I miss those Southern vowels that spread out like the Mississippi Delta, with all the time in the world to get where they're going and it's too hot to hurry anyhow.

I pick at my romaine. "Mom, why do you think he did it?" The words are out of my mouth before I can temper them.

She looks at me, bewildered.

"Commit suicide," says Mitch. "Let's just say it, for Christ's sake." The heads at the next table turn as we give them something to eavesdrop on.

Mom flinches, her casual demeanor instantly transformed by pain. Her eyes fill with tears that reflect the candlelight. "I keep thinking if we could just rewind the film and do it all over, maybe we could get it right," she says in a trembling voice. "I know I'm partly to blame. But I think he was headed for it his whole life long."

I stare at our miniature reflection in her eyes. "Why do you say that?"

She flashes me a look. "Your father . . ." She pours herself some more wine, takes a long swallow. "Your father was a brilliant man, so vibrant and full of life when he was young — ah, and so handsome." Her gaze goes to the ceiling as her tears fall. "But such a hard childhood. Then he compromised himself early on, and it never stopped eating away at him. It whittled away at the underpinnings of his soul."

I look at Mitch, but he too seems clueless. "Mom, what are you talking about?"

"Frances Marie, I cannot get into this — not here, not now." She scrapes back her chair and throws her napkin in her plate. "Besides, what's the point? It's all too late."

Chapter Five
Masks

Back at Bernie's house, Hannah and I sit cross-legged on the living room floor after Mitch goes to bed.

"Just like old times," she says.

"The digs are cushier, though," I say, petting the upscale couch. "Better wine. And I wasn't an orphan then."

"Oh, please."

"I'll wallow all I want." I sip my merlot, thinking how well it matches the pattern of the Oriental rug. "Can you smell my armpits? Deodorant doesn't do a thing."

"All that emotional clearing. Breathe."

I look at my cousin, my old soul sister. Her thick red hair has a few gray streaks, but on her it looks good. She still owns the health food store and café she opened right out of college, now a venerable institution in Boulder. She never did let go of all the transcendental stuff everybody fooled around with back then. She's a member of a Buddhist community and meditates and goes on retreats and keeps her soul squeaky clean.

"Can I be just like you when I grow up?" I ask.

Hannah hits me with a pillow.

"Now tell me all about you and Bernie — you're obviously in love."

"Am I? Whatever that is." Hannah scoots down to lay her head back on the sofa. "I didn't 'date' " — she makes quotes with her fingers — "for nearly ten years. I'd decided romance was too much trouble. And then Bernie showed up at the store one day and looked me straight in the eye, as if he could see inside of me. It was instant chemistry."

"Watch out for that," I say, recalling J.P. at the Jazz Fest.

Hannah chuckles. "How are you and that Cajun wild man of yours doing, anyway?"

A series of images flashes through my head — dancing a slow waltz, our last lovemaking. "We're good."

"You're happy with your life down there?"

The faces on the wall await my answer. "The decor is staring at us. What are all those masks for, anyway?"

Hannah smiles affectionately. "Oh, fertility, power, protection from evil. They're from all the places Bernie's studied shamanic cultures."

"Just what exactly does that mean?"

"Shamans — you know, who journey into other realms to do healing. Bernie teaches workshops in sort of a modern version of it. It's very empowering."

"Other realms, huh? Do you get to choose a mask?"

"Don't worry. You're already wearing one." She looks at me sideways. "You know, you changed the subject."

"About being happy?" My head hurts. "How am I supposed to answer that? Do you mean, happy like we used to think we'd be when we grew up and fell in love and had a house and children and a dog, and a man who really loved us? Or happy every minute of every day? Then the answer is no." I sip my wine. "Or do you mean overall, do I have a good life that means something to me? And do I have moments of sheer happiness, when I'm dancing a waltz with my husband, or really listening to one of my children, or whatever? Then the answer is yes."

Hannah nods thoughtfully.

I stare at the mask of a man's face with a

little red bow mouth topped by a mustache, and a third eye painted between large slanted eyes and heavy eyebrows. A cobra curls from beneath each ear, and on top of his head, another coils around the figure of a woman, her eyes pointed heavenward. "What's that one?"

"That's Shiva, the Hindu guru of all gurus, and his counterpart Shakti."

"Tell him to stop staring at me." I close my eyes, but they pop open. "I wish I knew what Mom was talking about. She wouldn't even let me in her room after dinner, said she had a sick headache. What the hell was this compromise she was talking about?"

"You're just the daughter, not the wife. Kids have a way of blocking out a lot of information."

"I never even thought of Daddy as depressed. Depressing, yes, but that was just the way he was. Somebody should've put him on medication."

Hannah reaches over to rub my neck. "Nobody could fix it but your dad, Frannie. He was responsible for his own life."

"It's just so cowardly of him — how could he be such a chickenshit?" I wince at the pain.

"What do you mean?"

"Come on, Hannah, for all we know this is the only go-round we get. You have to be able to take what life dishes out. He didn't even have a terminal disease to make it noble — he just gave up! And everybody at that funeral home tomorrow is going to know it."

Hannah leans toward me. "Who are you worried about, him or you?"

"Oh, shut up." It's my turn to hit her with the pillow. "So what do you think happens when you die?"

"Buddhism has a different take on it. It says that most of us condemn ourselves to suffering through endless rebirths until we finally wise up and wake up. It's totally up to each of us. Until then, past karma is constantly ripening and future karma is being created every minute, right now — it's called samsara."

"So there's no question that you're born again — you just don't know on what level?"

"Right, at least as long as you're still caught in samsara — in which dying is as much a part as living. But you can choose a downward or an upward spiral. Or you could choose once and for all to wake up to your own perfection, your inherent

Buddha nature. Then you'd only come back by choice, as a bodhisattva, to work for the benefit of all sentient beings."

"What about suicide?"

Hannah sighs. "Probably not the best way to launch yourself out of here. How you leave one life, as well as how you deal with your forty-nine days in the bardo, or in-between state, affects your next birth. I've asked the members of my community to repeat the inspiration prayers to try and help him along. But there are no absolutes."

"That's good of them — he can use all the help he can get. According to the Catholics, he may never get out of purgatory." I rub my hand over the rich pattern of the rug. "But what if it's all just a comforting fairy tale? What if there *is* nothing else?"

Hannah snorts. "You mean we're as good as it gets?"

She has a point.

One thing Cajuns know how to do is throw a good funeral, like when Pop Broussard, J.P.'s father, died a few years back. Everyone knows exactly what to do. First they come into the funeral home across from the church, sign the "guest" book, and head straight for the open casket in the front of the room. There's no question of what prayers to murmur or what to say to the widow, and everyone gathers eagerly around the coffeepot to repeat the details of the passing. The rosary gets recited every so often, and the room drones with "Hail Mary, full of grace, pray for us now and at the hour of our death. . . ." Sometimes people who didn't even know the deceased stop by just to see what's going on. Then they all come home to have a highball or two, to taste everyone else's covered dish, and to support the widow in her grief. And maybe boil some crawfish.

That's what this spiffy Denver home o' funerals needs: an urn of strong coffee, some ritual words, and a little boot of bourbon. Instead we all stand around trying to find meaning in the paneled walls and the paisleyed carpet.

The Stewarts are here, and a few of Daddy's other neighbors, and his old boss, Stan McPhee, with some cronies from his Aloco office, the odd friend or two. Messages of condolence and regret from several acquaintances or associates who couldn't be here. Not much to show for a whole lifetime.

In the front of the hushed blue room

looms the polished pine casket, its lid meaningfully closed. At the back of the room Mom has fallen into the role of unofficial hostess, for which I'm grateful. That leaves me free to stare at the white lilies on the ludicrously large spray of flowers sent by Aloco.

There's a tense moment when Daddy's second ex-wife shows up, having driven in from her family's ranch on the western slopes of Colorado. Edith looks down-to-earth in her gray pantsuit and low shoes, especially next to Mom's designer black. She heads straight for the casket and kneels down, and I see her shoulders shake. When she finally rises, she hugs Mitch and me and blows her nose.

"It's too sad," she says finally, clutching my hands. "It shouldn't have come to this."

There's an echo of Mom's sentiment in her words. "Could I talk to you about it sometime?" I ask.

She reaches into her purse for pen and paper and jots down her number. "Absolutely. Call me. Anytime."

"Thanks," I say. "It'll probably have to wait till after . . . we're taking him home to Tennessee."

"I heard," she says. "I'd like to see that

place — it might help me to understand him better."

Beyond her a man walks into the room, a familiar silhouette framed by the glare of lights behind him. My bruised heart falls to the floor. It's my old beau Neil Peters.

He crosses to me, and soon I'm looking into the gray eyes that used to be the first thing I saw every morning. We're in the bedroom of his treehouse apartment, a sand candle in a vague gonadal shape hanging by a leather thong over the bed and throwing crazy shadows on the walls. Joni Mitchell's plaintive voice sings of blood and holy wine.

A flush of my cheeks brings me back to the present, as Neil talks about my dead father.

"Thanks for coming," I stammer. "How — how did you know?"

"Actually I heard it at work. Our law firm has done some work for Aloco. I'm so sorry, Frannie — I know how close you were to him."

"Apparently not close enough." I stare down at my fingers, which are grasping each other, and blink aside the pictures that want attention, a slideshow of memories of the two of us. I'm not ready for this.

Mom approaches just in time. "Why, Neil Peters, what on earth? I can't believe my own eyes!" They hug, and I can feel the how-could-you-have-let-him-get-away oozing from her pores. "It's so good of you to come — I know this means the world to Frannie." Then Mitch shakes his hand, and we're all hunky-dory, like old times.

"You look like you could use a breath of fresh air," Neil says to me, and just like that, we're walking out a back door and into the parking lot. The stars wink at us as we sit on a stone bench.

"It's good to see you, Frannie. You look great."

My gaze flits up to see if he means it. "So do you."

He runs his hand through wiry brown hair that's cut short, close to a skull I never saw under all the long locks he used to wear. He's tanned and healthy, and the crows have been kind to his eyes. His crisp white shirt runs smoothly into the waist of his pants, which hang off his hips like they were made for him. The body looks the same but the accoutrements have been upgraded.

"I heard how he died," he says. "I'm sorry. He always did have something of the tortured soul about him."

I look at him in surprise. "Did he?"

"Something just behind his eyes. How long will you be here?"

"We leave for Tennessee in the morning." I suck in a breath. "Then I guess I'll be back — there's his house to take care of and all."

In the silence Neil props one ankle on his other knee and fiddles with a thread on the hem of his pants.

"Twenty-four years." There's a cautious note to his voice. "So how's your life down there? Are you happy?"

There's that question again. I nod. "I teach in an arts high school. We have an old farmhouse out in the country. The kids — Neville and Maggie — are grown and gone now."

"What's your husband like?"

"J.P.? He has his own construction business, hunts and fishes. Salt of the earth."

"Hmm. That's more than you told me when you left." I can think of nothing to say. "Is he good to you?"

"Yes, he is." My eyes flicker to his face, then away. "But tell me about you — I heard you're a corporate lawyer?"

"Yeah, made partner last year."

"How's your wife?"

"We finally went our separate ways a few

years back — or made it official, anyway."
"Kids?"
"One, a boy. He'll finish at the University of Colorado next year. He just took off for some backwater place in Mexico to study how they play the fiddle. I hope he'll come to his senses soon." He picks invisible lint off his pants. "So . . ."
"What?"
"Did that Cajun make you happy?"
I fill my lungs with the sweet, cool air. Just then Mitch calls us in to the service, giving me an excuse not to come up with an answer.

The undertaker asked me to select some music for the service. I'd flipped through the generic hymnal, having no earthly idea which ones my father liked. When my eyes fell on "Abide with Me," he nodded as if it were the wisest choice in the world.

A young, baby-faced minister stands beside the casket, his face pleasant and earnest. He takes my hand and coos words of comfort as he guides me to my seat in front. He's dressed in street clothes, no purple robes or incense here. He says a prayer but the words won't sink in.

I give myself a mental shake and concentrate as we turn to the Twenty-third Psalm.

I'm drawn into the rhythm, the comfort of the beautiful old words. But soon they're over, and the poor minister gropes for the appropriate things to say, since he didn't know "the deceased" from Adam.

I remember years ago seeing a photo in a *Life* magazine of a hockey goalie. Through trick photography, all the injuries he'd ever sustained to his face were superimposed one over the other to show what he would have looked like if he'd gotten them all at once. That's each of us, I think, full of invisible scars that we alone know are there.

Mitch jostles my elbow to stand for the hymn. Darkness deepens; comforts flee. Life's little day ebbs; earth's vain shadows flee.

How can we hope to abide with one another?

Chapter Six
DNA

This 727 has become my father's hearse and he my Addie Bundren, the Faulknerian corpse that gets dragged all over Mississippi on the pretext of burying her with her family. Mitch's bony elbow juts over the armrest as he snores softly beside me. He's not in a good mood. His boss called to say he'd missed out on a big contract.

The continent rolls by beneath us, its vast plains plowed into submission. We cross the Mississippi, that great shining jugular vein that carries the continent's waters to Louisiana and out into the Gulf. Then the hills, green upon green, roll toward my ancestral stomping ground, the Cumberland Plateau, gentle mountains older than the Rockies.

The plane touches down to earth on the Nashville runway and a trim, white-haired man greets us with a sign: ALDREN. Yes, that's my name, Aldren. Broussard is a name that was added later, like sprinkles on a sugar cookie after it's cooled.

He'll pick up the casket, he tells us in long, slow vowels, and drive it up to Willow Grove to meet us there tonight. He has us sign some papers in case he drives off a cliff with Daddy's body, then disappears.

"I wonder what the hell all this is going to cost?" mumbles Mitch as we head for yet another rent-a-car counter.

"Don't worry, dahling. I'm an heiress now." I can't help but push his buttons. "It's almost time for J.P.'s plane. I'll go wait for him at security."

The numbness in my head is slowly evolving with familiarity. It could be someone else's hand that lifts to wave to my husband. He encases me in his strong arms, smelling like Louisiana air, thick and sweet. He peers into my face. "How you holding up, *bébé?*"

I shrug and surrender to his arm around me. The airport is hip, with reminders of Nashville's music scene at every turn, interspersed with colorful, whimsical sculptures.

"Maggie called from Santa Fe." The name jolts me, reminds me I'm a mother besides being a discarded daughter. "She can't get here till tomorrow morning — I'll have to come back and pick her up." Santa Fe. "And I finally got a message through to Neville. He called back last night, pretty broken up about it. But there's no way he could get a leave."

My arms suddenly ache for my children.

"And Vera — I about had to tie her in her chair to keep her from coming. You need to call her."

There are a lot of things I need to do.

The Tennessee hills rise and sink in emerald waves, their curves a silent solace. I've spent so little time here where my father grew up, yet I must carry its memory in my DNA.

I've left the front seat to the men, who've fallen into easy conversation. In this land of hollows, ridges, creeks, and coves, lights are going on in the scattered houses we pass. I strain to catch glimpses of these people, to see what their lives look like. They gather round the table for their daily bread, or bask in the blue light of the day's catastrophes on the evening news. But what goes on in their hearts?

Mitch tells J.P. he's dating a woman with three children, that he was passed over for a promotion, and that he may be transferred to the East Coast. That's more information than I've gotten out of him in years. J.P.'s routine cheeriness as he recounts his latest business deals galls the hell out of me.

At last our headlights sweep up the drive to Aunt Lena's house. In the dusk the roofs of the steep front gables look like a pair of quizzical eyebrows. A tremor of excitement runs up my ribs just as it did when we came for visits during my childhood. I would watch my father revert to a smiling baby brother, and the stories and jokes and memories would pour forth from him like water over the Cumberland Dam.

Aunt Lena bursts through the screen door and trundles down the porch steps, wiping her hands on her apron and throwing her arms wide as if to embrace the whole rental car. Tall and plump, with pure white hair, she opens my door and sucks me to her, her voice choking on the "Frannie honeys." On the night air rides the scent of rich fields and some sweet, invisible flower. When I look into her tears, her eyes are the exact blue of Daddy's, and I know I've done the right thing for my father.

"Oh, just look at me, standing here like a fool," she says in her slow drawl. "Mitchell

Aldren, come over here and give your Aint Lena a hug. You look like you could use some of my peach cobbler. It's just terrible what it takes to get you all to come see me. And J.P., you remembered the way all right? I'm right glad you could come." She hustles us into the house.

Uncle Lex is watching the news in the living room. We used to count the words he'd say in a day, never more than a couple dozen. Now that he's battling prostate cancer, his smile makes deep gullies in his sagging cheeks. He pats my hand and says, "Mighty sorry to hear about your pa, Frannie Marie. It's a shame, that's what it is, just a shame."

Aunt Lena shows us to our rooms upstairs. The old cherry four-poster is covered with a hand-crocheted spread, and a doll with a knitted pink skirt and bonnet leans smiling on the pillows. Fireflies blink cheerful lights in the tree outside the window, and I look forward to bedtime when I can stare at them until my eyes can't stay open. J.P. clatters around behind me, stashing his clothes in an empty drawer.

"I love it here," I say to the tree.

"They're good folks," J.P. says, putting his arms around me. "If your daddy would've just come back here to his people, maybe he could've set himself straight. A tree won't live if you cut its tap-root."

"Maybe this is where he was headed. We'll never know." I change into jeans and a T-shirt before going back downstairs.

Aunt Lena waves us into chairs and bustles around putting on a spread — a tureen of steaming chicken and dumplings, bowls of butterbeans and carrots and Jell-O salad. She passes a jar of the famous pickled beets that won her a blue ribbon at the county fair, her deep laugh jiggling her double chins.

"How are the boys?" I ask. My three cousins, Junior, Russell, and Scottie, all live within shouting distance, each keeping up his share of the farm. Aunt Lena launches into a recitation of the successes of her grandchildren, her voice mixing with the succulent chunks of chicken and the rich gravy over the spongy dumplings. I close my eyes, and for just that little while, my heavy burden of grief eases.

As I dry the last dish, Aunt Lena pulls off her apron. "I fixed some sandwiches and a thermos of coffee for the funeral parlor. Does Mitch want to go?"

Funeral parlor. Come into my parlor, said the spider to the fly. Welcome to my nightmare.

"Tonight?" I ask. "What's going on tonight?"

Her head rears back. "Why, honey, we got to go set up with him. You don't want to leave him alone all night!"

Why not? He's left us alone forever. But I shake my head and go upstairs. J.P. is stretched out on the bed.

"Aunt Lena wants to sit up with Daddy," I say, rummaging in my suitcase for a sweater.

J.P. springs up. "I'll come with y'all."

"No, J.P." He shoots me a bewildered look. "I just — it feels like something Aunt Lena and I need to do together."

"OK, I understand." His hug brings no comfort, and I don't know why.

Downstairs Mitch is protesting half-heartedly at being left behind. "There's no need for all of us to be there," says Aunt Lena, patting his sunken cheek. "Good night, Lex honey. I'll be back before breakfast."

Uncle Lex blows her a kiss and we're out into the sweet air.

The road to town runs past fields of fireflies dancing their courtship tango just above the grass. What a clever romantic Mother Nature must have been, plotting how each life-form would attract its mate and outwit its enemies. They say the life force is so strong that it shows up in the most inhospitable of environments. Anaerobic bacteria thrive deep in the ice of Antarctica; tubeworms survive in the crushing depths of the ocean. And now they think there's life on the moons of Jupiter.

And yet with all that teeming going on in the universe, I wend my way through country roads to a small brick building where lies the corpse of my father. Somebody up in that starry sky has got to be shaking a finger with a *tsk tsk*.

Aunt Lena reaches across the seat and covers my hand with her warm and doughy one. "We got some figuring to do, Frannie. I still cain't seem to wrap my mind around this. But right now let's just do what we got to do to get him in the ground."

I nod.

Armed with her bulging satchel, she raps on the side door. A slight figure opens it. "Come on in, Lena. He just got here a few minutes ago — that fool driver got hisself lost."

"Fred, you remember John Franklin's girl, Frances Marie. Fred Cummings."

Fred Cummings shakes my hand. "Why, you're all growed up. I remember when you weren't but a little girl. Your daddy and I went to school together, you know, and I never could beat him at fishing. I used to think he talked those fish onto his hook somehow." When he drops his eyes, the crown of his head shines in the dim hall light. "He always said he'd come back, but I never thought it'd be this way."

"Come on, Fred," says Aunt Lena, "show me my baby brother."

We follow the undertaker down the dim hall and into a back room of shiny linoleum floors, white cinderblock walls, and bright fluorescent lights. In the middle of the room stands the casket I know too well, jacked up on zigzag folding legs.

"That gent from Nashville said it come off the plane with this scratch down the side. I was just fixing to get out my plastic wood and patch it up."

Aunt Lena holds her hands above the wood as if to warm them, then lowers them gently and begins to caress the surface. "John Franklin," she murmurs. "Oh, John Franklin." Her voice comes from deep within her like an alley cat's purr.

I turn away, her grief too raw. My eyes fall on the sink, the steel cabinets, the hint of instruments that cut and slice and probe. The glare of the lights is too strong. Mr. Cummings' hand is on my elbow.

"Come on out here and sit down," he says in his gentle voice. "I wished I'd got him in place before you all got here." He leads me into a room lined in dark paneling, the upholstered chairs covered in the same shade of blue as at the Denver funeral home. I sink into one and, alone for the moment, try to suspend my thoughts.

"Do you want to see him, Lena?" I hear Mr. Cummings say from the back. Soon the shadows ring with muted weeping.

"You just never can tell about these things," he goes on. "I've known this boy since we were in knee pants, and I never would've guessed that could happen."

"Does the whole town know?" Aunt Lena blows her nose.

"All they've said is carbon monoxide poisoning. Why don't we just leave it at that? And don't worry. We won't dig his grave to the north — his head'll be to the east like all the rest of the Aldrens."

"But there'll be lots of questions, and I don't want to lie about it. I'm not ashamed of him."

"Of course you're not, but let's make it easy on everyone." I hear Aunt Lena sigh before Mr. Cummings goes on. "That girl's the spitting image of her grandmother, ain't she? Why don't you go out there with her, and I'll wheel him on in."

I'd forgotten the stages a sleepless night goes through, the shiftings of depth. The first one happens around one o'clock, when your body realizes you're not going to put it to bed and goes into overdrive. Another happens around three, the beginning of the heart of the night, the absolute and resolute opposite of day. And then there's the still, gray, wretched period just as the light begins to seep back into the world, when you're not sure you want it to come back because you've gotten used to the dark, the shadows, the tricks of spirit, and your eyes ache at the thought of noon.

The ham-and-cheese sandwiches are things of the past, the thermos of coffee long empty. The coffin looms over the dim room, topped with a VA flag and two photographs of Daddy, one in his Marine uniform and the other a studio portrait taken ten years or so ago. In the first one, he looks rugged and tough, ready to take on the world. The same features are there in the later photo, but the face under the beard is fleshy, the half smile forced. I've finally seen what Neil was talking about, a look in his eyes like a hungry coyote that remembers the rancher that shot his father and the bear trap that got his grandmother and the poison that took his sibling, and he wants to eat that rabbit he's found dead but he fears a trap.

"Aunt Lena" — my voice makes us both jump in the hollow of the night — "what was it like when you were kids? It must have been terrible, losing your mother so young."

She draws a deep and ragged sigh. "Poor, poor Mama. She held on as long as she could."

"What do you mean? Nobody's ever told me exactly how she died."

"We didn't used to talk about such things — but it was female plumbing. Your daddy was such a big baby, and after he was born, she just bled and bled. It got worse every month till she couldn't get out of bed anymore, and finally she just left us."

Her words hang in the air. "She hemorrhaged for five years?"

Aunt Lena pulls on her earlobe. "Back then, these country doctors didn't know what to do about it." Aunt Lena's eyes are gray in the dim light. "She wasn't young when he was born, especially for those days. So I had to take over for Mama, Papa depended so on me. I practically raised John Franklin." She says John Franklin with the emphasis on the Frank so that the John is just a footnote. Her eyes are seeing a past that I can only guess at, her private load of baggage.

She heaves a ragged breath. "Your daddy took it so hard when Mama passed on. She spoiled him so, knowing she wouldn't be around long. But he was so cute, you couldn't help it. He used to sit on her bed and make up stories about doodlebugs and salamanders and I don't know what all. Her face would just light up when he was around." I see her lying under the smooth white sheet, the spreading of the secret red stain.

That's when it hits me — my grandmother gave her life to bring her son into the world, only for him to toss it away. Indignation boils up in my throat. I rise and stride over to his picture.

"You cheat, you dirty rotten thief!" I have the urge to punch the shallow smile off the face in the photograph.

Aunt Lena's by my side. "Now, honey,

that won't do a lick of good — you know it won't."

"But it's not fair! If he didn't care about us, at least he could've cared about her — she *died* for him!"

Aunt Lena's arms are around me and I'm sobbing into her soft shoulder. "You cain't look at it like that, girl. It'll only bring you grief."

I pull away. "He's a coward and a cheat, and he finked out on us all, on you too!" I run out the side door and into the steely predawn light.

A moment later Aunt Lena's plump hands set a sweater on my shoulders. "It's all right, baby. You're just exhausted. Let's get on home now."

I let her lead me to the car. But it's not all right, and it never will be.

J.P. snores softly in the pale morning light. I can't make myself get into bed yet. I'm drawn instead to the window, where a cool breeze brushes my cheeks, my ragged eyelids. As I drop to my knees, my hands take up the position that's supposed to make me pray. I close my eyes and try to find the words to beg for help, for comfort, for a morsel of clarity.

But the words refuse me, and so do the

answers. The admittedly thin image that I'd constructed of a God who could be troubled to give a damn about me seems to have receded into shadow.

Chapter Seven
Broken Circles

The clock reads ten o'clock; can that be right? It's light outside, and the house is quiet; maybe they're all gone and I can climb on the old mule in the pasture and head off into the hills. Instead I rise and pad down the hall to the bathroom, to face my ghastly reflection in the medicine cabinet. Pale, with puffy pouches like Silly Putty under my eyes and a network of fine creases that get deeper when I scrunch up my eyes. Oh, God, talk about baggage.

It's as I step into the shower that the thought of my grandmother's death reappears, and the indignation roils up again. She never had a chance to let her hair go gray, to let life etch its footprints into her face, and all because she brought my father into the world. A red anger washes through me, painting over the black of the pain and the mud-colored guilt.

I towel off and dab on foundation, eyeliner, mascara, blush. Thank heaven for small favors, but the camouflage is tenuous at best.

In the kitchen Aunt Lena has left me a huge breakfast in the oven, coffee on the stove, and a note that says to call the funeral home when I'm ready to come over. There's another from J.P. saying he's gone to Nashville for Maggie.

Clutching a cup of coffee, I let my eyes follow the curves of the horizon, a palette of greens from the pasture to the willows along the creek to the pines and hardwoods ascending the slopes. I wonder why Daddy ever left this place.

"He was a fanciful little boy, always coming up with the wildest tales. The other children loved him." Daddy's ancient grade school teacher, her white hair pulled into a high bun, her cheekbones protruding like sails in the wind, is the fourth or fifth person to tell me a similar story. Around here they don't forget.

I make the rounds of the flower arrangements and potted plants, politely reading strangers' names on the little white cards. The Geology Department at Aloco has sent another ostentatious spray, and the yellow roses are from Neville. Good boy.

The others are from local people I don't know, from that part of his life before I existed.

They're all here, first and second and third cousins, aunts and uncles, playmates, teachers, the storekeeper, and the "colored man" who used to work for the family. I love their drowsy, wide-open accent, the one Daddy used to lapse into at odd times. They remind me of the Cajuns, these hill people, with all the complex tendrils of their family trees, their steadfast independence yet reliance on each other, their stubborn refusal to give in to the outside world.

Their scraps of remembrances slowly add up to a collage of a young boy I do not recognize. John Franklin as leader, prankster, defender of the weak. Where was that little boy buried inside the disheartened man? Must adulthood extract such a price?

My cousins Junior and Russell and Scottie have just highjacked me into a corner and are intent on making me laugh. Junior's telling the tale of how I once insisted on riding their stubborn mare who'd recently foaled, and how I ended up on the wrong side of a barbed wire fence with my calf in shreds. "Yeah," says Russell, "and when we told her you had to get the tetanus shots in the stomach, she hollered all the way to Doc's office."

I am actually laughing when the outside door opens, letting in the blinding light of the summer's day. It's J.P. striding over to me, his mouth a thin, straight line. "Would you please come talk some sense into your daughter?" he hisses into my ear.

"Where is she?" In answer he grasps my elbow and steers me toward the door. The light shears into my head for a moment before I can focus on the rental car in the parking lot, Maggie hunched into the corner of the front seat.

"She refuses to take that goddamned ring out of her nose," says J.P. "I'm not letting people see her like that."

I open the car door. Behind the thick black eye makeup and the garish hair the color of boiled crawfish is the face of my daughter, the fruit of my womb. She looks so pitiful trying to look obstinate that I have to smile. It takes a moment for her pout to dissolve, and then she's in my arms, a little "Mom" escaping like the mew of a kitten.

"How are you, sweetie?"

"I'm OK, Mom. I'm sorry about Granddad."

"I'm just glad you got here."

J.P. snorts impatiently behind me. “Frannie, tell her she’s got to get rid of that thing. These people will think she’s from Mars.”

Maggie’s hazel eyes meet mine for just a second, then drop to the gravel of the parking lot. She’s wearing a black T-shirt cinched at the waist with a silver conch belt over a long black skirt. Thankfully her sleeve covers her tattoo. I can’t look at the ring without wondering how she blows her nose, but there it is.

“She looks like who she is right now,” I find myself saying. “She has a right to that.” Besides, I don’t have the stomach for a battle.

Maggie’s face lights up, her mouth breaking into a smile. She squeezes my hand. “Thanks, Mom.”

I slip my arm around her waist, and as we head for the door, she stops and removes the ring from her nose.

Heads turn as I lead her over to the casket. She draws a ragged breath as she takes in the two photographs of her grandfather. She was always a favorite of his, never letting his reticence stop her from climbing up his long legs and into his lap. She leans into my shoulder and sobs until at last I tissue off the remains of her streaming eye makeup.

"Come on, let me show you off." She sniffs and nods. Mustering my roster of new acquaintances, I begin to introduce her around. "This is my daughter, Magnolia."

"Mag," she says once or twice as she extends her hand. They look for familial features in her face and pronounce that she looks like everyone from her great-aunt Lena to her great-great-grandmother Aldren. Maggie falls into a measured politeness.

J.P. finally comes back in the door, walking straight to the coffin to kneel and cross himself. I give a little inner chortle, wondering how these staunch Protestants will like having these Catholics in their midst.

We're listening to a family tree of sorts from one of Daddy's cousins when Mr. Cummings hands me a fax. I stare at its military logo for a moment before my eyes skip to the bottom. It's from Neville, written in his neat and careful script.

> *Mom, So sorry about Granddad. I won't make it in time for the funeral, but they've given me a leave anyway. I'll be home next week.*
>
> *Love, Neville*

★ ★ ★

Aunt Lena and Maggie and I grasp at each other's hands as we follow the six pairs of pant legs flapping in the summer breeze. Junior, Russell, and Scottie bear the pall, along with Mitch and J.P. and another cousin.

The church next door to the funeral home, where Daddy went as a child, is a stark white frame, its bell in a modest steeple tolling a mournful clang. The preacher, dressed in a plain dark suit, reminds me by stark contrast of the Catholic priests at home in their purple-and-gold finery, surrounded by gilt and incense. I wonder if God has a preference.

"Fellow brethren," he begins, "we gather here today to mourn the loss of our native son John Franklin Aldren. Son of John and Mattie, brother of Lena Aldren Sparks, father of Mitchell Lane Aldren and Frances Marie Aldren Broussard." By saying our names, he has stretched a cord around the lot of us and gathered us into a tight bunch to which I've often forgotten I belong.

The windows are tic-tac-toed with colored glass, red and yellow and blue. The choir box is filled with a dozen or so men and women, mostly Daddy's generation, one young pregnant girl. They open a collective mouth and sing of circles unbroken in the sky. J.P. reaches for my hand. Words are spoken, more songs sung; Maggie snif-fles beside me. Then somehow we're in the rental car following the not-so-new hearse driven by Mr. Cummings.

The leafy trees wave gaily at us, the birds careen in the sky and call to each other, and my business this day is to fill up a hole in the ground. J.P. guns the engine up a steep rutted lane and we're at the Aldren family cemetery on top of the hill. I last walked here with my father as he talked in hushed tones and pointed out the names of his father, his mother, his grandparents, and their parents. And now the hole gapes at the end of the row, the dirt piled up waiting for him.

We stand around as the coffin is brought forward and they lower him in. I put one of Neville's roses on top of it and take a fistful of soil. It's rich red and warm, and Daddy would tell me its geological makeup. I drop it into the hole and it plunks onto the box. He's part of the hill now, part of the line that brought him into the world, and I know he'll like that.

As the others retreat and the shovelfuls of dirt begin to fill the chasm, I drop to my knees and water his grave with my tears.

★ ★ ★

"Why don't you all stay on a few days?" Aunt Lena is dishing out thick slices of ham, tuna casserole topped with crushed potato chips, and creamed peas. "You've come so far and it's been so long. Besides, we've got to eat up all this food." The refrigerator is full of platters and casseroles that friends and neighbors have brought.

"Don't tempt me," says J. P, forking scalloped potatoes into his mouth, though I know he's wishing for some red pepper to spice them up.

"I've got to get back to work," says Mitch. "I'm already way behind."

A longing to stay in the comfort of these green hills like soft sweet breasts washes over me. "I'd love to," I say, and watch J.P. shoot me a quick look. "How about you, Maggie, want to stay?"

She's picking at the peas. Her version of vegetarianism usually means pizza without the pepperoni. "I wish I could," she says, surprising me with the wistful note in her voice.

"Why can't you?" I look into eyes that are naked and vulnerable without the makeup that she's cried off.

"I just got a job — at a health food store. They're holding it for me till the weekend."

"I thought you were going to travel all summer."

"Well, my money was going a lot faster than I'd planned. Plus I really like Santa Fe, and I've met some cool people."

I smile across the table at her. "Your cousin Hannah would be proud."

"Well, that just leaves you and me and all this food, Frances Marie." Aunt Lena's chins jiggle under her tired face as she reaches out to squeeze my hand. "Lex don't eat enough to keep a bird alive."

"You're not coming home?" says J.P. forlornly when we're alone in our room.

"I'll be back before Neville gets home next week. It's been years since I've been here, and I think Aunt Lena needs somebody right now."

"I need you, too," he says, pouting.

"Oh, J.P." The fireflies wink from the tree. "Besides, it's too hot at home, and I feel like getting away for a while."

I wink back at the fireflies before finally stretching my weary bones in sleep.

Chapter Eight
Points of View

They're gone. Maggie put the ring back in her nose, Mitch promised to meet me in Denver later on, and J.P. left wearing his hangdog expression. Waving to the dust the car kicks up, I feel a spaciousness settle into my chest.

"Now I've got you all to myself, what would you like to do?" Aunt Lena puts her arm around my waist as we walk back into the house, the cool air funneling through the hallway.

"We don't have to do anything — it's enough to be here with you."

"In that case," she says, "there's a peach tree out back that's just feeding the squirrels. It's high time I got busy and made my peach butter. There's nothing like work to get your mind off your troubles."

Armed with baskets and broad hats, we push a wheelbarrow through a fence and a pasture to a gnarled old peach tree loaded with small, rosy fruits. The air smells of sweet decay, and the ground under the tree is littered with rotting rejects, manna for the flies. An old ladder leans against the trunk, and Aunt Lena sets to work plucking with a vengeance, as if loath to let another one go to waste.

"Lex's grandmother planted this tree," says Aunt Lena. "For the life of me, I've never figured out why she put it way out here. It sure makes it hard to haul the harvest to the house."

Climbing the ladder, I find myself suspended in a leafy amber world. The peaches hang in a fuzzy haze, their cheeks rosy and oozing sugar where borers have made their homes. I reach out to pluck one from its site of origin — bud, blossom, growing fruit until it has reached this state of utter perfection in my hand. A choir of angels strikes up as I bite into its meaty flesh and the juice, warm and sweet, runs down my chin.

Aunt Lena chuckles from below. "Don't appear I'll get much work out of you today." Her basket is nearly full.

Making quick work of the rest of my peach, I set to plucking and pulling so as not to bring shame on my side of the family. Before long we trundle back to the kitchen, loaded with perfection and utilitarian purpose. I realize that my grief has indeed loosened its grip on my guts for a little while, has risen up and out the top of my head.

Stretching out to take a half hour "lie-down," I sink into a heavy and peaceful sleep, so that when I wake the light is slanting through my tree and I hear Aunt Lena in the kitchen downstairs. Sure enough, she's sitting at the table behind a huge blue bowl half full of sliced peaches.

"Don't you ever sleep?" I ask.

Aunt Lena hands me a knife, the fatigue showing under her eyes. We work in comfortable silence for a while before she says, "How's your life with J.P.?"

I look up in surprise. "Fine," I say automatically.

"He seems to set great store by you."

"He does."

"And you by him?"

"Yes." I slice into a peach and the juice dribbles down my forearm.

"But?"

Here's the third person in as many days to want to know exactly what my marriage is like, a question I never think to ask myself.

"But nothing. We're very different, but

he always makes me smile. Every once in a while I wonder what the heck he's doing with me." I spear a pit from the rusty red center, the flesh reluctantly letting it go.

"I think everybody feels like that from time to time." Aunt Lena's bowl is nearly full. "You take me and Lex — did you ever see two more different people? There were times in my life I thought if he didn't talk to me, I'd rip the wallpaper right off the walls. But we filled up the house with all those little boys, and they made up for Lex's silences."

"What about after they left?"

She chuckles. "By then I guess I was glad for some peace and quiet. Besides, they haven't gone far. Then along come the grandkids." She shakes her head. "And since Lex took sick, I swear I can't find nary a thing to be cross with him about. When I think that I might lose him, too . . ." Her bottom lip begins to tremble. Wiping her eye with her apron, she gets up to dump the sliced peaches into a heavy pot on the stove and starts measuring in cups of sugar.

Thrashing about for something to say, I hear myself begin to say things I've never voiced before. "At first, nobody could understand why I married J.P. But I felt like he had something that I needed, a rootedness that I never saw in people when I was growing up. I mean, our street in Denver was brand-new when we arrived there, carved right out of the prairie, and people moved in and out of that neighborhood like it was a glorified hotel. And there was J.P., surrounded by his family, still so close to all of them, and to his roots, and to . . . I don't know . . . to the way things were supposed to be."

Aunt Lena stares at me while she stirs the pot. "You realize you're talking about just exactly what your daddy gave up when he left here?"

"I've been thinking about that since I got here. Whatever made him leave?"

"Oh, your daddy. The outside was always a pull for him. When he was a youngster, he was so blamed smart. He just couldn't get enough of school learning. He loved studying those rocks and figuring out what made them. Plus they were drilling for oil around here by then, and ever once in a while they'd strike it. Then folks'd carry on like the circus'd come to town. And then they built that atomic bomb right over at Oak Ridge."

"How did y'all feel about that when it killed so many people in Japan?"

Aunt Lena looks like Midas hoarding a dripping bowl of golden fruit. She peers over her glasses at me. "We felt it saved the lives of a whole lot of our fighting boys. And that's what got him interested in the uranium end of things."

"Even after he saw what it did?"

"In them days we all thought that nuclear stuff" — she pronounces it "nucular" — "was the be-all and end-all. It won the war for us, didn't it? It was the perfect crusade for John Franklin."

"Crusade?"

"He got in on the tail end of the Korean conflict, then went on to college. I remember a letter he wrote me from there. Said there was going to be cheap energy for everybody forever, and nobody would ever have to lose their land to a dammed-up river again, like so many folks around here did with the TVA. He thought it was the noblest cause in the world."

"If you ask me, it's caused more problems than it's solved."

She sighs. "You asked me why he left. He went off to school to learn all about that yellow rock, and never really came back."

I take the paddle from her and stir the peach butter. It's beginning to cook down into a rich amber slush. "Do you think Daddy would've been happier if he'd stayed here?"

Aunt Lena heaves a sigh and drops into a chair, fanning her flushed face. "Frances Marie, do I look like a fortune-teller? I cain't give you no answers. All I know is that John Franklin wasn't a happy man, not for a long, long time. I could see it but there weren't nary a thing I could do about it." She twists her apron in her hands. "I never in a million years thought it would come to this. If I did I would've dragged him kicking and screaming back here with me to try and straighten him out. But I didn't know how bad it was, and I blame myself for that."

"Oh, Aunt Lena, how can you say that? You were always so good to him, and he counted on you so much."

"Don't you dare stop stirring, young lady. I know that, and that's what I'm talking about. He counted on me, and I let him down. I never even got around to calling him for his birthday. We took the grandkids to Nashville and didn't get back till late that night. I'll never forgive myself for that. I guess I'm just going to have to live with it." Aunt Lena sniffles. "But I don't know how."

"What about me? I talked to him right before he . . . died. I keep trying to remember every word he said to see if he was trying to warn me. He was so down."

"He must've had good reason." She hoists herself up to scald the jar lids, her lips pressed together.

"Well, goddamn it, that's the most selfish thing I ever heard! He's just bailed out and left us to torture ourselves over how we treated him or what we could've done to save him."

"Watch your tongue in my house." Aunt Lena ladles the thick, hot liquid into jelly jars.

"And what kind of example does that set for the kids? What if we all went around doing that?"

"Wipe that rim real good." She's shaking her head. "I think you're being mighty uncharitable. John Franklin did right by everyone he knew all his livelong days. You know he must've thought long and hard about what it would do to all of us. We've got to take pity on him and forgive him."

"But that's just it — I don't want to have to pity my father. He's supposed to be strong for me and for Mitch and for the kids, if not for his own pride."

Aunt Lena *tsk*s at me. "Maybe he

thought you were a grown-up woman now, and he could finally lay his burden down."

"He didn't lay it down. He passed it on to me, and to you, to all of us." I screw the lid on the first jar, which I wouldn't mind slamming against the wall.

"The good Lord doesn't give us more than we can bear."

"Oh yeah? Tell that to Daddy."

Our labors finished, we're sipping iced tea on the front porch when Uncle Lex calls to me from the living room. "It's your ma on the phone, Frances Marie."

"Right nice talking to you, too, Annie," he's saying as I come up behind him. "Bye now."

"You might have called me to tell me how the funeral went," my mother fumes at my hello.

"I'm sorry, Mom. I just didn't think."

"Well, thank goodness your brother called. At least he remembers me."

"I'm sorry, Mom. It was a lovely service. I'm sorry you weren't here."

"I wouldn't dream of horning in on Lena's territory. She's finally got him back."

Aunt Lena rocks gently on the front porch.

"I don't think it's like that, Mom. Can I talk to you about it later?"

"Of course, don't let me disturb you. I hear you're staying on for a nice long visit."

"Just a couple of days. Then Neville's coming home for a short leave." My heart makes a joyful little leap. "After that, I'll go back to deal with the house." How absurd that I end up doing that duty when the man had two wives. "I'll call you from Denver."

"Frannie?" Mom's voice sounds suddenly like a little girl's. "Did they do right by him? Was it a nice service?"

"Yes, Mom. It was."

Back on the porch, I resume my rocking. "How's your mama?" asks Aunt Lena, her voice pinched.

"I think she's taking it harder than she wants to let on."

The implied *hmph* doesn't come out, but my aunt's jawline has gone tense. Swallowing my cowardice, I ask, "Why didn't you and Mom ever get along?"

"We got along just fine," says Aunt Lena.

"You never liked each other very well."

"That's none of your affair, young lady."

I look out at the road that winds past the driveway and soon curves out of sight around a hill either way you look. My tea tastes watery now. "Aunt Lena, I wish you'd give me an answer. I'm tired of not understanding things until it's too late."

Aunt Lena glances my way, finally shaking her head. "You want to know why your daddy was unhappy? Well, you don't have to look much further."

I stare at her profile, where her chins have compressed themselves into a mound of scowls. "You blame Mom?"

Aunt Lena drums her fingers on the arm of the rocker. "She wasn't the woman for him, that's all. I could tell from the minute I laid eyes on her." She stares into the distance. "That boy lost his mama too young, and he needed loving in the worst way, just pure-D— what is it they call it these days? — unconditional love. That's what would've pulled him through this life. But your mother was too selfish for that."

I try to grasp her view of things. I lived in that house with my parents, and I know it's not as simple as that, though I can't find the words to define it.

"Ambitious, too," she goes on, "wanting him to learn how to talk better so he wouldn't sound like a hillbilly. To make more money and buy a bigger house, cocktail parties and fancy clothes and all. We're just plain folks, and your Daddy was, too."

"That wasn't just Mom, Aunt Lena. Daddy was ambitious, too. What you're saying about this crusade of his explains a lot — I think he wanted to be the top dog, to find the biggest vein of ore, to beat out everybody else. He was gone from home a lot."

"Trying to support your ma in the style she wanted, more than likely. Only to have her run off with this other fellow. Why, he never got over it." Aunt Lena glares at me with a look that would fry an egg. "She should have stuck by him and tried to work it out. Every marriage has to weather bad times."

I stare her down. "I know that, Aunt Lena, but people go through things like that all the time without . . . doing what he did."

"Are you defending her, Frances Marie?" Aunt Lena hefts her bulk out of the chair and stomps over to the screen door. "And your father barely in the ground."

The screen door slams behind her, resounding on the horizon's hills.

Russell and his wife, Christine, arrive with their brood. Shortly after come Junior and Elaine, and Scottie and Cora. Junior's a year older, Russell a year younger than I am, and Scottie's the baby. In my childhood we visited here often, much to my mother's chagrin, and we kids ran the fields in perfect stepping-stones. Where Junior was the rabble-rouser and Scottie the eternal prankster, Russell tended to be serious and stalwart. Now here we are, a bevy of middle-aged cousins trying to remember how to play together.

The boys tease me about the heathen influence of Louisiana, pressing for details about Bourbon Street, Mardi Gras, and the latest trials of our ex-governors. Their wives poke them under the table and try to keep the conversation civilized. Next they want to know all about the state of the sugarcane and soybean markets, subjects about which I have little enlightenment to offer.

Aunt Lena keeps busy warming plates of food. She's still in a huff, and tiredness has settled in around her eyes. Christine finally shoos her off to bed, an order she doesn't argue with.

"She'll wear herself right out if you let her," says Christine, up to her elbows in soapy water. Her hair is cut stylishly short, and her cigarette-slim pants contrast with the pervading denim fashion statements of the rest of the crew.

"She does love to do for people," I say, taking up the drying towel.

"She needs to be needed," says Christine. "An enabler if I ever saw one."

"Your psychology degree is showing." I chuckle.

"It gets plenty of practice around here," she agrees with a laugh.

"She's mad at me for implying my father wasn't perfect."

"Ooh, don't mess with her babies." Christine scrubs a pot. "You'll never win on that one. Her heart's in the right place, though."

"I know. Have you ever regretted coming back here with Russell?" Ten years ago Christine married Russell, her high school sweetheart, after her first husband died in a Nashville car accident. Russell chucked his job with the U.S. Forest Service to come back to the farm. Now here they are, nearly my age with three grade school kids coming up.

"Thank God for satellite dishes and the Internet — that's all I can say." Her smile slackens. "But no, this place is right for us. We just finally quit fighting it. And I've gotten into spelunking with Russell lately — when I can get away from the kids. It's magical, something you can't imagine in the city."

"Caves? I remember Daddy talking about one around here."

"Russell's the one to talk to about that. He guides some of these university people around to look at them. There's even some cave paintings in one."

"You're kidding. I'd love to see that."

"I'm sure Russell would jump at the chance to take you over there. But right now, don't think you're getting out of drying these dishes."

Sleep will not come. At last I pull on my robe and pad down the creaky stairs into the living room. In the dim glow of an air-freshener night-light, the furniture looks like a bevy of plump old friends, each dressed in a prim hand-crocheted antimacassar. A little liquor cabinet in the corner offers me a drink like a discreet butler serving from the sidelines of the party. After pouring myself a tumbler, I curl into Uncle Lex's chair, its seat hollowed out by his bony butt, the color of the worn Naugahyde matching the whiskey.

It's good Kentucky bourbon, corn mash miraculously transmuted into a mind-altering elixir. Just as it begins lighting little fires on the way down my throat, a shadowy figure floats into the room. My heart stops a second before I realize it's Uncle Lex.

"Mind if I join you, Frannie girl?"

His voice reminds me of rich cherry wood that's been scratched by the years. I grin sheepishly. "You caught me."

"Far's I know, you're of age." He gets a tumbler from the butler and pours a prudent inch.

"Did I wake you? Here, I'll get out of your chair."

"Naw, you stay put. I'll see what the world looks like from Lena's side of the room." He sags into the overstuffed armchair with the worn, cut velvet upholstery the color of garnets. "Not bad." He chuckles. "I do believe hers is softer'n mine. The old girl's been holding out on me."

Laughing, I remember how, after my failed attempt at prayer, I'd slipped into bed beside J.P. in the early light. How his arm had come around me automatically, how his warmth had felt at my back. Who are these creatures called men, I'd wondered, and what would we do without them?

Uncle Lex is gaunt in the shadowy light, little more than a bag of bones. "I have trouble sleeping most nights now," he says. "I'm mighty glad to have some company tonight."

Sipping whiskey, I marvel at the stream of words that has just come out of his mouth. Maybe he's only talkative at night, and the rest of us miss out on it.

"How're you feeling, Uncle Lex?"

He swallows. "Oh, you know, I've quit fighting it, and that makes it easier. It's gonna get me in the end anyhow."

I dare the bourbon to make me weepy.

The hall clock ticks away several minutes as we sit in comfortable silence. Then his cheery voice says, "Don't mind Lena, honey. If ever a soul on this earth means well, it's her. She's just a might set in her ways, that's all."

"I know, Uncle Lex, I know."

"It's hard for her to lose her baby brother."

My chin trembles as the clock strikes one, its tidings echoing through the house.

"I had a brother, too, name of Emmett. Two years younger'n me. Died when he was twelve."

"I never knew that, Uncle Lex. What happened to him?"

"Scarlet fever." His sigh puffs across the room. "I give it to 'im 'cause I'd went over to a boy's house where I wasn't supposed to go to, and caught it there. I didn't have it bad. But it kilt Emmett. *I* kilt Emmett."

Unable to look at him, I stare at the silenced eye of the television. A cricket sets up a dainty chirrup from under the sofa.

"Then one night, about a month after we buried him, I woke up in the night, and there he was setting on the foot of my bed, just as plain as you're setting right there. 'Lex,' he says, 'don't you worry 'bout me. I'm all right.' Says, 'Just wait'll you get here, Lex. You're gonna like it. Tell Mama and Daddy not to worry 'bout me. I'm all right.' And just like that, he faded away."

He drains his glass and gives a satisfied smack. "I do believe I can sleep now." He lifts himself out of the chair and comes over to pat my hand. "What I'm saying, Frannie girl, is that your daddy's all right. There's no call to worry about him now."

And then he's gone like he came, a bare-bones phantom already haunting his own house.

Chapter Nine
Degrees of Darkness

Christine was right: my cousin Russell's ears perked up when I asked about going spelunking. "How about tomorrow morning?" he said. Now here he comes in his rattletrap farm truck. Lanky and loose-jointed, with an angular face and pointed nose, he barely shows his age.

"Come on in, son," says Aunt Lena, "and get you a cup of coffee. There's nothing in that old cave that won't wait a spell."

"Naw. Christine's on a jag about caffeine."

Aunt Lena grins. "I won't tell if you won't."

Russell's John Deere cap ducks. "Mama, you got yourself a deal."

Before long, coffee and a thick biscuit sit in front of each of us on the kitchen table. Russ aims his deep-set gray eyes at me. "And what, may I ask, prompted this interest into the great art of spelunking?"

I stretch out my hands and survey the wrinkles around the knuckles, my narrow gold wedding band. "I don't know. It seems like it might be a comfort somehow to go down into the earth, like it might be getting toward the center of something."

"You pass. That's the feeling all us insane cavers have."

Aunt Lena lets out a "Pshaw," but the dark circles under her eyes betray her weariness and need for some time alone to mourn. She hands us a bag of sandwiches and a thermos of coffee, her answer to any out-of-the-ordinary circumstance. "Have you got spare batteries for them bat lights?"

Russell pecks her on the cheek. "Don't worry, Ma. I'll get her back before dark so you can feed her again."

"Want to go by the old homeplace where they grew up?" asks Russell as we jostle along the twisty road in his extended-cab pickup.

"Oh, Russ, I'd love to."

He turns off the paved road onto a lane overhung with thick branches until we're stopped by a padlocked gate. "We'll have to climb over. The place was sold again a few years ago, but the new owners don't mind if we visit." Picking our way along, we skirt a pond and round a bend until a modest two-story house comes into view. The roof sags on one end and the porch is falling in.

"It's showing its age, like the rest of us," says Russell.

"Didn't you boys ever think of buying it?"

"Nope. I've got plenty to do. Besides, it's better to let things die a natural death."

You can say that again.

We made a pilgrimage to this place every time we visited Aunt Lena in my childhood. Daddy would show us where his mother's bed was, the one she died in, and the loft where he slept. I could see him replaying in his mind scenes of a childhood scarred by illness and death. The sadness still feels tangible in the walls, and I turn back toward daylight. "Which one's the John Franklin tree?"

"That one." Russell points to the smaller of two massive maple trees in the front yard. My grandfather planted them along with the afterbirths of his children on the days they were born. I always meant to do that with my own children, but somehow forgot when the time came.

Picking my way through the tangle of

to the darkest black imaginable. The air is suddenly cool and clammy. Water drips into my face from the low ceiling, causing a breath of fear to scuttle through me. But when I switch on my headlight, Russell's lean haunches are there in front of me, squeezing into a tiny opening at the back of the cave. Taking a deep breath, I duck in after him. We're in a narrow passageway, my thighs immediately feeling the strain of the crouching position I'm forced into.

"The first keyhole's right up here," says Russell.

"Now I know how toothpaste feels," I grunt as he pulls me through the narrow opening.

"You get to crawl through this part," he says, his wide grin glowing in the eerie lamplight. "Through a stream."

"Oh, boy! I see why you and Daddy got along so well."

"Yep, he was one of my heroes."

Now we're sloshing on hands and knees through a shallow trickle of cold water. Russ' light cuts into the dark ahead, leaving even blacker black around its beam. My headlamp casts a deformed shadow of my cousin, like a pudgy dwarf with a stout head, onto the rutted stone wall ahead.

weeds, I lean into the trunk of the tree. My arms go around the thick, rough trunk as I press my chest into its warmth. The branches rock gently in the breeze, the leaves whispering soft words in my ear.

Scattered on the ground are the tree's fruits, looking like pairs of translucent wings made to float on the breeze, each bearing a small seed of the future. I slip one into my pocket.

Back in the truck, we swing west toward a chunky red bluff in the distance. As we nose into a pullout in the narrow road, I put on heavy boots and a jacket borrowed from Christine. A hard hat with a carbide light completes my ensemble.

After stashing the sandwiches and coffee in a grungy backpack, Russ heads off on a faint trail that rises and dips toward the bluff. I hustle to keep up with his long strides. "Christine tells me you're the local expert on this place."

Russell shrugs. "I guess I am now. Thank God it's on private property, or it would already be Dolly Parton's Cave-land."

I'm out of shape and out of breath. "How come there's all these caves around here?"

"All the right conditions, that's all. Take some stratified Mississippian limestone, add some carbonic acid, some seasonal flooding of underground streams, and you've got the perfect setup. Water has to run somewhere, so it hollows out a drainage network — the same geological principles that work on the surface."

"A network? You mean caves connected to other caves?"

"Sure. Didn't you hear the big news a few years back, when they found the connection between Flint Cave and Mammoth Cave up in Kentucky? It's a whole peneplain drained by a system of channels."

"I must've missed the news that day." Another man obsessed with rocks. I envision a subterranean tangle like the grass in our lawn, runners creeping out in all directions. "And there's cave paintings in there?"

"Glyphs, not paintings. Etched into the mud walls."

"Oh, excuse me. What do they look like?"

Russell shakes his head. "It's better if you let them take you by surprise. That's what Uncle Frank did when he showed them to me."

"Daddy? He knew about them?"

Russell slows to let me catch up. "Yo didn't know? I thought that's why yo wanted to see them. He found them whe he was a boy — kind of claimed them a his own, since no one else ever went fa enough in to find them. He only showe them to me after I started studying forestry." He swats at a fly. "After I saw them, I wanted to switch to anthropology and do my thesis on this cave, but he wouldn't let it go public — thank God."

As we approach the bluff, the cave looms a third of the way up the face, a black sideways hole like a mouth open to speak. We scale the side of the ridge and follow a narrow ledge to the opening. "Stop right there," says Russell, pulling a camera out of his pack.

"No," I protest, "I look like shit." I can feel the bags under my eyes and my hair pulled back in a sloppy ponytail. But he snaps it anyway, me being eaten by this giant mouth.

"You ready?" he says, his voice bouncing back at me as he ducks into the opening. "It's pretty rugged here at the beginning — that's what's protected it so long."

Bending down, I follow him in. The sunlight penetrates only a few feet, giving way

"Not much farther now," he says, his voice bouncing off the walls.

I crawl a little faster to catch up. "Does anything live back here?"

"Oh, bats, worms, some blind crayfish."

"Crawfish? Don't tell the Cajuns — they'll get out the boiling pot."

Russ chuckles. "So how's life down there in the swamps?"

Why does everybody keep asking me that? "It's good, it's great. How about you? Are you happy?"

"Yes, ma'am, I am. It took me a while, but I finally got it together." His words reverberate like the voice of God.

"I haven't seen you since you moved back home. What made you decide to quit forestry?"

"I got disillusioned with the whole thing. The U.S. Forest Service is just another branch of big business these days. Finally I realized what was right under my nose: that contentment — for me, anyway — lies in nurturing the land, not in exploiting it. I'd resisted farming like the plague, and here it was the answer all along. But if I'd stayed here to begin with, I would've missed Christine again. She was living in Nashville when I ran into her after her husband died."

"And the rest is history. Lucky you."

"Luck, yeah. But she felt more like a reward."

"Huh. You really think it works that way?"

"Yep. I do."

We slog on in silence. The air is cold in my lungs, but thin and close. "Anybody ever die in here from lack of oxygen?"

"Don't know. Did you forget your canary?"

"I feel like I'm crawling backward in time." Faced with only degrees of darkness, I feel as if the outer world must have ceased to exist, or at least to matter.

"I like the way the Indians looked at things." Russell's voice startles me. "The whole pineapple as a living, breathing system. If you kill off part of it, it all suffers."

"Codependence without the twelve steps."

"Heap big White Man, we've got to conquer, possess, change things. Look what we've messed up in two hundred years that had done just fine for several millennia before that. The Indians look farther ahead than their own lifetimes. They consider that every single act we take will have repercussions for seven generations."

Seven generations. That's Neville's and

Maggie's great-great-great-grandchildren, way on down the road.

A wave of fatigue washes over me, and my knees feel as if they're on the wrong end of a meat cleaver. Briefly I consider the possibility of curling into a tight little prenatal wad and going to sleep in this blissful dark.

But it's too damn cold.

We've been ascending a gentle slope for the last few minutes, and the little creek we're crawling along is running faster. Russell's headlamp slices the darkness like the Luke Skywalker light saber that Neville used to sleep with when he was little. Russell the Jedi, fighting back the Dark Side.

"Ta-da!" he sings out. "Squeeze through here, and you're in the cathedral."

"You didn't tell me we were going to church. I might've had second thoughts."

"Too late now. Didn't you know that was holy water you were crawling through?"

I groan but worm into a rough opening after him. When I stand up my light cuts greedily into a huge dome-shaped room. The chilly air spreads out, easing the pressure in my lungs, and the creek fills the space with a cheerful trickle punctuated by steady *plink, plunks* of dripping water.

Overhead my light refracts off colors on the ceiling, a ceiling adorned with thousands of long, parallel stalactites like giant soda straws.

Russell digs into his pack and lights two carbide lamps, one of which he passes to me. I swing it around, trying to get a feel for the shape of this space beyond the shadows.

The center of the room is dominated by a great dripping shape, like a gargantuan ice-cream cone that's melting faster than you can lick it. It towers above Russell's head. "The altar," he says in a stage whisper. "Takes a hundred years to build up an inch of this puppy."

Beyond the cone and at odd places around the sides are columns and stalagmites delineating areas that could indeed be naves and chapels. The whole is fashioned in shades of pink and amber and gold.

"Oh, wow," I say, turning round and round. "Pass the collection plate."

"There's no charge if you can make it this far." Russell's voice is dancing. "And you know what's wild — the cathedrals were built upward to amplify the energy. And I'm sure this place does the same. Don't you feel it?"

Looking around, I don't know what I feel. Lighter, maybe, and sort of heavier at the same time.

I shake my head, wagging my beam around the walls. "To think of all this beauty buried down here in the dark. I feel as if we might be the first humans to lay eyes on it."

"And all formed drip by drip by slow drip." Like Cajun coffee.

My jeans wrap their wet legs around my knees. I dry my hands on my thighs and zip up my jacket. Even the tip of my nose is chilled. "Is this where the glyphs are?"

"A little farther on." He's digging into his bottomless backpack again. "Feel like tanking up? Must be getting on toward noon."

"Noon? What's noon?"

Throwing me an approving look, Russ breaks out the thermos and hands me a cup of coffee. My frigid fingers wrap around its warmth. As I bite greedily into a sandwich and wander around, my headlight illuminates anything I turn my head toward.

The stream dribbles out of a deep pool with water so clear that light bounces off the sides ten or fifteen feet down. Beyond it, my beam falls on a cluster of sculptural shapes like twisted sagebrush. I hop the stream to investigate.

"Helictites," says Russ. "Ain't they beauties?"

The bizarre form sprouts from a low ledge in the wall and stands chest-high. It seems to grow on a central branch, like a coral, but from there spreads out into tiny humanoid shapes, each three or four inches long, like something dreamed up by William Blake. Their smooth and curvy arms, legs, shoulders, and haunches wind in grotesquely convoluted poses. I can't tell if the figures are climbing or falling, but there is the distinct look of arms reaching upward.

Then I know. Purgatory. That's what it is. All those suspended souls pleading for mercy, for another chance.

A cry leaps from me into the darkness, and Russ is beside me in a heartbeat. "It's a crime how grief can sneak up on you like that," he says gently.

I nod blindly and turn my back on the apparition, leaving it to disappear once more into the primordial darkness. Perhaps I only dreamed it.

Or perhaps it dreamed me.

Russell turns to the back of the room,

aiming his light into a cleft in the wall. “We have to squeeze through here, then do a little climbing.”

“Aw, shucks, no more crawling?”

Russell’s breathing is the only answer, or maybe it’s the walls of the cave exhaling. I follow the crunch of his boots until he makes a steep right turn, and then we’re walking on something like soft turf. Ahead, the lights show a spilling wall of mud blocking the passage.

“Careful,” he says, “it’s slick. Put your feet in the toeholds.”

“Did you make these?”

“No. They were here long before me.”

The mud is soft and silky, like the clay slip on a potting wheel. There are no handholds. My calves clench as I balance on the balls of my feet in each miniature cave of a step.

“This cave used to fill up with dissolved limestone during the spring floods,” says Russell, his light reaching far back into the shadows. “Over the centuries it silted up the walls. It’s always cool and damp in here, so the clay stays soft.”

When at last I reach the top, I again have the sensation that there is nothing left of the world but this rock that surrounds me, nothing but this moment. And when my headlamp falls on the wall beyond, I see the glyphs.

A narrow room stretches black beyond the powerful beams of our lights. At first glance it looks as though a succession of kindergartners has been given free graffiti reign on its walls. I turn slowly to my right, my beam dancing over lines, circles, and squiggles cut into the walls of the same silky mud we've just crawled up.

"Basically it's just like it was seven hundred years ago, when they drew the glyphs," says Russell. "A natural art gallery as long as a football field."

Awestruck, I follow the wall, flashing my carbide up and down. Arcs, lines, and squiggles, drawn with a stick or a finger, all with a vigor, a passion, an energy that leaps out of the clay. I can almost see the artist rubbing and poking and stroking the clay, working hurriedly, urgently, before whatever vision is driving him down here into the guts of the earth can fade from his sight.

"Who did all this?"

"Probably Indians from the Mississippian Period — most likely members of the Southern Cult Dallas culture. Maybe ancestors of the Creeks or Cherokees."

There's a throaty burr to Russell's voice, as if he's caressing the information. "Check out this snake."

I shine my light along reptilian curves that slither down the left mud wall. Its entire length, maybe fifty feet, is decorated with complex layers of design — parallel squiggles, concentric circles, free-form undulating lines ending in a small circular head. The snake's tongue laps out at the darkness to get its bearings, to test the environment, to find its way.

No downfall of the human race in this serpent. No threats, no punishments. Only a searching, a questing, a getting closer to the answer.

"It looks like this cave was used strictly for ceremonial purposes," continues Russ, his hands punched into his pockets, "or even just for a simple recording of spiritual experience."

A large winged figure, almost as tall as I am, holds me spellbound. It has a long rectangular body decorated with parallel lines, loops, and holes. Above that is a melon head with huge half-moon ears. Its eyes are holes jabbed into the clay, each with an inverted V-shape extending below it. A large, vague, oblong mouth, which looks as if it has been poked at in anger or frustration, cries out at the violation of the darkness.

"Why all this poking at his face?"

"I have a few theories," says Russell beside me. "Who needs eyes down here anyway?"

"Like the crawfish."

"Right. And he doesn't look like he has a hearing problem. Maybe it's about listening."

The arms are sets of parallel lines on either side of the body, raised in a graceful arc toward the roof of the cave, as if pointing or praising or simply acting upward. The whole figure has an airiness to it, a floating à la Chagall, that invites me to rise along with it like a child's lost balloon taking off for the unknown skies. What is it up there he's reaching for? And what is he doing way down here in the dark?

I move slowly down the wall, trying to find my way through to the questions. There are profiles that look like the half-moons of children's drawings, some with tiny bodies walking or running beneath them. There are geometric figures, rectangles filled with abstract designs, and graceful arches as if imported from some Gothic cathedral, some with a Picassoesque dismantling of elements.

I'm filled with the import, the weight of what my eyes are taking in. Yet each drawing is only one person's record, what one person left behind of what he knew. He may have been a holy man, a seer, a medicine man, yet he was still mortal and has long since perished. Was he so different from the rest of us, or did he just put more effort into the search?

"Tell me what Daddy told you when he brought you here."

Russell's hand swipes across his face. "He told me to try and think what it was like to come all the way down here with nothing but a cane torch — he even lit one that he'd made. The flickering light somehow brought the figures to life, sort of like the early silent films. The most amazing thing."

Russell's chest heaves noisily in the dark. He squeezes my hand hard before he goes on.

"I remember he told me to think about these figures, to try to dream about them, and above all to listen to them. That's all I've ever tried to do. That's where the answers come from."

I squat in the middle of the chamber,

trying to listen. Switching off my carbide, I stretch out on my back. The clay is cool and welcoming, and my helmet lamp shoots up to the rocky ceiling until I reach up and switch it off, too. From the far end of the cave, Russell cuts his lights, and the blackness closes in and presses on my skin.

The silence whooshes around my brain, but I know the figures are there in the void and I'm not afraid. I fill my lungs with heavy air as damp as the clay beneath my back.

As I breathe out, it feels as if my lungs have decided to keep on expanding. In fact my whole body is pressing outward, filling like a huge balloon in a Thanksgiving Day parade. My molecules spread until they bump into the ceiling, and I'm somewhere among them but also everywhere, caressing the silky walls and the figures and the floor all at once.

I'm afraid to move for fear of breaking the spell, and yet the floating is discomfiting.

Russell switches on his light. "You about ready to go?"

I pop like a pricked balloon, reluctantly shrinking back into my body. I don't know what just happened to me, but I hate to have it end. I feel as if I'm not just *in* the cave, but have *been* it.

My head wheels as I sit up and cut on my light. "OK?" he asks. I nod in silence.

He lowers his head so his lamp shines full on my face. "And now, Frances Marie, there's something I've been saving to show you."

"What now?" I ask dizzily.

"This way." He leads me back past the footprint I saw at the beginning, to the entrance to the gallery. Reaching for my hand, he kneels and aims his lamp at a tiny corner of the wall. My eyes work at focusing on the small figure he's pointing out, a miniature of the other, about the size of my hand. An oval head, a rectangular body, arms reaching upward, "weeping" eyes, legs planted wide apart. At its heart is a series of concentric circles, a spiral.

"What is it?" I ask. My voice reverberates behind me and through the opening ahead.

Russell shines his beam. "Look," he says, his voice again a stage whisper.

I lean closer. Three tiny geometric symbols — no, letters — inscribed into the soft clay wall at the junction of the entrance and the floor. I catch my breath. J.F.A. John Franklin Aldren.

"He did this?" My voice has gone trembly. "When?"

"When he was a boy and didn't know any better. I think he was mighty embarrassed by it when I found it twenty or so years ago. He was ashamed of having defiled this place — asked me to wipe it out for him."

"Oh, no. I'm glad you didn't."

"I know what he meant. It's just this kind of thing that can put big question marks on the authenticity of a site."

But I see the sweet motherless boy earnestly incising this picture into the clay and giving it his name so that he might belong. The figure is staring at me with its big round eyes, its heart a swirling vortex that would pull me into its depths.

A painful pressure bears down on my chest, and the hollow cavern roars in my ears. I drop to my knees and reach toward the figure in the silky clay, as if to scoop it up and swallow it. It would ride around inside me and I could chew on it, gnaw at it like a dog at a marrow bone, until I understood.

Chapter Ten
Concentric Circles

Sloshing back on hands and knees through the tight tunnel of rock, we let the cathedral and cave of the glyphs settle back into their ageless void. I am humbled and silenced by where I have been, and the daylight that glints up ahead seems harsh and cold.

Crawling through the last opening into the broad mouth, we emerge into the stippled light of day, which turns out not to be cruel after all but late-afternoon hazy. A fine warm rain is falling, and the tang of wet green leaves mingles with the thick humus of the forest floor. On the ledge, with the dark and secret wisdom of the cave at my back and the surface of the earth before me, I stretch my arms up toward the soft gray of the sky.

As the truck jostles us back the way we came, I ask my childish question again.

"What do you think happens to you when you die?"

Russell keeps his eyes on the winding road ahead. "I don't know, but I'm pretty sure it's good."

"You mean if you've been a good person?"

"Ah, there's the rub." The truck bounces over the narrow road zigzagged with long shadows. "All I know is there's some kind of system, some kind of checks and balances — maybe karma, maybe reincarnation, maybe heaven and hell."

I study his jagged profile. "How can you be so sure of that?"

He looks at me to see if I'm serious. "Just look around you. The whole thing's an intricate system, so minutely engineered we can't even begin to guess how complex it is. Look at these trees. We need oxygen; they need carbon dioxide. We breathe in what they breathe out, and vice versa. It's all interwoven. I'm sure the plan is just as elaborate for when we die."

The trees nod in agreement. "Well, the fact that we die, we rot, we furnish nutrients to the soil — that makes us a part of the system." I'm not sure if I'm just playing devil's advocate or not. "Plus we're carried on in our children."

"Whoa, is this the Catholic convert talking? Don't they teach you any better than that?"

"It was a conversion of convenience, I assure you." I tuck my chilled fingers under my armpits. "I remember when I was little and came up against the idea that God gave us life just to take it all away. I used to lie awake at night and imagine myself in a coffin, rotting. It still seems terribly cruel, doesn't it?" No answer from Russell. "I feel like I'm back there again, asking those same questions. I mean, I'd like to think we live forever. I'm just not sure if I really believe it, deep down."

He squints into the low sun that peeks out from under a cloud, his silence egging me on.

"So if there's a heaven and hell, what about suicide? The Catholics call that a mortal sin."

"Screw the Catholics," says Russ vehemently. "That's bullshit."

My wet jeans rub on my sore knees. "How do you know?"

Russell pulls over to the side of the road and lays his arm on the back of the seat. "Uncle Frank has not gone to hell, Frances Marie."

"Maybe he's in purgatory, suffering until

he's purified and makes amends."

"Oh, please."

My shoulders hunch. "It's possible. Checks and balances, like you said."

Russ lays his hand on my knee. "Frannie, if anybody deserves a happier place after this life, it's him."

"Why do you say that?" I stare at the groove between his eyebrows. "A lot of people have hard lives, and they don't all go around killing themselves. That's certainly not part of your system. Why couldn't he just get over it — whatever it was? I mean, look at the people in Kosovo or Afghanistan or Sierra Leone — now *they've* got something to complain about. You don't see them committing mass hara-kiri, do you?" Heat rises to my cheeks and I yearn to be back in the blissful darkness of the cave.

Russell looks out the window into the gathering dusk. "So you've decided your father was just weak?"

"Well, that and depressed. I mean, a little Prozac probably would've fixed everything."

He shakes his head. "That's a foreign language to the folks around here. Pioneer stock. They pride themselves on being able to weather anything without help."

"I wouldn't say that worked very well for Daddy, would you? And besides, he wasn't from here anymore."

Russell swings his eyes at me, their whites glowing in the fading light. "Is that what you really think?"

"It's been fifty years since he left."

He reaches for my hand. "Honey, this place never leaves you. If you've grown up here, that rolling horizon is burned onto the backs of your eyeballs. I'm sure it was like that for Uncle Frank."

"So the best years of his life were here? Gee, thanks. I like to think of the birth of my children as a high point in mine."

"That's not it at all" — *a'tall,* he says, impatience seeping into his voice. "It's just that whatever it is you learn as a child is what you take as the standard. And I think you're always yearning to go back to it. You know how much it meant to him to come home and visit."

"Yeah, I know." It's my turn to look out the window. A fat squirrel arcs its body, followed by its tail, along a low branch, then makes a flying leap onto the branch of the next tree a good five feet away. A leap of faith, I'd say. "Then why the hell didn't he just move back?"

Russell glares at me. "It's not that simple

and you know it." His voice cracks in irritation. "Why don't you give him a break? A little compassion wouldn't kill you."

His smugness galls me. "Goddamn it, Russ! It wasn't your father who killed himself. It's easy for you to keep him up here on this caveman pedestal. You have no idea how it feels for him to abandon, to betray you. So don't go preaching goodness and mercy to me!"

His head ducks toward his scrawny chest. "People kill themselves in all kinds of ways, you know. His was just a little more obvious than most."

I glare at him, then swerve my gaze out the window again. "Would you just drive?"

Russell puts the truck in gear and swings back into the road. My head hurts again, all across the right side of my skull. Soon we're pulling up the lane to Aunt Lena's. He opens his door and comes around to me, putting his arms around my shoulders in a hug that's warm and sweet. It feels good, but I don't want to cry, so I break away and busy myself with untying my soggy boots. My strength is suddenly gone, and my fingers can't remember the motions to untangle a shoelace.

Inside, Aunt Lena's wide smile and the

brightly lit kitchen stab at my head. Excusing myself, I take three aspirin and crawl into the dark bed upstairs.

Turning onto my back, I put a pillow over my face. The soft feathery weight of goose down covers my mouth. But the old gray goose is dead. If I don't move my mouth soon I will run out of oxygen. I leave it there as my chest and throat start to tighten. A panic begins in my solar plexus. Then something like a gag reflex chokes my throat, and I yank the pillow from my mouth and turn on my side.

The firefly tree stares at me reproachfully, most of its little lights having turned in for the night. It sends some fresh oxygen my way and I blow out some carbon dioxide, but I'm in no mood for mystical rhetoric. The headache slams into the side of my head with renewed vigor, and I hug my knees to my chest, pull the sheet over my head, and retreat into total darkness.

I am moving through the tight tunnel again, coming out in the glyph room. There is Daddy's stick figure glaring at me with cartoon eyes, enormous ears, and those weeping marks like a sad clown. The flickering light brings him alive in jiggling jerks like a loose-jointed puppet. He's reaching upward because my father is under the ground and wants back out, regrets what he's done, wants another chance. He begins clawing at the mud. . . .

Gasping myself awake, I lunge for the fresh air at the window.

The bright sun painting the horse pasture doubles my regret at leaving, except that I'm going home to see my son.

"About the other day," says Aunt Lena. "I know I talked out of turn. . . ."

"Don't be silly. You don't know what it's meant to me to be here. You and Uncle Lex and everybody — it's been like a balm to my soul."

"I wish you could come to church with us. Everybody'll want to see you before you go."

"You'll tell everybody goodbye for me," I say gently. "Have you gathered the eggs yet?" She shakes her head. "Mind if I do it?"

"There's the basket." She points to a rusty wire globe hung on a peg by the door. "Just watch that old banty rooster."

I step outside and turn my face to the butterscotch sun, taking in the smells of livestock, green fields, and family. I check out the garden, Aunt Lena's tomatoes a good month behind the ones I left at home. The corn is chest-high, the pole beans' tendrils greedily grasping the neat trellises.

My eyes adjust slowly to the dark recesses of the chicken house. The hens make suspicious clucks and glance nervously at one another; the rooster is nowhere in sight. I reach gingerly under the ruffled feathers for the warm fruits of their wombs. Or do chickens have wombs? Whatever they have, I thank each of them for the gorgeous eggs in shades of tan and brown, and turn to leave.

That's when the rooster emerges from the shadows, his puffed-up plumage glowing iridescent red and green. He charges me, first on his feet, then with a flying leap. Ducking through the door just in time, I close it behind me.

"Good for you, old boy," I say through the slats. "You keep on watching out for your wives and families."

The kitchen is filled with the warm baking soda scent of biscuits, but Aunt Lena sits at the table wiping dust off a rectangular wooden box. She sniffles, then looks up and motions me to her.

"Here's something I think should go to you, honey child, being as the good Lord didn't see fit to give me a daughter. It was your grandma's."

I look from her to the box. Its grain is dark and marbled, with the initials M.L.A. carved in the top and stained black.

"It was Mama's. Daddy made it himself and give it to her on their first anniversary."

I stare dumbfounded at this piece of family history from the grandmother I never knew.

"Go on, open it."

I swivel the tiny latch and lift the lid. A snug tray fits inside, and under that lies a treasury of mementos from another time: mini Christmas cards, pressed flowers, children's drawings, baby teeth, and tiny snips of silky hair tied in bits of ribbon.

"Aunt Lena, I can't take this — it's too precious."

"Go on now. I'll warrant Mama would want you to have it."

I pull out a small scrap of yellowed paper. In a beautiful flowing script is written:

This is the day that the Lord hath made.
Let us rejoice and be glad in it.
MATTIE LAWTON ALDREN

My fingertips caress the richly grained

wood, the inlaid initials. "Thank you, Aunt Lena." I clench her soft bulk before she pushes past me to rescue the biscuits.

I glance back at the blurry figures waving sadly from the porch. At last I trust my voice long enough to say, "Could you take me by the cemetery on the way out?" Russell, my chauffeur to Nashville, turns dutifully down the dirt road and waits by the truck as I climb the rutted hill to the lines of graves.

The red dirt is still raw over the long rectangle, and I drop beside it, willing the grass to cover this place quickly, reaching roots deep into the soil to take hold and prosper on this uncommon compost.

There's no more melodrama in me now, just a need to sit beside my father and remember his presence in this world. The hills roll off in the distance, blue-green under a soft blue sky. I breathe in the scene, the light breeze, the sun's warmth on my face, and it's not peace that comes to me, but the knowledge of a peace that perhaps I'll be able to find. I tell him goodbye and walk back down the hill.

We turn out onto the highway to Nashville, people rushing by in cars in such a hurry to get wherever their day is taking them. I wonder if I'm ready yet for the real world.

"I'm sorry about yesterday, cuz," says Russell. "I had no right to light into you, especially at a time like this."

"It's OK, Russ. Small price to pay for what you gave me. That cave was one of the most exquisite experiences of my life."

"Watch out. It'll hook you."

"How often do you go back down there?"

"Not as often anymore, what with the kids and all. But it's always right here" — he touches his temple — "and I tap into it all the time. You'll see how it is — it kind of haunts you." When he smiles, the crow's-feet deepen around his eyes. A few yesterdays ago we were kids running the fields together. I wonder how long it will be before we see each other again.

The horse farms whiz by, their miles of pristine white fences holding back fields of minty grass and gracious, long-legged quarterhorses. Too soon we're following the city signs to the airport.

"Don't come in with me," I say as Russ pulls over to the curb. He nods and gets out to hoist my bag from the pickup bed. A skycap hovers as I fish out my ticket with shaky fingers. "Thanks. Thanks for everything." I bury my head in Russ' shoulder and his long arms come around me.

"It's going to be OK, Frannie," he says, pulling back to look into my eyes. "Just go forward."

I nod and turn away. In the light-flooded airport, I move through the line and board the plane with my fellow human beings, each of whom has a story to tell and losses to count. I store my grandmother's treasure box in the overhead bin. Then the big jet bird soars into the heights as the sweet hills of Tennessee roll themselves up behind me.

Part Two

Igneous

Igneous rock is rock formed by the hardening and crystallization of molten material that originates deep within the earth. This material, called *magma,* is usually a mixture of liquid rock, gases, and mineral crystals.

Chapter Eleven

Home in This World

Following the rivers west and south, I finally land back in Louisiana, where I started. But before that, my journey began in the Rocky Mountains, and before that my ancestors dug roots deep into the hills of Tennessee. A great triangle that I run around this summer like a dog on a track.

J.P. waves eagerly from behind the plate-glass wall of the airport terminal, and I can't help but smile. J.P., who never met a day he didn't like — how I envy him that. He looks so solid in his compact frame, so sure of his place in this world. He watches my approach, and then his arms go around me.

"Ah, there she is." He plants a kiss on my lips, which I do my best to return. "Let me go get the car," he says, "and I'll come back for your bag." I nod, happy to have someone to look after me.

Trailing behind him, out the automatic

doors and into a solid wall of heat and moisture, I struggle to take in air, to orient myself into this place, into this life. I have the feeling that, though I'm standing here clutching my suitcase, I'm lost somewhere between here and there.

Soon his red truck pulls up to the curb in front of me, and when I climb in, J.P. pulls me by the waist until our bodies are pressed together. "I'm taking you to Don's for dinner," he says, kissing my cheek. "Would that cheer you up?"

At my answering nod, he puts the truck in gear and hits the streets.

Don's Seafood and Steakhouse, which claims to be Lafayette's original Cajun restaurant, is an old and trusty standby in the regional cuisine battle. I follow the waitress to a small table under a print of a plantation house under moss-draped oaks, but J.P.'s been snagged by somebody he knows and is laughing loudly across the room. What's so funny? I wonder.

J.P. finally arrives and orders us vodka martinis, which arrive in huge tumblers adorned with painted-on crabs and crawfish.

"Here's to my baby coming home," says my husband, clinking my glass. I take a stiff gulp and immediately feel the oily taste mixed with the salty olives hit my bloodstream, the muscles of my legs.

"So you had a good visit with Aunt Lena?" J.P.'s sun-browned skin looks nearly as dark as the paneling behind him.

I want to recount my days, the peaches, the visit to the cave, and the great gift of the box. But the task of doing it all justice seems impossible, and I don't have the steam.

"I'll tell you when I'm rested," I answer. "What about Neville?"

J.P. swells with pleasure. "He gets in at three tomorrow afternoon. T-Will and Vera are having a barbecue for him. Then I figured we'd take him to the camp for a couple of days, really take our time like the old days."

"Great," I say, but am thinking how I hate to share my son with the whole family on his first night home.

I take in a ragged breath and try to calm my nerves. It must be the flight, the weather, and everything else that's happened since I set foot here last. Maybe a fishing trip is just what the doctor ordered.

"Got any lump crabmeat?" J.P. asks the waitress as she offers a plate of hush puppies.

"Honey, I got enough crabmeat to feed the legislature," she answers, pulling a pencil from behind her ear.

"Now you're talking, Joyce," says J.P., reading her name tag. "That's your favorite, huh, babe? I'll have the frog legs. And two cups of seafood gumbo."

Suddenly I'm starving, and can already taste the chunks of white crabmeat sautéed in butter. "Uh-huh," says J.P. "You're hungry for seafood. They don't have that where you've been."

"No, they don't," I say with a smile, popping a warm hush puppy into my mouth.

After bread pudding and thick black coffee, we're out into the night. The temperature must still be in the upper eighties, and the heavy scent of ginger blossoms cloys at my overloaded senses. The stars I saw so clearly a few nights ago are veiled in the humid air.

As we pull into our gravel drive, J.P. keeps saying he's glad to have me back, but I'm not sure I'm here at all. The soybean fields are shrouded in the dark, but I know they're there, dense with knee-high plants, each one sinking its roots into this fertile alluvial soil, midway through the cycle of flowering and fruiting and dying to make way for the next generation. And there sits my home in this world, full of the stories of the four of us, mixed in with the stories of J.P.'s relatives and the others that lived there before us.

Pistache comes out from under the house and practically pees on himself at my return. As I kneel to rub his favorite spots, he regales me with a look of such adoration that I feel guilty for all the days that have gone by without my giving him a passing thought.

"Hey, save some of that for me," says J.P., lugging my suitcase into the house. Yes, he adores me, too, as long as I rub and scratch him in all the right places.

The house — my house — smells of cypress wood and coffee and years of sweat equity and daily chores. It welcomes me back as the door closes behind me and J.P. steers me into the bedroom.

His hands are warm and sure as they trace their usual routes over the pleasure spots of my body, and for a moment I have a sense of being present and whole. But as he joins his body to mine, even as my body responds to the sudden thrill, I seem to split away until I'm floating on the ceiling, spying on a scene of two strangers in the bed.

J.P. doesn't seem to notice.

* * *

Vera's at the door the next morning by the time I pour my second cup of coffee. J.P. went off with T-Will to buy meat for the barbecue, and I'd hoped to have a few minutes to myself. But Vera's hug is like a warm chocolate chip cookie.

"I know it's early, but J.P. said you were up," she says, looking fabulous in a yellow shorts outfit that complements her dark skin and eyes. She cups her hands on the sides of my face. "You look like you've been run through the cotton gin."

"Thanks a bunch." I laugh.

"Hey, nobody said losing a father doesn't take its toll on you." Vera's father dropped dead of a heart attack at the race track a few years back. She pours herself some coffee and sits across from me. "So tell."

I still don't have the fortitude. "Oh, God, Vera, I don't feel like talking about all that now — I'll tell you later, I promise. It's too good to be home."

Leaning back, I run my fingers through my long, scraggly hair.

"You need a haircut."

"Did you bring your scissors?"

"No, but yours will do. Want me to?" Vera is the official family stylist, having been to beauty school before she married T-Will and took up bookkeeping for the construction firm.

I pull a long strand in front of my eyes. Boring. "Yeah. And I want you to cut it short."

"You're kidding, right?" Just what she's been wanting to do for years.

"No, I'm not kidding. I'm tired of being me."

"Ooh," says Vera. "What'll J.P. say?"

"Don't get cold feet on me — it's my hair. Besides, if we hurry, we'll be done before he gets back."

"Are you sure?"

"I'm positive. Cut it really short. But cute."

Vera's eyes widen. "Like Halle Berry? That'll look fabulous on you. Wanna put a new rinse on the gray, too?"

I think of a woman I saw in the Denver airport. She was about my age, but her hair was gone mostly gray, which gave her a nobility and surety that kept me staring at her. "Nope," I decide on the spot. "I've earned these gray hairs, every one of them. I'm not going to hide them anymore."

"I'll have to work on that one later," sighs Vera. "Sit right where you are. I'll be back before you can change your mind."

She rummages through the bathroom and returns with towels, shampoo, scissors, clips, the dryer, and a can of mousse. She washes "them" — my *hairs,* that is, since Cajun English kept the plural version of the French *les cheveux* — in the sink, then expertly parts and clips it into sections.

A little *shoomp* and a clump of my plural hairs falls to the floor. *Shoomp. Shoomp.* Vera won't let me look in the mirror till she's done. A blast of cold air from the ceiling vent hits my bare neck. She works her way around my head as piles of hair build around me on the floor like the winter coat Pistache sheds in the spring.

She palms on some mousse, then turns on the hair dryer, twisting and fluffing sections with her fingers. When she finally stands back to survey her handiwork, a smile spreads across her face. "Come on," she says, pulling me up and into the bedroom. She puts her hands over my eyes until I'm standing in front of the little vanity that belonged to J.P.'s grandmother. "Ta-da!"

I suck in a little gasp. Standing before me is someone I don't recognize, someone cooler, thinner, maybe surer of herself than the woman who usually looks back at me. My hands go up to feel the lack of hair on my head. Vera's left little wisps down the nape of my neck and in front of my ears, but the rest is short, really short, releasing the bit of natural curl that's been weighed down for years.

"I love it!"

Vera lets out a breath of relief and claps her hands. "You look mah-velous, dahling. And at least ten years younger."

"Oh my God, I can't believe this." I ruffle my head as if I'm rubbing in shampoo, and it still looks the same. Vera gets a big hug. "Why didn't I let you do this ages ago?"

She rolls her eyes and grins.

J.P. hasn't yet recovered from the shock. All the way to the airport he keeps throwing me glances and saying things like "My wife won't like me sleeping with you tonight." I have to keep touching my new coif and looking in the visor mirror.

In the terminal we stare out the same glass windows where I spotted J.P. yesterday, and watch each figure as it emerges from the door of the small prop plane. At last comes the one I'm waiting for, and my hand clasps my mouth to stifle a cry. Dressed in his fatigues, his hair cropped close to his skull, he's tall and long-limbed like my side of the family, but with J.P.'s dark hair and eyes, and that squareness in the trunk that looks so steadfast.

Neville raises his eyes and sees us, gives us a big wave. J.P.'s arm goes around me as we wave back, and I see my husband surreptitiously brush at a tear in his eye. I kiss his cheek and help him wipe it away. And then Neville strides through the security checkpoint, looking at once like the boy I raised and like a stranger whom I can't quite place. The three of us do a group hug, mother, father, and the fruit of our womb and loins grown into someone who is of us, and yet is himself and no one else. The magnitude of it could blow you away.

I wish I could sit down and look into Neville's eyes, touch his cheek, hold his hand until I know who he is again. But J.P.'s herding us down the escalator to the baggage claim, patting Neville on the back over and over, telling him about the barbecue, the camp, the fishing forecast. And for the first time, in the face of Neville's robust youth, I see the years showing on J.P., see the crinkles at his eyes, the lost elasticity of his skin, the tiniest hint of a stoop to the shoulders. My hand goes up to feel my hair, as if the simple act of cutting could have stopped the seepage of time.

"You've got a new hairdo, Mom," says Neville. "I've never seen you with it short. It looks great."

"Yeah, she snuck around and did that this morning. Don't know what's gotten into her."

Neville puts his arm around my shoulder. "Change is good," he pronounces unexpectedly. I look up into his tanned face. "How you doing, Mom?"

"Fine." I nod. He hugs my shoulders and pats me as if I were the child here. That thought makes me smile.

Neville looks too big for his old room, for the house he was born into. Fortified with cool glasses of tea, we move onto the porch and Neville sits beside me on the swing.

Pistache, abruptly switching loyalties, has attached himself to Neville's leg and is staring up at him with moony brown eyes. Neville scratches him and calls him "old buddy," making me wish I could be as overtly adoring as the dog. We make small talk about the house, the crops, the heat. The enormity of what there is to catch up on in one another's lives seems insurmountable, so we communicate through the most mundane of topics.

Our glasses are barely drained before J.P. is urging us to get ready to go to T-Will and Vera's. "Is this OK with you?" I ask Neville. "You've barely walked in the door."

"Sure," he says, with a wink that says he gets my drift. "Might as well do it now. I'm anxious to see everybody."

We walk down the road in the retreating heat and turn in at Vera's yard. Her flower beds are manicured to perfection, and the smell of Jack Miller's barbecue sauce wafts over the breeze. We're soon spotted, and a horde of Broussards swarms around us, hugs and kisses given all around. Mom Broussard, T-Will and Vera, Paul and Connie, all the nephews and nieces, assorted cousins and aunts and uncles and godparents — every one of them looks respectfully at Neville and sorrowfully at me. Suddenly I want no sadness to intrude on this reunion, and take my clue from the pink-and-yellow four-o'clocks planted alongside the porch. It's time to be happy.

I can't help but compare this scene to my last family get-together, Mom and Mitch and me at odds around a chichi restaurant table, with the fourth side of the table empty always and forevermore. Watching the commotion centered around Neville, I am grateful that my children have this shelter, this web woven of all these interrelated lives that they can fall back on, wherever they may roam.

I've gnawed the last sparerib clean and licked the crumbs of fried okra from my plate. Across the yard Neville rubs his belly, and I wonder what he's been eating for these last months, looking at what kind of view, with what kind of people for companions.

The men lean back in their folding chairs as the women dump paper plates and tablecloths into trash bags and troop inside with the leftovers. I find Mom Broussard in the living room resting beside the cane she's taken to using since I last saw her.

Over the years my mother-in-law and I have reached a truce of genuine admiration and affection. While at first she distrusted me immensely on the grounds that I, an *Américaine* and non-Catholic, was taking away her favorite son, I have, little by little, worn down her defenses and forced her to get to know me. My greatest triumph was the oil portrait I gave her for her seventieth birthday, which she keeps hanging in her living room. I like to think she has now modified the template for the perfect wife for J.P.

"I tell you, Frannie, this diabetes is a curse."

"Not feeling too good, huh, Mom?"

"No, no. My doctor says I got to stick to my diet or I'm gonna lose dat toe." Mom has never quite adjusted to English, the foreign language she was forced to adopt in her traumatic first days of grade school. Hers was the generation of Cajuns that was made to feel ashamed of who they were, a trend only recently reversed when the food and the music began to gain national attention in the 1980s.

I shake my head sympathetically, then reach for the plate in her lap. "I better get rid of that lemon cake for you then."

Seeing my stifled smile, she playfully slaps my hand. "Not on your life! Sit down. I got to talk to you." I obey and take the recliner beside her. "You got the prayer plant we sent?"

I nod dutifully, though unless someone else remembered it, it was abandoned at the Denver parlor of funerals. "And thank you for the novenas."

She nods. "Now tell me w'at happened wit' your daddy."

I stare into her dark eyes, not sure how much she knows.

"Did he kill himself like they say?"

I wince. "Yes, he did."

"*Cher pitié*. That's a shame. Why he did somet'ing like dat?"

I pull in a breath of air-conditioned cool. "He couldn't find a way to get happy, I guess."

She lifts her plump hands and drops them back onto the arms of her chair. "Happy, huh? What's dat got to do wit' it? The *bon Dieu* don't say life's going to be easy. But when He takes something away, He always gives us something in trade. Not right away, maybe, but sooner or later."

Before my fumbling brain can come up with a reply, she goes on. "Me, I done lost J.P.'s daddy, and my *chers vieux* Mom and Pop" — her eyes lift to the ceiling — "and my sisters and my brother, and so many of my friends I can't count dat high. But I got all you children and all my grandbabies and before long maybe some great-grandbabies. It's never the same thing, but I t'ink it evens out the scale."

She pats my hand. "I'm sorry about your daddy. But you got J.P., and you got those two beautiful children. And just you wait, *le bon Dieu* will make it up to you in time."

I give her soft cheek a kiss and take her plate to the kitchen.

Outside, the party's still in full swing. Vera has lit citronella torches all over the backyard, and a kissing cousin has brought out an accordion. Neville leans on a post in the fuchsia shadow of a crepe myrtle.

"They're about to wear me out," he says.

"I tell you what. One quick dance with your old mom, and we'll sneak on home."

His teeth shine in the shadow. "You got it." He spins me out on the patio in moves nearly as smooth as his father's.

"I still find this hard to believe," I say into my son's chest. "It hasn't been long enough since you were learning to walk. Or since I was your age, for that matter." Neville chuckles, but I know he doesn't believe me. He'll find out soon enough.

When the song ends, we sneak out of the circle of light and into the darkness.

I'd hoped for a mother-son talk, but Neville's quit trying to swallow his yawns. With a bear hug and an "It's good to be home," he goes off to bed. I find myself with the solitude I'd wished for earlier in the day.

The bottled-up air-conditioning makes me feel cloistered, so I douse myself with insect repellant and head for the front porch. Pistache cuddles up to me as I sit on the top step. Faint strains of accordion music drift from the party down the road as the stars glow feebly through the Gulf Coast humidity.

As if in accompaniment, a mockingbird sets up singing in a nearby bush. They say mockingbirds have a song of their own, but amuse themselves by imitating others, often with a repertoire of up to fifty songs. As its clear voice veers wildly in the dark from one song to the next, I chuckle at the thought of it adding the accordion to its bag of tricks.

The things that have happened are jumbled into a giant tangle in my mind, and I'm too tired to figure them out. Instead I slip into a place that is as narrow and as wide as each breath I pull into my body. It's as if I've fallen into a gap between yesterday and tomorrow, a gap where nothingness is the rule. I am simply sitting, the porch boards under me, the tree in front, the stars above, and there is nowhere and nothing besides this moment.

It seems a long time before J.P. strolls up the drive, whistling a waltz, without seeing me on the shadowed porch. I do nothing to get his attention, unwilling to break this unexpected spell of peace. He follows the drive to the back of the house, and from a great distance I hear the toilet flush, lights click on and off, and then silence.

At last the mosquitoes break through my defenses. I pull myself back into my fingers and toes and muscles and skin and, patting Pistache, go inside to lie beside J.P.

Chapter Twelve
Chain Reaction

Soon after sunup we are trucking along I-10 headed east. Beside me, J.P. is electric, charged with the great pleasure of the adventure. He greeted me in the dim dawn with a cup of his special wake-up brew, sweet and so strong you could stand a spoon in it. I tried to roll over and go back to sleep until Neville's voice in the next room propelled me to my feet.

Now he sits on my right in the pickup, not as wired as his father but alert and large, a male animal in the prime of life. I like it here, sandwiched between my two men.

Neville's smile encompasses the pale sky, the fields of tall sugarcane, the tranquil Bayou Teche as we cross its muddy waters. The exit off the interstate takes us winding along the levee, the great mound of dirt erected by the Corps of Engineers to try and tame the snaking currents that flow through Louisiana. Despite the levee's bulk, the waters are forever threatening to go their own way, to reassert their rushing wills and obey the laws of nature.

The town of Butte LaRose sits on the edge of the great Atchafalaya Basin, its name probably testament to some small rise that had great significance in this sea-level landscape. The people here look as if they've been formed from silt and fish emulsion, patted into stocky rubber-booted forms and fired in the sun. The narrow road is lined with a colorful assortment of camps, from the makeshift to the grandiose, with names like "Paradis," "Lagniappe," and "Papa's Pad When Mama's Mad."

J.P. turns onto the canal-side drive of what must be his favorite place on earth. Sandwiched between a faded aqua trailer and a stilted cypress one-roomer that barely clings to terra firma, J.P.'s "camp" is really a docked houseboat that he built in his early twenties. Its original plywood walls are covered now in white vinyl siding, its deck glimmering with a new coat of marine paint.

"Wow, you've really spiffed up the place, Dad," says Neville.

"You ain't seen nothing yet," says J.P.,

beaming. “Let’s unload the truck and I’ll show you.”

Crossing the shaky gangplank, I pull open the screen door and duck into the cabin. The usual smells of dead fish and stale beer have been replaced with the tangy scent of Pine-Sol, and all surfaces fairly gleam in the morning light. The bunked beds are freshly made, the linoleum floor is spotless, and even the windows have been washed.

I turn a smile on J.P. as he hauls in an ice chest.

“What you think?” he says.

“I approve.”

“I had to have something to do while you were gone,” he says.

Neville smiles from where he’s stowing gear under the bed. “Thanks for this, Dad. This is just what I need.”

As I set to unloading food into the cabinets and stashing the ice chests under the counters, J.P. practically dances out the door and toward the back of the boat. “Now for the *real* surprise,” he crows.

After a moment, the crank of a motor makes Neville and me exchange a look of surprise. It coughs a few more times before sputtering to life, and Neville lets out a whoop. “I can’t believe it, Dad. You rebuilt that old engine?"

"You bet your bippie I did. We're going cruising, son." J.P. throws it into reverse, and the bank begins its retreat. Soon we're chugging past the fringes of civilization and into the open water of the Basin, our valiant vessel churning the deep at a good ten miles per hour. Thankfully the bass boat is in tow behind us, just in case.

Neville throws back his head and howls, "Ai-eee!" J.P. beams.

The huge expanse of view and the thick warmth of the air fill my lungs. Long-legged cypress trees topped with feathery limbs mirror themselves in the water, reaching out to the jagged remnants of their brethren who fell under the logger's ax during the clear-cutting fever back in the twenties. The gentle slant of sunlight turns the weathered stumps into exotic sculptures. In the distance runs the pale ribbon of Interstate 10, suspended on improbable concrete legs over the venerable secrets of the swamp.

"I never come out here without wishing I could've seen it like it once was," laments Neville. "You could drive a car into some of these stumps — the trees must have been hundreds of years old. It's hard to believe they needed lumber that bad."

The Seven Generation Rule would've covered that. "We never know what we've got until it's gone," I offer.

J.P.'s teeth gleam into the breeze. "I thought we'd tie up at Beaver Cove," he says. "Then we can take the *bateau* from there."

Neville nods, pure happiness shining from his eyes. But something else flickers behind them, and I wonder what story he has to tell, and when he will tell it.

J.P. backs us into a deep cove, causing a chain reaction of turtles plopping into the water from fallen logs. Dropping anchor, he fills a small ice chest with sodas and throws in a bag of chips, then loads the fishing gear into the bass boat. "You coming, Mama?"

I know they need some time together. "You guys go on — I've got some reading to catch up on."

The two of them, so alike but so different, climb into the boat. "Suit yourself," says J.P. "We'll be back before lunch."

I reach into the ice chest for a Coke, and head for the swing hanging from the square porch. The stack of magazines that accumulated in my absence lies unopened as the last ripples of the boat's wake smooth themselves out, and stillness descends on the little cove.

I find myself sitting on the edge of the deck, staring down into the thick brown water, sunlight sparkling off its surface. They say this basin's water used to be clear, that it had its own filtering system. But now the Atchafalaya has lost its self-purging habits and silted up, making solid ground a relative concept.

The turtles begin to reemerge from the depths, clambering slowly back onto fallen logs smeared with bright green algae. Turtle Island is what some tribes call this planet, Mother Earth having been formed by a turtle who volunteered to let the otter pile mud onto its back until the land was born. Thank you, turtles, for that — life is slippery enough as is.

A great blue heron, its long neck preceding its arcing wingspan, cuts through the thick branches and lands just inside the trees. It takes in my presence and the houseboat with a dispassionate black eye, then rises into the air again and disappears.

The water beckons me, draws me down, as if I could curl into it and sink to the bottom. What the hell? There's no one around and J.P.'s not here to tell me I'm crazy.

I slip out of my clothes and off the side.

The murky water is surprisingly warm, only cooler deep down where my feet stir up the depths. Keeping a wary eye out for snakes, I make a cautious circle around our floating refuge. I can't see below my buoyed breasts, and the thought of creatures lurking in the depths sends a shiver through me. But the water feels good sliding along my skin, as if it would wash away the recent past and leave me cleansed and holy.

Braver now, I try sneaking up on some turtles, two huge ones and a baby lined up on a broken log. The big ones lunge forward and disappear. The little one turns its bullet head on its leathery neck and eyes me, in defiance or fear I can't tell. But it makes its decision and hangs tough on the log.

Turning back to deeper water, I make several wide circles around the boat until my breath runs out, then emerge onto the man-made solidity of the houseboat, ready to sprout the buds of limbs and adapt my gills into land-locked lungs. It's hotter now, but my skin is cool, and suddenly I know that even a fixed concept like summer heat in Louisiana is only relative.

* * *

The sandwiches are made by the time I hear the *putt-putt* of the outboard motor and step out to greet my returning tribesmen. Their catch is meager but their spirits undaunted as they wolf down lunch and sprawl on the double bunk beds to sleep off the midday heat.

I wander back out to the front deck, sweat trickling down the sides of my rib cage. The turtles, no fools, have retreated to shady logs. The swamp lies still as a bleached-out negative, stunned by the white heat of midday.

Something fidgets inside of me, keeping me from sitting still. Finally I make my way around back to the flat-bottomed bass boat. It's been a while since I've driven one, but the well-tuned motor purrs to life. My hand takes the rudder and remembers the backward trick of steering in the opposite direction from where I want to go.

I putter aimlessly for a while, back down the canal toward Butte LaRose, mesmerized by a flock of egrets overhead and by the shimmering heat. When a shady cut to the left beckons, I nose into an opening barely wider than the boat and so overgrown that branches fumble for my face, causing me to duck one way and then another. J.P. would say you're never supposed to drive under an overhang, that a snake could drop in and bite you before you know what hit you. But fool that I am, I keep going.

My skin soon cools in the deep shade. The motor runs barely above idle, and my rudder hand quickly learns the subtlety of movement needed to thread my way. A brown commotion a few yards ahead turns out to be a huge owl awakened from his slumber. He lights on a branch farther on and turns his mud-colored head to eye me, taking off again in a huff as I near. We play this game of tag for a while until he veers off into the thick tangle of woods and out of sight.

A sharp turn, and the cut opens into blinding sunlight glancing off the surface of a narrow lake ringed by a dense jungle of vegetation. With no fellow humans in sight, I am just another link in the food chain, a member of the gang, a piece of the picture, like the mullet that hurls itself sideways across the water.

Duck blinds dot the area, a few deer blinds on what passes for dry land. The heat is so oppressive that if I think about it, I have trouble breathing. Pulling into a little cove, I cut the motor and drift into shady stillness.

Drowsiness seeps through me, and I stretch out awkwardly on the life jackets in the bottom of the boat, soaking the seat of my shorts in fishy puddles of water. The faded sky seems far away compared to the willow branches that droop their narrow, delicate leaves over me, and a trumpet vine with bold orange flowers blasts its color from the treetops. Tiny yellow-and-black birds flit across my vision, and three renegade egrets fly in formation high above.

The boat bumps the bank beneath a large cypress, whose trunk narrows gracefully as it reaches for the sky. A chunk of the top has been sheared off, by lightning or disease, but replacement parts are busy making up for the damage.

I raise my head to peek over the side and find myself in a miniature forest of knobby cypress knees decorated with water hyacinth, whose pale violet blossoms belie their rampant choking growth. A whisper of ripples turns out to have a head, then a long body arcing slow S's. I find myself staring into the black eyes of a water moccasin.

Before my heart has had time to finish lurching, the snake swims past me, around the back of the boat, and disappears.

Lying back in the boat to catch my breath, I find myself snorting with relief, then laughing out loud. Now this Eden is complete, this primordial ooze from which indeed life must have originated. The very earth here is composed of the slow piling-on of generations.

The impulse not merely to survive but to prosper, to multiply, to triumph is so strong here as to make the idea of the self-destruction of any individual an unheard-of possibility.

J.P. suppresses his irritation at me for going off by myself, and in his boat. But he's forgotten it by the time the late-afternoon haul is cleaned and dipped in corn flour and the oil is heating over the butane burner. He kisses my neck as he hands out cold beers to go with supper. Neville, though, seems so serious, so preoccupied, that as I heap our plates with fried fish, cole slaw, and French bread, I try again to get him to talk.

"What do they eat in Kosovo?"

He shrugs. "Stews and potato pancakes, mostly. So much of the land was blown to smithereens, it's hard to tell what their normal life used to be like."

"Well, just hurry up and get the whole damn thing settled so we can get you boys out of there," says J.P.

"The big boys could have pulled us out a long time ago if they wanted, Dad." Neville shakes his head slowly over his plate. "I think, as long as we've got an excuse, we'll stay there. The Balkans are a pretty plum piece of real estate — all that Caspian Sea oil, mines, refineries. . . ."

J.P. puffs up like Aunt Lena's rooster.

Neville looks him in the eye and subtly squares his shoulders. "I know what I'm talking about, Dad. It's not nearly as cut-and-dried as they want you to believe. Look at the strategic location between Europe and the Mid-East."

"I'm sure the military brass know what's best," says J.P., his voice gruff.

"Oh, come on, Dad. They can tell the press anything they want, and nobody's going to contradict them. Now we're in there backing the Kosovo Liberation Army, and the crimes they've committed in revenge are just as bad as anything the Serbs did."

J.P.'s eyes narrow, and his voice comes out in a strange hush. "You shouldn't even be there if that's what you think," he says. "You're a danger to your fellow soldiers."

"My fellow soldiers don't need me to put them in danger. We've got our own government for that job. What used to be Kosovo is now a litter heap filled with our leftover cluster bombs, and depleted uranium, and the mess in the Danube that affects everybody downstream. I can't believe the American people have fallen for the whole sham."

My ears ring as I stare at my son. "Depleted uranium?"

J.P. leans toward Neville. "Now what are you talking about?"

The veins on Neville's temples stand out. "You haven't heard this yet? The U.S. military in its infinite wisdom is tipping bullets and tank shells, even land mines, with radioactive material — depleted uranium from the leftover tailings of uranium mines and power plants. The government's found a cheap way to dispose of a huge problem back here at home — just give it to the military. It makes the ammo denser, heavier, so it goes through tanks and armor like a knife through butter."

Neville punches the air with his fork. "On impact, when the stuff burns, it oxidizes and releases particles of radiation onto whoever's anywhere around and downwind. It contaminates the air, the food, the water — probably for generations to come. And it's *us,* our country's valiant fighting forces, who got prime exposure to it. They didn't even bother to tell our boys to stay out of the zones where they dropped the stuff."

J.P.'s face has darkened.

Neville presses on. "It's true, Dad. I wish it weren't, but it is. If you question it, they tell you it's 'depleted,' so there's no radioactivity to it. But that's bullshit. They used it in Desert Storm, and they *know* it's part of the Gulf War Syndrome. The guys who fought over there are dropping like flies with cancer, leukemia, kidney, and reproductive problems, you name it — and a lot of it won't show up for another fifty years or so. I'd been hoping to pick Granddad's brain about it. . . ."

The sweet taste of life has deserted my mouth. "Are you certain about this, Neville?" I ask, though I know from the grim surety on his face that he's telling the truth. He only nods at me, but when his eyes lock on mine, my stomach churns with dread.

"What's being done about it?"

Neville lets out a frustrated puff of air. "Oh, there's been studies and reports. But mostly it's one big human experiment, and nobody really knows what the long-term consequences are, to human health or to the environment. The Europeans are pissed at what it did to their forces. Meanwhile we're selling the DU to the rest of the world because it works so fucking well. . . ."

"That's enough, Neville!" J.P. barks. "Until you've finished serving your tour, you suck it up and do your duty."

Neville sets his plate carefully on the deck and stands. "Thanks for listening, Dad." He strides past us and down the side deck. Shortly we hear the bass boat's motor spring to life, and Neville roars past us, leaving the houseboat rocking in his wake.

The crisply fried fish eye me coldly from their platter.

"But suppose he's right, J.P.? Why would Neville make this up?"

"Don't *you* start, Frannie." J.P.'s anger is rare but vehement.

I'm taken aback by his stance. I'd forgotten how opposite our opinions were on the subject of Vietnam, how J.P. would have joined up straight out of high school if not for a slight heart murmur. By the time we met, it was so obvious what a fiasco the whole thing had become that it never was much of an issue between us. But a prideful strain of soldiering runs through the Broussards, all the way back to the ancestor who wounded Sherman's first lieutenant in the Civil War. And he's always been a sucker for patriotic rhetoric.

But that doesn't mean he's right, and it's an argument that's more than theoretical if Neville's life and health are at stake. I force a calm voice. "We don't have a great track record of looking out for our own soldiers. And this one just happens to be our son. Why would he make this up? Can't you at least hear him out?"

J.P. stares into the dusk.

Darkness has long since settled over the swamp and the nearly full moon risen high when I hear the hum of the boat motor and feel the houseboat sway. Beside me J.P. snores softly as Neville washes up and climbs into the bunk above us. The old mother's worry antennae satisfied of his safety, I drift off to sleep in a blitzkrieg of swamp sounds, mostly deep-throated bullfrogs and owls hoo-hooting to each other across the water.

Sometime later, in the deep of the night, I wake to Neville climbing down the bunk ladder and sliding open the screen door. I extricate myself from J.P.'s nocturnal grip and follow him out. He's rocking gently on the swing.

"Can I join you, son?" He smiles and pats the swing beside him. I can't help it: I cup his face with my hands and give him a kiss on the forehead, wishing for all the world I could make it all better like I used to. "I don't know what to make of what you told us," I say quietly.

"I didn't tell you everything, Mom," he says. I catch my breath. "I'm involved with a girl over there — her name is Aida. She's half French — from her mother — but her father's ethnic Albanian."

It takes me a minute to remember that, in this case, the Serbian Christians were the bad guys. Which means we're talking about a Muslim.

"I'm in love with her, Mom. And I've got to get her out of there."

I take my son's large, callused hand in mine, surprised to find his palms sweaty. "How did you meet her? You wrote us that you weren't allowed to have much contact with civilians."

"We're not supposed to. But I'd been sent out to the countryside on minefield duty, and she was doing a story on it. She's a journalist, one of the few who had the guts to stay behind and keep broadcasting during the worst of the war. She — she's beautiful and passionate and brave. And Mom" — he heaves a breath and turns to look me in the eye — "she's carrying my child."

I stare dumbly at his mouth as his words hang in the thick air between us. Finally, as they sink in, my arms reach out to enclose Neville in a large embrace.

His shoulders shake with the weight of unleashed tears.

As the moon dips low in the water and the owls tire of their conversations, Neville tells me he means to marry the girl. Then he'll try to get her a green card and send her back to us until he gets out of the service. "If you'll consider letting her come home, that is."

My mind resists. After all, we just got the house to ourselves. But I give myself a shake. *That's your grandchild you're talking about, fool.* A tiny new life — my grandchild — riding around in this girl Aida's belly, as if we are joined like a set of Russian nesting dolls, one inside the other inside the other unto an eternity of generations.

Neville watches my face closely, so I take a deep breath and say what's on my mind. "Son, are you sure you want to marry the girl and not her cause? You sound pretty taken up by the politics over there. And are you sure she doesn't just want that little green card?"

A little smile cracks his austerity. "No, and no, not a chance. Just wait till you meet her, Mom. You'll love her — she's a lot like you."

Tears spring to my eyes. "Wow, there's a line if I ever heard one." Though from the sounds of it, I'm not even on the same planet as this brave girl who risks her life for her principles.

Neville squeezes my hand and stares into my face.

"You know we'll take care of her, Neville. Although you haven't exactly gotten off to a good start with your father."

Neville's head droops. "I know it, Mom. It just pisses me off that half the reason I went into the service was to fit the myth of the Broussard fighting man. I had to find out the reality the hard way, and now I'm stuck."

I shake my head. "You made that decision, Neville. You can't blame it on anyone else."

He looks up at the fading stars. “I know, I know. But why won’t he even listen to me?”

“Because that’s the way he is. But tell me how you plan to get this girl — Aida, I mean — over here.” I roll my eyes. “And a Muslim, the way things are these days?”

“I don’t care how things are. She’s a person, not a religion. . . .”

“Listen, Neville, you’re going to have to cool off if we’re going to get anywhere. Just because you’ve gone off and learned another reality doesn’t mean people around here have. Cut them some slack — it’s the only way.”

He nods.

“Now what’s the plan?”

“I was hoping I could get the chaplain to marry us before I left, but he has orders not to perform any weddings over there. So it might have to be a Muslim wedding on the sly. . . .” He looks sideways at me to gauge my reaction.

To his astonishment, I burst out laughing. “Won’t we be an ecumenical bunch? The Broussards had a hard enough time with me being a Protestant!” But inwardly I groan at the trials ahead for my son. “What will it take to get her a green card?”

"Get who a green card?" Neville and I start in fright.

J.P. is standing at the screen door.

Instinctively I try to think of a way to cover for Neville. But like the man that he is, he opens his mouth and delivers the news. "I'm going to be a father, Dad. And I want to get my girl out of Kosovo."

My heart suspends its beating as J.P. rubs his eyes, then the stubble on his chin. "What the hell are you talking about now?"

Neville briefly repeats what he's told me.

"And you want to marry this girl?" J.P. asks incredulously.

"Yes, Dad. And not just because she's pregnant," says Neville. "Although that does make it a little more urgent."

"Jesus Christ. Didn't you ever learn where babies come from?" J.P. turns back around and disappears inside.

Horrified, I wish I could rewind the moment and cover my ears so as not to know this about my husband. But I do. And I can find no words to cover the gap between us.

The pain in Neville's face doubles my own. I can only think to be practical, and repeat my question, "What will it take to get her a green card?"

"That's what I have to find out this week." Neville's voice sounds crushed. "I guess I'll start with the Immigration Office in New Orleans. But I can't do anything till we get married."

I pat his leg. "I'll do whatever I can to help, but I have to finish up in Colorado."

"Thanks, Mom. I knew I could count on you, at least."

I take a stabilizing breath. "Don't get me wrong. I think you've chosen a hard road for yourself — not the one I would've wished for you. But since it seems to be your road, all you can do is keep to the straight of it."

His forlorn expression breaks my heart. "You know what your grandmother told me?" I offer. "She said when the good Lord takes something away, He always gives us something in trade. I lost my dad, and now you're making me a grandmother."

He hugs me and goes off to bed.

It's not till I'm by myself that I realize what the additional churning going on inside me is. Besides Neville's bombshell, and J.P.'s appalling reaction, it's my blood boiling from the idea of our own military putting radioactive particles into the air, particles that may traverse the frail uterus that's incubating my grandchild.

Particles that my own father may have helped extricate from the depths of the earth.

Chapter Thirteen
Holy Water

The next day J.P. wakes up declaring that the trip is ruined and we're going home.

"J.P. . . ." I venture.

"Don't talk to me about this, Frannie" is his curt reply.

As the three of us line up in the pickup, it feels as though we've divided into two against one. Something fundamental has shifted. The joy of the monumental knowledge that I'm going to be a grandmother, added to a growing fury at my husband, fear for my son's welfare, and my fresh grief, has formed a wild roller coaster of emotions.

Soon after we get home, Neville takes off for New Orleans. On his return, he confides to me that it's not going to be easy, either with the military or the immigration red tape, to get Aida out of Kosovo. It's not hopeless, though, and I can see his eagerness to leave mounting as the days wear on. When he's not sleeping, he gets together with all his old friends and goes out to the bars.

J.P. stays away from home, too, working from sunup to sundown. Ping-ponging back and forth between the emotional extremes of outrage and commiseration, I try to keep busy cooking, cleaning, and going to movies with Vera, to whom I say nothing of our family rift. Meanwhile I make my return reservation to Denver for the same day that Neville has to leave.

J.P. will have to work it through in his own time; there's no rushing him. The same stubborn boundaries that have kept the Cajun culture safe from the reach of outside influences for several centuries sometimes keep it locked in its own myopia as well, and there's nothing I can do about that. After all, that's part of what appealed to me about the man in the first place.

My studio beckons, and at last I face my fears and open the door to the enclosed side porch. The air conditioner in the window drones on, beating back the fierce heat.

Having no clue where to begin, I decide to go back to basics, rooting around until I find a nub of charcoal and an old drawing pad, which I prop up on my easel. My hand hovers indecisively until I take pity and give it permission to do anything it wants, regardless of the outcome.

The charcoal begins to move in slanted vertical swings, putting down two long parallel lines, which then become a rectangle. Above that it draws a large melon-shaped head, adding big half-moon ears like the cartoons of G. Dubya Bush. Then eyes atop inverted V's like tears running down its face, and an elongated mouth. My cheeks flush with the realization of what is emerging onto the paper.

Two sets of parallel lines arc up to become arms reaching skyward, and crude wings give it the air of rising like a child's lost balloon taking off for unknown skies.

As I stand back to survey the picture, I am as satisfied with it as with anything I have ever drawn.

Suddenly I know what to do with my grandmother's box. Opening its inlaid lid, I carefully place the nub of charcoal in the tray over the precious treasures, then add in my favorite paintbrushes. Last, from my purse I retrieve the winged maple seed from the John Franklin tree, wrap it in a scrap of blue velvet, and add it to the brittle souvenirs in the bottom of the box.

On Saturday I join the short line of the faithful waiting to make pre-Mass confession to Father Préjean. I step into the small room at last, grateful for the screen between me and the priest.

I don't feel like confessing anything. In fact, I've come here for answers. My mouth opens and closes like a baby bird greedy for nourishment until finally I get it out. "*Mon père,* my father recently took his own life. I was wondering where you think he is now, in heaven or in hell? Or in between?" In the place where bodies writhe in supplication?

There is a heavy silence, followed by the sonorous voice asking, "Was he in a state of grace?"

How should I know? "He wasn't a churchgoer."

"The Church has taken a compassionate stand on this issue in recent years. If he dealt in his last moments with the sins of his life, if he made his peace with our Father, he may have avoided purgatory."

"Then he could get into heaven?"

"That is not for the Church to decide, my dear."

"But you said the Church has gotten more compassionate. Does that mean God agrees?"

"I would not presume to speak for God the Father."

I look at the shadowy profile of this member of a profession that's made a tradition of harboring its own bevy of child molesters. "But you do presume to speak for Him all the time."

After a shocked silence, the voice goes on in a studied calm. "My dear, perhaps you would like to schedule a visit with me at a time when we could discuss your doubts at length."

With a flash of blinding surety, I know that it's not for this mortal man, or any other, to sit in judgment of my father, to forgive him or to bless him. It's between him and his maker.

"Yes, maybe so. Thank you, Father."

But I know he's not my father.

I dip my fingers into holy water, touch it to the cross of my body, and steal into a pew midway down the nave. The kneeler clanks onto the floor and I am on my knees, humbling myself in the vastness of what I don't know. I half listen to the Mass and am mumbling responses by rote until we get to the Lord's Prayer.

Our Father, who art in Heaven,
hallowed be Thy name;
Thy kingdom come, Thy will be done
on earth as it is in Heaven. . . .

"Thy will be done . . ." Is that what happened to my father? God's will was done to a lowly sinner whose only crime, besides being born heir to Adam and Eve, was to be orphaned, set adrift in the world, and left to feel unloved? Who died by his own garden hose, thereby making himself the one who gave his own strings the final yank? It probably really pisses God off when an uppity mortal decides his own fate. But if my father was a good boy, and turned his eyes upward as the carbon monoxide filled his lungs, then maybe he art in heaven. Otherwise he's caught in never-never land until he finds a way out, and what are the chances of that?

Rancor rises in my chest, and I stand and retrace my steps to the doors, past the surprised glances of my mother- and sister-in-law. I stumble back out into the sunlight, the heavy church door clanging shut behind me.

On my last afternoon home, I concoct a peace-offering gumbo with some shrimp from the freezer and okra, bell peppers, and a few sorry tomatoes that have survived the scorching days in the garden.

I take a bowlful down the road to my mother-in-law to tell her goodbye. After her usual litany of health complaints over a demitasse of sweet black coffee, she levels her gaze at me.

"How come you walked out of church?"

"I — I wasn't feeling well."

"And what's troubling J.P.?" she barks. "He's not himself."

"You'll have to ask him, Mom."

"And Neville?"

I take a deep breath. "I think he's seen too much of how the world really works," I answer, wishing I could confide in her. But Neville asked us to keep his situation to ourselves.

"No, there's more to it than that. He's as lovesick as I ever saw a soul. I remember once when his daddy came back from New Orleans with that same look on his face." She drains her tiny cup. "I knew he was a goner for sure."

Chuckling, she reaches over to pat my hand. "Neville will tell us when he's ready."

When I arrive home, J.P.'s truck is already in the garage. He sits hunched over the computer in the living room. "Come see," he says without turning.

The printer whirs as I peer into the screen. "What is it, J.P.?"

"I looked up this thing about depleted uranium, just to see," he says. "There's all kinds of stuff here. Neville might just be right."

I sit next to him. "Tell me."

J.P. shakes his head. "You sure get two different stories. It's the isotope U-238, leftovers from the nuclear fuel for reactors and weapons after they take out the fissionable U-235. Dense and heavy. The M1 Abrams tank uses only DU-tipped shells and has protective armor made from the stuff.

"The military says it makes our tanks nearly impenetrable, and there's no danger unless you're up close and personal when the shells explode and burn. Then the DU vaporizes into a fine dust that might be poisonous if you breathe it. They've been refining it since the Gulf War. But the other side says it's toxic and carcinogenic — has a half-life of 4.5 billion years. Plus it sure looks like they tried to keep it quiet for a long time, and there's veterans and doctors and Europeans saying there's huge jumps in cancers, especially leukemia, where it's been used."

J.P. takes off his reading glasses and rubs his eyes. "One VA study says sixty-seven percent of kids in Mississippi born to Gulf

War vets have severe illnesses or birth defects."

"And yet they're still playing Russian roulette with it? With our own soldiers?" My blood churns at the thought of Neville's health and that of all his progeny in danger. I wonder what Daddy would say to this turn of events.

J.P. shrugs. "I don't think anybody really knows what it'll do."

Vera and T-Will arrive for supper bringing a fresh blackberry cobbler.

"Hey, Frannie," says my little brother-in-law with the same mischievous grin as my husband, "what's a seven-course meal to a Cajun?"

"I don't know, Will, what is it?"

"A six-pack and a dozen oysters."

J.P. laughs for the first time in days.

Neville doesn't show up until halfway through the meal, and excuses himself as soon as he can get away with it.

Vera and I are loading the dishwasher when she says, "OK, Miss Frannie, let's have it. What the hell's going on around here?"

"What do you mean?" But I know she knows us too well.

"J.P.'s pouting, Neville acts like he's got

ants in his pants, and you go storming out in the middle of Mass."

"I just couldn't handle it — I'm pissed off at God right now. And Neville had the nerve to question our military presence in Kosovo, which amounts to treason in J.P.'s book. Plus Neville and I are both leaving tomorrow, and that's got him all out of sorts."

She says nothing until the last dish is loaded. "I wish you felt like you could really confide in me."

With a quick hug, she's gone before I can answer.

I hear J.P. and Neville deep in conversation as I pack my bag to leave. When J.P. finally comes to bed, he lays his hand gently on my hip and is soon snoring.

The next morning I corner Neville in his room. "Well?"

"Now that Dad's read some official reports about the radiation danger, he's beginning to believe me." Neville looks as despondent as I've ever seen him. "But did he say anything about Aida? Not a word."

I pull him to me. "He'll come around, honey. Give him some time." I only hope I can make good on that promise.

* * *

At the airport I clutch Neville's camouflage-shrouded shoulders as if my mother love could protect him from the danger and pain that lie ahead. I have to force myself to let him go, to release him to step off into his life. He promises to call me at Hannah's as soon as he makes any progress.

Then it's my turn to board the jet. My husband's eyes are dark pools, the irises nearly as black as the pupils.

I take a stab at getting him to voice his feelings. "You know I have to deal with Daddy's house, J.P. — not because I want to. And I need to understand what happened."

He stares at his steel-toed boots, uneasy in the land of sentiment. "It feels like you've turned against me, Frannie."

Tamping down my incredulity, I say, "Not at all, J.P. We have a major situation here, and Neville needs our help, that's all. I'm not going to abandon him now. I'm sorry you think that means I'm turning on you. I wish we were on the same side."

I remember his repressed fear that my stay in his life is only temporary. Added to this is the knowledge that J.P.'s mother never slept a night away from his father in all the years they were married. "I'll be back as soon as I can, J.P. I'll know more after I meet with the lawyer about the will, and Mitch will get there later in the week to help with the house."

He stares into my eyes with an intensity that leaves me feeling naked. Then, with a hard kiss to my lips, he is gone.

Buckled into another plane seat, I reflect on what a different place I'm in from the last time I left home, numb and grief-stricken, the pain so great I could barely breathe. By now the sorrow for my father has settled into my heart, a weighty ache that must make room for the needs of a new generation ahead, a life that carries the seeds of its grandfather into the future.

I can only hope that J.P. and Neville will patch things up. But for now I resolutely leave them behind to deal with my own private calamity.

Late that afternoon I let myself in with Hannah's doormat key, feeling like a rag doll with the stuffing pulled out. Years ago she bought this stone Victorian cottage on a steep street near downtown Boulder, the kind that sells in the high six digits now. The place is every inch her: sunlight pouring in large windows and glancing off impeccable wood floors; fat furniture in vibrant colors, plants thriving at each window. *Cheerful*, it shouts as I make my way to her guest room. With the backs of my eyeballs burning, I close the curtains and sprawl on the futon.

The dream comes before I'm even sure I'm asleep. *Crunching along a dry creekbed through a barren prairie landscape. Red cliffs rising on either side, some jagged and angular, others worn smooth like giant loaves of homemade bread. Shoulder-high sagebrush pulls at my clothing, scratches my face, letting off a sharp acrid scent. A hawk, wheeling in the impossible blue of the sky, screeches at me. The creekbed, dotted with round stones of purple, red, and orange, twists and bends.*

Something pulls me forward toward a destination. Finally the cliffs part, the land opens out, and light glints off the surface of a smooth river in the distance. My feet lead me in a left turn, toward a towering overhang, like a giant sandstone band shell.

I climb shelves of red and ocher rock to arrive at a precarious ledge. The wide mouth of a cave gapes at me. There's something there I want to see, that wants to see me. But as I drop to all fours to crawl into the opening, a dried-gourd-seed rasp stops me. My heart knows what it is before I find myself looking into the face of a diamondback rattler, an arm's length away. Its head is pulled back into the gray-brown S of its neck, its split tongue taste-testing my body warmth.

I stare into the lidless eyes, the jutting jaws, the pits on either side of its head. From the center of its coiled body rises its rattle, shaking now like a metronome gone wild. Still it doesn't strike. My eyes adjust to the dim room beyond, and there on the walls are pictures — still lifes of hunters, big-horned sheep, buffalo. Off to one side, near the bottom, is a familiar winged figure, a signature in code, flanked by the initials J.F.A.

And then I see that the snake is the guardian of this place, and that it will not let me pass. Slowly I crawl backward as if pushing against a resistant membrane, one leg, an arm, another leg. When at last I've backed out of striking range, I rise.

But now I notice the ledge is littered with rattlesnakes, and I must decide whether to stay still or to move. Finally I pick my way through their coiled bodies, warnings shaken at me from all sides. The creekbed, too, is now alive with snakes, as if they've staked out their territory and are herding me back the way I came.

As I retreat, the secret of the cave sits large within me like a newly swallowed egg.

* * *

The shadows are long when I wake, feeling strangely calm. I find my cousin on her deep front porch overlooking the tree-lined street. She motions me into a wicker chair and pours me a glass of iced tea — herbal, of course.

Hannah listens intently as I recount the momentous events since I saw her last — the funeral, the cave, the fishing trip, and finally Neville's big news.

"You're going to be a grandmother?" She throws her hands in the air and dances a little jig.

I grin at her. "I can't tell you how good it feels to say that out loud. But I'm so worried about this depleted uranium business. Is it possible they would really screw around with that stuff at the risk of our own soldiers — not to mention the people that we're supposedly saving?"

"Honey," says Hannah, "I'd believe anything. That weapons plant down at Rocky Flats near Golden has messed up the land for the next couple of millennia at least, and they want to turn it into a park! Nobody really has a clue how much radioactivity it's safe to leave in the soil, but you can bet it's a lot less than they'll admit."

I shake my head in disbelief. "Who

needs foreign terrorists?"

Dabs of light tap-dance between leaf shadows in my lap. Boulderites wheel by in Lycra shorts and helmets, in European cars, in pricey footwear. A kid in baggy shorts that droop on his ass and a tie-dyed shirt slumps by like a scene from another time.

"Why does it feel like the sixties never ended here?" I ask.

"Probably because this is a self-proclaimed never-never land. Anything we baby boomers can dream up to want, the People's Republic of Boulder will supply — gorgeous scenery, state-of-the-art, hi-tech, designer shopping, organic underwear. But you'll pay a price for it."

I shoot her a look, surprised by her cynicism. "At least people here have some sort of conscience about what we have to do to protect the planet."

"Don't kid yourself, Frannie. You could pick your poisons anywhere." She props her feet on the porch rail. "And a jazz festival here wouldn't have half the soul of the one down there. I can still hear those drumbeats, feel the heat — as if life itself was being created."

"I hate to tell you, but life in Louisiana is not one long Jazz Fest. I've never been to another one like the one we went to."

"It was cosmic, for you to meet J.P."

"I'm not sure he would agree with you right now." I chuckle, looking over at my cousin. Her red curls glow in the sunset, her short dress showing off her trim shape. "I've been meaning to ask — how'd you get to be so perfect?"

She turns sharply. "Don't be ridiculous."

"But you are — you're so damned together."

She leans fiercely toward me, shaking her finger. "Listen here, I struggle every single day I live on this earth. And every morning I have to start all over again."

My chin tucks into my neck. "What are you talking about?"

"You want to know what I'm talking about? You really want to know?"

I nod blankly.

She sighs. "I was a freshman in college, but looked older, and I knew a little place where this guy would sell you beer without an ID. So I bought a case, and my best friend, Julie Arnbacher, and I took it way up Left Hand Canyon. She had a couple of joints, too. We proceeded to get totally snockered, and she wanted to go back to her dorm because her boyfriend was coming back from an out-of-town football game. I'd had way too much by then and was barfing my guts out, so she got behind the wheel and we took off down the canyon in my little VW."

Hannah's hand trembles as she waves away a fly. "She swerved wide around a curve, and I saw the lights of the pickup coming at us. I grabbed the wheel and jerked it to the right — into perfect position for the truck to hit Julie."

She looks toward the mountains. "It crushed just about every bone in her body. When I came to, she was a pile of bloody pulp beside me. I had broken a leg and a couple of ribs. The truck driver broke an ankle." A car goes by, the deep bass booming rap music. "If I hadn't grabbed the wheel, we might've gone off the road — or it would've hit us both."

I reach across and touch her arm. "I'm sorry, Hannah. I never knew. I remember you were in an accident, but . . ."

"Oh, I know. You were still in high school." Her cheeks are flushed, her eyes fierce. "My parents didn't want anyone to know."

I wish I had some profound words to offer her. "It could've happened to anybody. We all did stupid things back then."

"Yes, but it happened to me, and there's

no way to undo the harm I've done." She points her finger at me. "So don't you dare say I'm perfect."

She rises and opens the screen door. "Bernie's bringing his famous couscous over for dinner. I wanted you two to finally meet."

He arrives a little later, a tall, slim man with a black-and-silver-streaked ponytail. He smells of ginger and saffron as he and Hannah go into a long embrace. When he turns his black olive eyes on me, I like him immediately. "It's great to finally meet you, Frannie," he says, giving me a hug. "My sympathies over the death of your father." His voice reminds me of dark-roast coffee.

"Thanks." I smile. "It was good of you to let us stay at your house."

He whisks tiny stuffed grape leaves out of a bag and onto a plate. I bite into one, its lemony rice tingling my jaws.

"I can't look at you without picturing your wall of masks," I say, wiping my mouth. "They're fascinating — but disconcerting, too."

Bernie chuckles. "I just think of them as my buddies. They usually have more to do with *un*masking — with being given permission to put on the faces that we would really wear if we weren't so constrained by society and our own egos."

"I liked the three-eyed guy with the snakes coming out of his head. What was his name?"

"You mean Shiva?" Bernie smiles. "That's an interesting choice."

"Why's that?"

"He's a very powerful god — part of the Hindu trinity, the guru of all gurus. His third eye once saved the world from darkness, but he can also reduce wrongdoers to ashes in a flash." He offers the plate of grape leaves, and I help myself. "But since creation follows destruction, he's also a great reproductive power, a symbol of regeneration. The snakes coming out of his hair represent the fertility of the Ganges River."

"And how do you think that relates to me?"

Bernie looks me in the eyes. "Well, your father's death has dealt you a huge blow — basically a destructive act. Life crises often afford opportunities for regeneration."

I knew it — they're going after my spirit. "I think I'm dealing with it pretty well, thank you."

"I didn't mean to imply that you weren't." He adjusts the heat under a big pot of stewed meat and vegetables.

I gulp some fresh evening air from the open window. "It's funny about the snakes," I say as if to the shrimp-colored clouds over the distant mountains. "They seem to be popping up all over the place."

Bernie turns. "They do? Come tell me while this is heating," he says, steering me into the living room.

"I had this dream this afternoon. It was surreal, but so real at the same time." I recount the journey to the snake-guarded cave, which leads me to the real-life visit to the mud glyphs in Tennessee and the water moccasin I saw in the Atchafalaya. Bernie fires questions at me, pressing for details, as Hannah watches him with an amused smile. "What do you think it all means?" I ask shyly.

"I just came back from Peru," muses Bernie. "My teacher there is a Kallawaya shaman. The Kallawayas are an ancient order of healers. They're called gypsies now, but they were doctors to the Inca kings and priests."

"OK, you've got my attention."

"The Kallawayas use basically the same methods as indigenous peoples all over the world. Usually drumming or some other sort of percussion, sometimes with the aid of hallucinogens, to enter an altered state — a parallel world, if you will, where higher information about this world is available. Cultures all over the world tapped into these methods, apparently independently of each other, which to me vouches for their authenticity. Not to mention the dramatic results I've seen."

"What kind of results?"

"A shaman's business is to travel to the nonordinary world to effect changes in the patterns of his patients' lives. They can heal physical, emotional, mental, psychological disorders — you name it, they can address it on a level that no typical Western doctor can even dream of."

"So they go into a trance and fool around in your . . . what? Psyche? Spirit?" I ask.

"Whatever you prefer to call it. It's nothing new. It's all knowledge that our ancestors possessed and that was taken away by the religious and political powers."

"So what does this have to do with my snakes?"

He shrugs. "I could journey for you. Or better yet, you could ask them yourself."

I stare dumbfounded. "Ask them what?"

"What they're trying to tell you. It's very significant that you've had three experiences with them lately. That leaves no doubt that they're trying to get through to you."

I look to Hannah, but there's no hope for sanity in this room. *Help! I'm being kidnapped by old-hippie New Agers!* I can only imagine what J.P. would think of all this.

Bernie goes on. "I'm offering a class next weekend. It's already full, but I'd be glad to make room for you if you're still here. All it takes is a day to learn the techniques."

"OK, Bernie," says Hannah, coming at last to my rescue. "Let's go eat."

I attack the couscous as if I've just woken up from hibernation, relishing every morsel. Plumped-up raisins burst amid the spicy lamb and tomato sauce, washed down by heavy Algerian wine.

Finally, leaving the two of them staring gaga into each other's eyes, I head to my room to sink into sleep, hoping not to meet any snakes.

Chapter Fourteen
Duck and Cover

For the first time since the morning I got the news that my father was dead, the grief doesn't ambush me the moment I surface from sleep. It's more a dark pool off to one side than a tsunami. The windows sit open on the Boulder morning like a Joni Mitchell song, no screens to keep out the bugs and a fresh breeze drifting across my cheek. To my amazement I feel my lips pull back from my teeth. I think they call it a smile.

But it's time to go to Daddy's house. Throwing on some clothes, I head out the door toward the past.

The memory of the smell finds me before I slip the key into the lock, and I wish for a sprightly yellow canary to send in ahead. The scene inside hasn't changed since that day — could it be less than two weeks ago? Since then I'm sure my molecules have all molted and exchanged themselves for a woman much older, weighed down by more of life's tests than I care to study for.

All other realities recede, and I find myself past the desire for solace, utterly alone with these walls and the story of what went on within them.

Gasping for air, I pull open the sliding doors to the backyard, where the sun still shines on the cottonwood trees. Next door is the Stewarts' yard, where their bomb shelter used to be.

"Duck and cover," sang Bert the Turtle cheerfully in the school "safety" films designed to prepare us for imminent nuclear holocaust. They showed a series of ever more terrifying scenarios that we were to take instruction from: a boy in a protective aluminum foil suit riding his bike for the community fallout shelter; a couple strolling down a street suddenly cowering against the side of a building; a schoolroom full of kids looking just like us, diving under their desks as a flash blinds them. "Duck and cover," sang Bert the Turtle cheerfully.

Much as I wanted to, I never bought the line they were feeding us: to duck and cover would protect us from the push of the button. By then we'd all seen the pictures of the skull-littered landscape of Hiroshima and of the survivors, their skin hanging in tatters and their mouths gaping in pain. Deep down I knew there would be no refuge from the fallout if it came.

This ultimate destructive force seems too big a responsibility for mere human political powers, with their inherent self-interest to handle. And how could it be that, knowing what we know, we would wish even a hint of that fate on innocent civilians and our own military? How could immediate victory over the enemy so outweigh the long-term consequences?

But I procrastinate. Back in the kitchen I raise the window to the purgative cross-breeze, then tune the living room television to a soap opera. The sound of human voices cheers me, their melodramatic follies just the right note for this surreal day. I turn it up loud so they'll follow me through the house.

Hannah has provided me with a number of tightly wrapped bundles of dried stalks, silvery-green sage and tough sweetgrass called *smudges*. She claims that burning them — sacred plants, she tells me — will cleanse the house of the chaotic energy left behind from the trauma of Daddy's death.

Now, feeling silly, I open the bag to a

pungent smell like wide-open places, like the vanished prairies, like my dream. Holding a bundle over the stove, I touch the tip to the burner's flame. When the bundle catches fire, I follow the instructions to blow it out, leaving smoke rising and tiny red points glowing on the ends of the stalks. The smoke bites at my nostrils, but I must admit, it does seem cathartic somehow. Like the gris-gris the Cajuns swear by, like the priests dispensing incense on all us lowly sinners.

I shake the smoke around the regimental kitchen. After Daddy's two divorces, all that's left are the bare essentials of an ex-Marine bachelor existence. Nothing that's not functional, nothing sentimental. We can get rid of it all.

I process down the hall to my old room, whose psychedelic yellow hurts my eyes. On the windowsill is the accumulation of chunks of quartz, pure white or tinged with pink or gold, that Daddy used to bring me from his geologic expeditions. Curtains that I tie-dyed myself. Posters of the Monkees and the Beatles, and later Janis and Jimi. My early attempts with acrylics. Peace signs and a lava light and my old gray phonograph. All the now-trite totems of the times.

After lighting a fresh smudge, I proceed through the other rooms, Mitch's beige one, the living room, the bathrooms. And finally to Daddy's bedroom.

The suitcase yawns from the floor, shouting the same question: where was he going? Shirts, pants, underwear, socks, bathrobe. When I stoop to pick them up, I uncover an accordion folder that matches the saddle brown of the suitcase. In it is a bound blue folder, the cover page stamped with a red CONFIDENTIAL.

Its title page is in the secret language of geologists, similar to all the other site studies I've seen in Daddy's lifetime: STRIATIONS OF RADIOACTIVE SHALE IN BLOCK 35, SECTION 114. I flip through the pages of unintelligible text and dotted and lined section maps, none of it making the slightest sense to me. I'll have to mention it to Stan McPhee, his boss.

I wave the smudge like a kid with a sparkler writing her name in the Fourth of July night sky. Above the bed where he and my mother slept away the nights of their joint lives. Inside the closet, over the dresser, around the head of the middle-aged woman who stares back at me from the mirror.

Then my feet lead me again to the garage door. Panic rises in my chest, but my hand is on the cold doorknob and pushing.

From the gloom, the car still leers at me, flaunting its triumph. I stare in feigned defiance at my own personal nemesis, dealer of vengeance and retribution. The air seems poised like a magnet to repel me, or else to suck me in. If there are negative spirits, this is their domain, winking at me from the garbage cans, rising from the snaking garden hose, sticking out their tongues from the backseat of the car.

This puny wisp of smoke won't be enough to triumph over this place. I fight the urge to bolt as I light a second bundle. My feet move forward and I walk around the car, waving my hands like an orchestra conductor. But my mind won't stop. Choking. Gagging. Too late. Gone.

Stumbling back through the door, I throw up in the kitchen sink, then collapse trembling onto the floor. When the wall phone behind me gives a shrill ring, my nerve endings explode.

"Hello?" I sound small and frightened.

"Frannie? Is that you?" Hannah's brisk voice is like a splash of cold water. "How's it going over there?"

I twist the spiral cord around my finger like the teenager I used to be. "I'm doing the smudging like you said . . ."

"Is it helping?"

"It's that damn car. I need a can of gasoline and a torch for that." Feeling weak and foolish, I try to stand. "Don't worry. I'm all right."

"Yeah, right. Don't try to do too much today. Take it a little at a time."

"You know, I think you're right. I've got to go see the lawyer this afternoon. I think I'll get out of here."

I'm ahead of schedule for my appointment with the attorney as I negotiate the canyons of the downtown Denver streets. The gold-plated dome of the capitol building winks in the smoggy air, testament to the hidden riches that have long lured humans to these mountains. Following the secretary's directions, I'm surprised to see that the lawyer's office is in the same building as Aloco's Denver headquarters. If I'm still up to it, I'll have to pay a call at Daddy's old office.

Brandon R. Fowler, Attorney at Law, lives high on the town, not at all the type I would think Daddy would have confided his dying wishes to. His glassy office takes in views of the purple mountains' majesty and the legions of faux–manor homes marching west toward Boulder. Fowler is younger than I, his handshake firm and friendly, his knit shirt surprisingly casual. But something about his too-bright smile, then the immediate frown of sympathy puts me on my guard. He leans back in his leather chair and presses his fingertips together.

"I understand your brother is unable to be with us today?" Light glints off his fashionable wire-rimmed glasses and slicked-back hair.

"Right. He'll be here later in the week, but I understood it was urgent."

"Not a problem. We'll express him a copy of the will. I tried to get in touch with the other beneficiaries as well, to no avail. Your father's will is pretty straightforward." He hands me a black legal folder labeled LAST WILL AND TESTAMENT OF JOHN FRANKLIN ALDREN. I press my lips together. "He left everything to you and your brother except for some nice trust funds for his grandchildren and" — his smile fades a bit — "a tidy sum to his ex-wife Edith Aldren."

It takes me only a moment to smile. "Good for him." This elicits a look over the rim of the glasses. *Don't try to read me, bud. You don't know a thing about me.*

"The urgency came in a small footnote." He flips through some loose papers in the folder. "Do you know someone named John Yellowhorse?"

I shake my head. "Why?"

"Well, your father called my office the week before his demise. I was out of town, but he talked to my secretary and told her he wanted to add this Yellowhorse to his will. He wanted to leave him ten thousand dollars. We drew up the papers, but he never came in to sign them. We have no more information than that, so basically it's a moot point."

"That's a name I would remember if I'd ever heard it — I have no idea."

"Well, we won't worry about it. Legally we're not bound to honor his wishes. Also, just to put your mind at rest, I want you to know that the cause of death is officially accidental. Stan McPhee insisted on this fact, rightfully so, in order to avoid any problems with the insurance policy."

"I see. Didn't the coroner have anything to say about that?"

Brandon Fowler purses his lips and shakes his head. "In a case like this, they can often be persuaded to spare the family further grief."

His words are meant to please me, but

now I really don't like him. I cross my legs and restrain my forked tongue. He walks me through the will, gently explaining phrases that tie themselves into legalistic knots, and then he's done with me, promising to be in touch as soon as the red tape is sorted out. Having shaken his hand and turned away, a ding in my head makes me turn back. His smile goes up again.

"You said you've been talking to Stan McPhee," I say slowly. "Do you represent Aloco?"

"Our firm does a good bit of their legal work. That's how I came to represent your father."

I nod and slowly turn away.

It's as I approach the elevator, lost in thoughts of Brandon R. Fowler, that I recognize the angle of shoulder, then the familiar profile standing in my line of vision, tapping an impatient foot. As he turns his head in my direction, my heart takes a ridiculous dive into the pit of my stomach. Dressed in a classy double-breasted suit, shiny loafers, and a silk shirt is Neil Peters.

Am I imagining it, or did his face just go pale? If it did, he recovers faster than I do. "Frannie — you've cut your hair." He steps over to me and presses the legal folder he's carrying into my back. "You've been on my mind. How are you?"

I look at my toes in their comfortable sandals. My toenails need trimming. "I'm making it, thanks. It's been rough." Slowly it dawns on me where we are. "Is *this* the firm you work for?"

"Yes, why?"

"I just met with Daddy's lawyer. You didn't tell me you worked with him."

"It's a big firm."

The elevator dings. Neil looks at his watch. "Listen, I'm late for a briefing. Going up?"

I shake my head.

He stares at me for a moment before he speaks. "Meet me for a drink after work?"

I look at the gray of the eyes I used to love. "Sure."

He steps into the elevator. "In the bar downstairs at six?"

I nod and raise my hand in a wave. The down elevator arrives, and I push ONE, my stomach lurching with the high-speed descent. I head for the coffee shop as if for refuge from the storm.

The froth of my double cappuccino parts as I spoon in sugar with a shaky hand.

That long-ago spring when I returned from my odyssey to New Orleans, Boulder seemed cold and gray at the tail end of an interminable winter. Even the mountains looked rigid and aloof after the warmth, the scents, the fecundity of Louisiana. And as I stepped off the bus into Neil's waiting arms, I felt myself losing the elasticity that had set into my muscle fibers with the gyrating pulse of that tropical music. Fueled by J.P.'s persistent phone calls and Neil's jealous tirades, I needed only a few weeks to make my decision to go back.

And now here I am living at the opposite end of the spectrum. I traded in the mountains for the swamps, the cold for the heat, the solid granite under my feet for the spongy humus of generations of rampant, reckless vegetation.

Neil next to J.P. — the pricey suit next to the camouflage coveralls; Stanford Law School up against the school of hard knocks; crisp diction versus *cher bébé;* cappuccino or a French-drip pot. I smile into my Zimbabwe brew with a flush of affection for my husband. He's never tried to make himself into anything because he's always liked who he is. Maybe he's got the key to the whole shebang.

So Neil and I will do a bit of catching

up, a little remember whening, and go on about our lives. Hannah would say that fate put him in front of that elevator, and that there's a lesson to be learned today.

Well, come on, karma, let me have it.

Since I have time to kill, I let the elevator whisk me back up to the floors that house the Aloco offices. The plush lobby is filled with large framed photos of offshore oil platforms, refineries and desert compounds — industry cum art. A blond receptionist asks to help me. I give my name, which doesn't seem to ring a bell, and tell her I'm here to see Stan McPhee.

"Do you have an appointment?" Her possessive tone irks me.

"No, but I think he'll see me."

"I'll have to check with his secretary." She talks into her tiny headphone. Her expression changes. "Go right on through," she says with a coy smile.

"Thank you ever so much," I say. *You were still in diapers the last time I was here, honey.*

I wend my way through the labyrinth of corridors to the geology offices.

Stan's secretary, Mrs. Amoss, has worked here for aeons, since the days when Mom used to dress us up for downtown shopping trips. We'd have lunch with Daddy at the Top of the Rockies, a revolving restaurant that slowly rotated 360 degrees as if it were a planet or a moon in its own peculiar sightseeing orbit.

Mrs. Amoss' bouffant hairstyle has changed shades over the decades, now being a crisp ashen blond belied only by her steely gray eyebrows. She hurries around her desk.

"Oh, Frannie, how are you, honey? Look at you — I remember you when you were this big." She makes a vague waist-high gesture. "I'm just as sorry as I can be about your dad. I wanted to make it to the memorial service, but my mother had just had a stroke, and . . ." Her eyes tear up. "I tell you, I still can't quite believe it."

"Thanks, Mrs. Amoss. Is Stan busy?"

"Not too busy to see you, I'm sure. Just let me buzz him."

"Could I surprise him?"

"Oh, I don't see why not." Her face droops. "But first, I have a little something for you." She pulls open a desk drawer and hands me a doorplate. On it are the words FRANK ALDREN. "I saved it for you."

The brass is cold in my hands, but the letters carved into it, nothing more than curves and lines, can attest to the fact that my father once lived and breathed on this earth.

"Thank you" is all I can get out. She blows me a kiss before retreating behind her desk again. Her fingers clacking efficiently over the computer keyboard make me miss the sudden *whooshes* and *dings* of her old Selectric.

I continue to the big office that Stan got when he was promoted over Daddy, who had trained him from a young whippersnapper just out of college. His door is open, and he's staring intently at a computer screen.

"Knock, knock."

He looks up with a frown, then a blank expression, before jumping to his feet. "Frannie! What on earth? Why didn't Mrs. Amoss tell me you were here?"

"I wanted to surprise you. Looks like I succeeded."

"It's a bit hectic. Hang on a sec. Let me get out of this." He pushes keyboard commands and stacks some papers before he comes around his desk to give me a hug. "How'd it go in Tennessee?"

I take the chair he offers. His view can't compare with the lawyer's but at least he has a window. "It was nice, as funerals go. Lots of family and old friends."

"Good, good. How are you kids doing with it?"

I pick at a hangnail. "I think I'm still in shock. But there's lots to be done, so I'm trying to concentrate on that."

"And your mother?"

"She's fine, thanks. I saw Brandon Fowler this morning."

His head bobs. "Everything go all right there?"

"You mean the cause of death? I thank you for that, even though it seems so dishonest."

"Oh, come on. Those insurance companies can afford it. You and Mitch are entitled to your benefits. Besides, the whole world doesn't need to know."

"To tell you the truth, I don't think the whole world cares."

The phone rings, and Stan looks relieved. During his brief conversation, I scrutinize his face. He's got to be in his late fifties, and the years are beginning to tell on him. His carrot-colored hair has stiff competition from the gray, and his freckles are pale compared to the old days when he mostly worked out in the field. He hangs up, folds his arms, and says, "What can I do for you today, Frannie?" I catch the note of impatience in his voice.

"I wanted to know if you can give me any clues as to what brought this on, Stan. I mean, I know Daddy had his bouts of depression, but I never, ever thought he'd take his own life." Stan winces. "You still saw him on a regular basis, didn't you?"

Stan picks up a gold pen. "He did most of his work out in the field, but he came in to the office every week or so."

"Did something happen, was there trouble here at work? Is there anything you can tell me?"

Stan spreads his hands, palms up, as if to receive a blessing. "It came as a shock to me, too. Of course, I know the split with Edith was hard on him. And lots of men go through a crisis when they retire — loss of purpose, that kind of thing. But that's been several years now, and we kept him plenty busy with contract work on those new uranium fields."

"New uranium fields?"

"Yes, ma'am. With the instability of the global situation, uranium's taking an upturn again. There's new activity out west, and if there was anybody who could find it, it was your old man."

The phone rings again, and this time when he puts down the receiver, Stan looks at his watch. "I'm sorry, Frannie. I've got a meeting. Let me walk you to the elevator."

"Thanks for seeing me, Stan." I wave to Mrs. Amoss, who's on the phone.

"Anytime. Wish I could be of more help. If there's anything, anything at all we can do for you or Mitchell, just let me know, you hear?" He pushes the DOWN button and gives me a hug. "Oh, by the way, have you come across anything in Frank's possession that belongs to us?"

"Anything like what?"

"Oh, like a brief, a report he might have had in his briefcase. I'd wanted to ask you, but didn't know how to contact you."

The brown folder full of gibberish in his suitcase. Face-to-face with Stan, I decide on impulse not to mention it. "Good thing I stopped by, then. I'll check for you."

"Get back to me on that, won't you?" The elevator doors swoosh open. He pecks my cheek. "Good to see you, honey. Take care."

I step in, then grab the door as it begins to close. "Stan, do you know somebody named John Yellowhorse?"

Stan shrugs. "Never heard of him."

Chapter Fifteen
Karma

I choose a stool in the upscale lobby bar and order a glass of wine to appease the moths flitting in my stomach. A parade of white collars marches by in variations-on-a-theme suits. Even the women wear pin-striped jackets over short skirts, their makeup elaborate and their hairstyles current. As for myself, high school teacher and backporch artist, I've dirtied my limited number of dressy outfits in the past couple of weeks and have fallen back on basic black out of necessity and mourning. Not so different from my early bohemian days when I first fancied myself an artist, and when I first met Neil.

All the years between then and now present themselves as one endless circle of seasons, of hectic school years and too-short summers. My children have grown, the fig tree has blossomed and borne fruit, and how far am I really from where I started?

With a light touch on my shoulder, Neil steps back into view. "Let's move to a booth," he says, loosening his tie. I follow him to a darkened corner and slide into an upholstered bench that hugs a dimly lit table.

Neil sits just far enough away for me to smell the citrus spice of his freshly applied cologne. The cocktail waitress appears promptly, asking what he's having this evening. "Does Henry make a mint julep?" he asks.

"Why, yes, Mr. Peters," she says, flaunting her cleavage as she sets coasters on the table.

"We'll have two of them — in honor of my Southern lady friend here." Neil turns to me and leans forward on his elbows. "So. How are you?"

"Doing all right. I —"

"Did your meeting with Brandon go well?"

I recall Fowler's fake smile, his false solicitousness. But I guess that's what they do, solicit. "It went fine."

"He's a good man," says Neil. I wonder what his criteria are.

Cleavage comes back with tall, thin glasses sprouting ludicrously large sprigs of mint. I hold up my glass for a toast "to old times," then sip the sweet bourbon.

"Is this what you drink on your veranda at home?" says Neil. If I hadn't once known him so well, I might not notice the touch of malice in his voice. A colleague stops by to shake his hand, and Neil introduces me as "an old friend."

I'm smiling when he finally turns back to me.

"What?" he says.

Another sip of sweetened bourbon. "It's amazing to see you now. So successful. I remember when you decided to go into prelaw. It was a big decision."

He nods. "I've done well."

"You were going to work for the ACLU to defend the poor and downtrodden of the earth."

"Yeah, and we were both going to move to SoHo so you could try out the art scene."

"Touché." He doesn't smile until I do, and I have the sinking feeling this was a mistake.

Finally he leans toward me, his arm on the back of the booth. "It took me a long time to get over you."

My head ducks under his stony gaze. "I'm sorry, Neil. I've thought of you often, wondering how things would have turned out. . . ."

"If you hadn't gone on that trip? Hadn't screwed that guy? Hadn't dumped me cold?"

"Whew." I lean back. "You're still angry."

"I'm not still angry. In fact, you rarely cross my mind."

I stare at him as if he's slapped me. "Obviously this wasn't such a good idea," I say, gathering up my purse. "A battle over ancient history is the last thing I need right now."

But as I move to slide out of the booth, Neil lays a cool hand on my arm. "Don't go, Frannie," he says in the softer, more vulnerable voice that I remember. "I'm sorry. I didn't know there was so much bitterness left in me. It just shakes me up to see you, that's all."

I hesitate.

"I know I've changed," he goes on. "Seeing myself through your eyes makes it pretty obvious. And I'm not so sure all this 'success' has brought me any great pleasure."

There he is, underneath the polished surface: the handsome, earnest, shaggy-haired college kid who could be ruefully honest with himself. I have to restrain myself from touching the little dimple in his cheek.

"All those roads we had to pick from," I offer, thinking of my own kids, "without being able to see very far ahead. And we were so young to be choosing."

"I've never admitted this out loud, Frannie," says Neil, staring into my eyes. "But one of the main reasons I went into corporate law was because I knew you would hate it."

I stare in disbelief, unable to fathom how I could have had such an effect on his life. I'm trying to find something to say when another crony arrives to congratulate Neil on his latest triumph in the courtroom.

When he's gone, Neil bends toward me. "I tell you what — there's a private lounge upstairs where we can talk without interruptions. I'll be good, I promise."

"All right."

In the elevator, I am keenly aware of the hollow in Neil's shoulder where my head used to fit. By the time we reach the top floor, some of the weighty years have fallen away, and I feel young and flirtatious. There's nothing like a guy claiming you ruined his life to make you feel good about yourself.

He ushers me through a door, to which he produces a credit-card key, and into a plush apartment that tries to feel cozy yet smacks of corporate. Not the "little lounge" I was picturing.

"What will it be?" he asks, stepping behind a well-stocked bar.

"Food," I say. Neil laughs and tosses me a bag of pretzels as he selects a bottle from a glass-fronted cooler.

He sets a stemmed glass in front of me and expertly pops a cork. The champagne bubbles catch the early-evening light, throwing little starburst reflections on the glass table. He kicks off his shoes, letting some of the starch out of his demeanor.

"To celebrate what we had," he says. I drink to that.

"What are you painting these days?" he asks, a question which makes me flinch.

"Not much. My art has taken a backseat to my life for a long time now. That was my project for this summer, to get back into it."

"You're kidding. You never used to be able to get through the day without working, sometimes all night. Every time I turned around you were drawing me in that little sketchbook of yours."

I remember that. Back when I knew the trick of seeing. The reality of it hurts under my breastbone.

"But you never did answer my question," he goes on.

"What question was that?" I sip the bubbly as he sits beside me on the couch. Rich, dry. Very expensive.

"I asked if you're happy with that Cajun."

I don't want to see J.P.'s face right now, don't want to think of my life at the edge of the continent. "Yes. For the most part, yes."

"That's too bad." His old smile softens the sharp angles of his face.

"Gee, thanks." I cock my head to one side. "What about you? Anyone special in your life?"

He takes my hand in his as he half nods, half shrugs.

"Tell me about her."

"Why?" He has that little frown above his left eyebrow.

"I'm curious, that's why. I bet she's young."

"Mid-thirties."

"That's what I thought. Let's see, a lawyer, too? Very attractive. Ambitious — almost as much as you are."

"Maybe. She's an assistant DA. Not interested in marriage, and neither am I. Works out great for both of us."

He goes on to tell me about his failed marriage and the ugly custody battle over the son he hardly ever sees anymore. I tell him about Maggie's newfound wanderlust and of Neville's unexpected career in the military, stopping short of getting into the present dilemma. The heady wine sends us chuckling over old times and catching up on news about old friends.

He rests his arm behind me.

"Tell me something, Neil."

"Uh-oh." He laughs. "Sounds heavy."

"Have you had dealings with Aloco?"

He shrugs. "I've done a little legwork for them. Not much."

"Did you ever see Daddy?"

"Nope. Contract law's not my department."

With a sigh of relief, I let the present drop. Instead I zoom backward in time, to Neil's treehouse apartment on the Hill, where I used to stare at the crazy shadows thrown by the sand candle hanging from the bedroom ceiling. Straight out of a bad movie, I lean my head on the back of the couch and look into his face.

He leans closer, his breath on my cheek. When his mouth brushes my lips, a charge zings through my body, and a demanding warmth flares in my groin.

It's been so long. It would be so easy. . . . It's as if I hear someone else saying, "Neil, wait."

"Frannie," he whispers. "Just for old times' sake?"

I'm still back in the space where I loved him. His lips touch mine again, his tongue slipping between my teeth. Here is this man who adored me when I was young and naive and full of spit and promise, who still wants me now, when so much, so much has faded.

But no. I'm no longer that girl.

I wriggle out from under him and stand, my head whirling. "Neil, I'm sorry. . . . I'm so sorry, but I just can't. . . ."

As I watch, pain flits across his face before it abruptly morphs back into that other, harder one. He shrugs. "Oh, well, it was worth a try." His voice has gone dry again. "But you know you wanted it, Frannie. We both know you did."

The truth of his words echoes off the walls as I slam the door behind me.

Emerging into the now-dark and nearly empty streets, I snatch a parking ticket from my windshield and rip it into a million pieces. I can't stop trembling as I drive up I-25, turn west on Highway 36, and pull numbly onto Hannah's street.

Mercifully she's not home, so I head for the guest room and stretch out on the bed. Uncertainty churns in my stomach.

You know you wanted it, Frannie.

My heart has no healthy tissue left. I dive into the dark of sleep.

I wake sometime later to the sound of a phone ringing, then Hannah's head appears in a crack of light from the door. "Frannie? You there?"

"Sort of."

"Maggie's on the phone."

I groan. *Go on, God. Rub my face in it.* Hannah holds out the cordless receiver.

"Mom? How come you haven't called me?"

"I'm sorry, sweetie. It's been a rough time for me — I guess I don't feel much like talking." I can feel her unspoken "Gee, thanks" through the phone. "How are you? Tell me what you're up to."

"I'm great, Mom. I met this guy — Jay — and he thinks I'm the coolest chick ever. I think I'm in love."

I cover my eyes and shake my head. How can I tell her to beware of the pure joy she's feeling?

I can't. I have no right to tell her anything. All I can do is give her a quick rundown of Neville's visit, minus the most crucial information, and beg off with a headache as an excuse, promising to call her back.

Hannah comes in and sits on the edge of the futon. "You OK?"

"You mean besides my life flashing before my eyes? Just hunky-dory."

"Always with the sarcasm."

"I almost made it with Neil Peters tonight."

She takes this in with such equanimity that I'd like to shake her.

"The strangest thing — he works for the same firm as Daddy's lawyer, who also works for Aloco. . . ."

"There are no coincidences in this world."

"Hannah, would you shut up with that crap?" I sit up, annoyance rising like bile. "Anyway, I ran into him, he took me up to a convenient little apartment, we talked over old times — and I could've screwed him in a second. In fact, I really wanted to."

The doorbell rings. "That'll be our dinner. I ordered Thai." Hannah leaves me in the dark.

As I wrestle chopsticks around the pad

thai, I try to answer her unspoken question. "To be honest, I guess I've never totally let go of Neil. I liked having him in the background, as if maybe I could go back if I ever wanted to."

"So you wanted to tonight?"

"It would've been so easy. God, sex was so good back then. He's the first guy who really showed me just how much pleasure I could feel."

"Then it's pretty natural you'd be tempted," says Hannah. "And you didn't do it, so ease up on yourself."

"I guess it always felt sort of unfinished — I mean, I *was* in love with him until the minute I met J.P." I chew a crunchy bean sprout. "So if you can fall in and out of love so arbitrarily, what the heck *is* love, anyway? Is it like a progression of people who meet our needs at different points in time? And if that's it, then maybe we should always be trading up in lovers to go with our presumably growing selves."

"The problem comes when we try to freeze the situation, grasp at the happiness," Hannah says. "Besides, you're assuming that it's someone else who's going to make you happy."

I roll my eyes. "Oh, OK, so I'm going to

become a nun and not need anyone else?"

"That's not what I meant. But just how much is it you're asking of your lover?"

"A lot, I guess." I look out the darkened rectangle of the window. "Sometimes I feel like I've lost myself somewhere along the way. Coming back here has made it all so obvious. That young girl that Neil used to love was so full of promise, so joyful and carefree. I don't feel full of any of those things anymore."

"Why not?"

"You grow up, I guess. Get serious. Get a life." I shrug. "He reminded me how much a part of me my art used to be. And here he is a corporate lawyer. It makes you wonder if any of us were sincere in all our ideals back then — present company excluded, of course." I close my eyes against the truth. "I guess I was just trying to get back to that girl."

"She's still in there, Frannie. But you're the only one who can find her."

"I'm not so sure."

Plunging my hands into the bubbly dishwater, I wish our blunders could be rinsed off as easily.

"The stuff you were telling me — about what happened to you," I say gently. "How do you handle the guilt?"

Hannah nods. "Buddhism teaches that we create our own suffering by clinging to the illusion of the past. Since it's just a memory, the only thing that exists right now is the present moment," says Hannah, wiping a plate dry.

"You mean, like it never happened?"

"No. It's just not here anymore. It's part of who you are, but not to be attached to. I have to accept it and live today for all it's worth. That's what you do in meditation, try to stay mindful of the here and now."

"OK," I say skeptically. "That sounds like a tall order."

"It's hard work, cutting through the ego's constructs. I still work on forgiving myself. I tell you what, though, learning Bernie's shamanic techniques has changed my life. Now I can have long talks with my Higher Self, my teachers, my power animals. They're the ones who help me the most."

"You mean, you really have conversations with them? What, in your head?" I stare in amazement. "So what do they tell you, all these spirits?"

"*They* are really *us* — it's really just an elaborate method of tapping into our own innate wisdom. It's about taking a higher perspective in order to see how things fit into the pattern of your life, your destiny."

"You mean it was your fate for those things to happen?" I scan her face for traces of humor. She looks back earnestly.

"In the accident, some kind of karma ripened on me, which I had done nothing to change. It's a free-will, free-choice universe. We make decisions all along the way, and each choice leads us further down one path or another."

"So destiny has nothing to do with it."

"It's something like this — at least the way I see it: each soul enters this life agreeing to try to accomplish a certain number of lessons. Ideally each lifetime brings us higher up the spiral toward enlightenment. So the opportunities for learning are presented, and it's up to us how we deal with them."

I palm a pile of soapy bubbles. "So in your way of thinking, Daddy's death happened for a reason?"

"Obviously he chose it, based on a long series of causes and effects. And he could have found a better way. But maybe he'd tried all the other doors and found them all locked, at least as far as he knew. And now it's part of *your* destiny."

"Oh, right, he had to kill himself so I

could get enlightened?"

Hannah snaps the dish towel at my backside. "We've all got crosses to bear. But his suicide has changed your life. The choices you have now are different than you had before."

"Do they make allowances for stupidity?"

Hannah laughs. "We can keep repeating the same mistakes for the rest of eternity if we prefer. But that's not what I want, and I feel like I've used up all my wild cards. Now I have to make every action count."

"Oh, is that all? Have you got some magic pills for that?"

"Nope. The only way I've found is to plant my butt on that cushion on the floor and come face-to-face with my own mind. It's hard work."

"I guess it's either that or 'duck and cover.' Sometimes I feel like Bert the Turtle taught me that lesson a little too well."

Before turning off the light on this baffling day, I feel the sudden need to talk to my husband, who, if anyone, is part of the lessons I'm supposed to learn in this lifetime. It takes several rings before he answers in a drowsy voice. I've forgotten it's an hour later at home, and he starts his day at five thirty.

"J.P.? Sorry to wake you. I — I just needed to hear your voice."

I can hear him smile. "It's good to know that." He yawns. "What happened today?"

If he only knew. I recount the parts that I can tell him, my narrative ending at a strategic juncture.

"I talked to Maggie a while ago," he says, waking up now. "I was going to call you in the morning."

"What's up?" I vaguely remember her call earlier, as if in a dream.

"She wants to take off for California with this boy she's just met."

The new love of her life she told me about. I must have cut her off before she could get to this part. "I thought she was short on money."

"I don't care if she has a million bucks. I don't want her taking off like that," says J.P. "We don't have any idea who this kid is."

Or who his daddy is, who his people are. That's the first thing you establish when a Cajun boy comes courting your daughter.

There you have it, the Gulf of Mexico between J.P.'s upbringing and mine. I could probably be talked into letting her go in the name of adventure, albeit with plenty of cautionary advice. But tonight J.P.'s paternal stance seems protective and downright sweet.

"Whatever you say."

"You'll stand behind me then?" he marvels.

"It's your call."

J.P. seems at a loss for words at his easy victory. I myself am concentrating on the warm fuzziness in my chest, hoping that it's not just guilt. "I'll let you get back to sleep. I love you, J.P."

"G'night, Frannie."

As we hang up, I realize that he didn't once call me by the usual "babe."

Now it's my turn to be awoken. Just as I sink into sleep, Hannah's holding the receiver out to me, saying, "It's Mitch." I swim to the surface and back into our turbulent tides.

After cursory apologies, my brother gets to the point. "So what'd this guy Fowler have to say?"

I recall the lawyer's office, the feeling of distaste, the sunlight glinting off his glasses. "He left it all to us, and our kids — a nice trust fund for each of them. And he left some to Edith."

Mitch lets out a gasp of exasperation. "You've got to be kidding me. She's half the reason he ended up like he did!"

"I'm just telling you what's in the will, Mitch."

"How much?"

"Twenty thousand. And another ten to someone named John Yellowhorse. I don't know who that is, but I plan to find out." I make a split-second decision not to tell him that this last bit was an oral request that we're not bound to honor.

A short silence while Mitch's blood pressure rises. Then his words zip through the phone lines. "That's ridiculous. I'm contesting the will."

"Oh, good Lord, Mitch, it's what Daddy wanted. Don't worry. There's plenty for us. He had a good life insurance policy, and he'd been buying stock in the company all these years."

"So you're saying we should just give away thirty thousand dollars without a fight?"

I scrunch my eyes, seeing Mitch needy, always needy, as if a black hole in his belly sucked up all the good that might sustain him.

"*We're* not giving it away, Mitch. Daddy did."

"Not if I have anything to say about it. I'll be there Friday."

That gives me a little time. I fish out my tattered address book and look up Edith's number. It's late, I know, and she probably gets up early on the ranch. Finally her groggy voice answers.

"Edith? It's Frannie. Could I come for a little visit?"

Chapter Sixteen
The Razor's Edge

"Anything to avoid working on your dad's house, huh?" says Hannah as I throw some things into a borrowed duffel the next morning.

I answer with a guilty grin. "Getting a handle on his suicide is every bit as important to me as packing up all the leftovers of his life. Edith just might have a different slant on it."

"Go for it, girlfriend."

I give her a squeeze. "Love ya, cuz. Here's her number in case you need me. I'll probably be back tomorrow."

I'd slept in a bottomless place and woken up feeling as if the air before my eyes had cleared. So when Maggie rang again to plead her California case, I was ready for her.

"Maggie, your dad has already given you an answer."

"Mom," she wailed. "That's why I tried

to talk to you first, but you were so whacked out last night. Can't you talk to him?"

She was so sure of her usual machinations, she couldn't imagine I wouldn't override J.P. "Not this time, kiddo. You're on your own."

"Thanks a lot, Mom," she huffed. "I never should have called Daddy."

"Are you trying to play divide and conquer here, Maggie? Because I'm not in any mood for games." And because your brother has beaten you to the punch, and because there's too much else I'm keeping from your father. I suppose it's never too late to hone my parenting skills — at least I'll have a grandchild to use them on. "Besides, I thought you'd run out of money."

"We have enough for gas. And Jay has friends out there we could stay with."

"You just met him, honey."

"Like you just met Daddy, in case you've forgotten."

Touché. As I said, how do we know when and what is love? "And he told you you couldn't go."

At that, my sweet Magnolia hung up on me.

Now I tank up the car and hit Highway

36 going north. There's a faster way to get there, via I-70 west, a route that smacks head-on into the Front Range. But I've been looking at these mountains from a distance for too long lately. I want to feel there's at least one thing I can get on top of. So I opt for the long high road through Rocky Mountain National Park and over Trail Ridge Road.

In Lyons I turn left onto Highway 7 up the South St. Vrain Canyon, remembering the backpacking forays Neil and I used to make. The road cuts across the Dakota Hogback, rising shelves of sandstone in tints of salmon to maroon. The river runs along the left of the road, at first wide and shallow, but gradually narrowing and deepening, its pleasant babble building to a roar. I'm driving like the flatlander I've become, clutching the wheel and craning my neck to take in the shifting 3-D landscape above me.

Near the top the highway rounds a bend, and suddenly a huge montane vista opens up, a place where Neil used to say Beethoven would have come up with an appropriate chord. And there's the Sleeping Indian.

I'd forgotten about him, one of nature's whimsies. His reclining form spreads over several miles, his well-fed belly the pyramidal bulge of Mount Meeker. His face in profile on Chief's Head Peak has a strong forehead, an aquiline nose, resolute lips, even an eye where the snow hasn't melted yet. A feathered rock warbonnet arcs gently southwest into Wild Basin. To the northeast are his knees, his feet formed by the diminutive Estes Cone. He lies there in his ceremonial rest, buoyed by the legend that when he wakes up, the Indians will take back their land.

On to Estes Park, set in a wide mountain meadow named for one of the first white guys to settle here, as if the Arapahos and the Utes hadn't used it for summer hunting grounds for centuries. What arrogant shits we "Americans" are.

The western end of the main street rises into the stunning beauty that is Rocky Mountain National Park. The peaks fan out in jagged and inchoate splendor, each with its own attitude and personality. My car follows the line of vacationers tilting up Trail Ridge Road in search of unexploited terrain.

At one point the traffic stops midlane for a cluster of bull elk on the side of the road, their antlers jutting out proudly above thick necks, the last of their winter coats clinging in thick clumps to their haunches. Video cameras whir, and a man in lime green shorts creeps toward them, his telephoto lens erect in front of his face.

Finally I climb above timberline, beyond the limits of survival for any tree. The road hugs the sides of the barren moonscape, dropping off into rifts so deep I dare not even try to see the bottom. I forego the RV-infested visitors' center at the top, twelve thousand feet above Louisiana's sea level. The road starts down the other side, with a whole new set of the endless wrinkles of the earth's crust opening out to the west, as I officially cross the Continental Divide.

The Divide of the Continent. The demarcation line for the Pacific and Atlantic watersheds. As a kid, when Daddy waxed poetic about it, I always pictured a razor-sharp edge of rock slicing the raindrops in half as they fell on that dividing line. Now I wonder if at some point there's a Continental Divide within each of us, where we get separated from our true selves, like conjoined twins separated by surgery.

And is it inevitable?

I blow a kiss to the water starting its long downhill run to the Gulf of Mexico.

Bypassing Grand Lake, where I have a

clear view of the magnitude of the heights I've just descended from, I turn west at Granby and follow the cut of the Colorado River through Hot Sulphur Springs to Kremmling. Then it's up and over again, this time over volcanic Rabbit Ears Pass and into Steamboat Springs. From there I follow the Yampa River and Edith's directions out of Craig, past the gashes of a strip coal mine, down a long dusty road, and onto the family ranch she's moved back to to help her sister care for their aging mother.

In the lee of a windbreak line of cottonwoods sits a two-story white frame house, its green-shuttered windows alert in the no-frills square of the building. Barns, sheds, corrals, and farm equipment, some old, some new, are scattered at seemingly random intervals, yet the whole gives off the impression of order and purpose.

Edith waves her arms at me from the ruins of a log cabin at the end of the compound.

She's let her hair go solid white and cut it into a short bob with a fringe of bangs. Her brisk hug is made of solid muscle and bone. Already she's pulling her work gloves back on.

"I like your new hairdo. Come on, give

me a hand here. Grab that end of the log — that's it — and place it in that notch."

The thing weighs at least a ton, and my shoulder muscles resist. "What are you building here?"

"I'm restoring my grandparents' homestead cabin. The pieces are all here. They'd just given up on anyone paying attention to them."

In her jeans, short-sleeved sweatshirt, and round-toed boots, and with her tanned face squinting into the sunshine, she could be the Norman Rockwell portrait of a ranch wife. "You look great, Edith."

"Thanks, honey." She puts her arm around me. "I've seen you looking better. It's still rough, isn't it?"

"Yeah. Rough. I'm glad you could see me."

"Hey, you got me out of a trip to town with my nephew. Instead I get to show you around the ranch. How long's it been since you rode on a horse, and how do you feel about camping out tonight?"

"Forever, and there's nothing I'd like better."

"Good. Thought I'd take you to a place your dad used to like to go. It's special to me."

★ ★ ★

Before long I'm perched astride an Appaloosa mare named Missy, riding into the afternoon sun. Edith's on a palomino and leading, of all things, a brown-spotted llama that hissed at me, then stuck its nose into my chest to be petted. Pedro is loaded down with bedding and food packed into dirt-colored canvas bags, which smell of old engine oil.

Following Edith's purposeful back ahead of me, Missy and I pick our way along a steep trail up a red slope capped with layered sandstone. We top the rise, cross it, then drop back down into a grassy creekbed. For a good half hour, we ride in a comforting silence dimpled only by the clomp of the horses' hooves, Pedro's daintier clack, and the tinkle of the creek. The sun enters the pores of my cheeks, generating warmth.

At last we dismount and tie up the horses. "This is it," says Edith, beaming at our campsite. Ten feet or so from the bank of the creek is a firepit surrounded by logs, and a flat sandy spot for the sleeping bags. Across the creek rises a cliff, stratified in red and orange and tan, hollowed out underneath by the bend of the stream.

Edith sets about unloading the gear, unsaddling our trusty mounts, and starting a fire. I follow her instructions on how to brush the horses, reveling in the beasty smell of their sweaty coats. Western bluebirds whirl and swoop overhead. Before long Edith hands me a blue enamel cup of coffee. "Sit down, cowgirl, and tell me about your daddy's funeral."

The shadow of the cliff has already snuck to the edge of the water. We lean against the logs and look in each other's eyes, ex-stepdaughter to ex-stepmother, though I never could think of her as anything but "Daddy's new wife." I take a deep breath and launch into an account of the all-night vigil with Aunt Lena, the visiting hours, the church service, the a cappella rendition of "Will the Circle Be Unbroken," and the burial beside my grandparents. Edith wants to know everything, from his childhood playmates to the preacher's eulogy.

When I've recounted everything I can remember, she shakes her head and stands, brushing the dust from her pants. Pulling a Dutch oven from a sack, she puts it on a rack over the fire, then dumps in some oil and some bloody chunks of meat from a packet of butcher paper. As the meat begins to sizzle, she cuts up an onion, carrots, and celery, throws in a sprinkling of flour, and stirs it all with a wooden spoon. Salt, pepper, some creek water, and she turns the lid of the pot upside down and shovels some coals from the fire onto it.

"No wonder Daddy fell for you," I say. Mom wouldn't know a Dutch oven from a frying pan.

"Do you know he made love to me for the first time right over there?" She points with the spoon to the spot where she has spread out the sleeping bags. This is more than I want to know. "He was the noblest man I've ever known."

Edith's words hang in the air and spiral upward with the smoke from the fire. She swipes at an eye with the back of her hand.

"Noble?" Not a word I'd have thought to use for Daddy, especially given his less than gallant end.

"Yes, noble. And kind and brave and generous and thoughtful. And handsome and sexy and gentle."

I have no idea what to say. If I had to list adjectives to describe him, they would go more along the lines of *depressed* and *distant*. "So you still loved him?"

She lets out a cough of aggravation. "Don't be a fool — of course I did!"

"Well, Edith, I'm sorry, but I seem to remember you're the one who left him."

She glares at me, then up at the blue sky tinting to rose. Her chin juts out, and she swipes at another tear before it can run down her cheek. "That doesn't mean a thing."

Oh. I see. You loved him but left him alone till he died of loneliness, and it doesn't mean a thing? "Then why weren't you still with him?"

She squints up at a hawk dipping overhead. "Because I didn't have any choice — that's why." Tossing the spoon to the ground, she stomps away, leaving me alone with the beasts of burden.

I rise slowly, retrieve the spoon, and rinse it in the stream. Pouring another cup of wood smoke–flavored coffee, I sit on my haunches at the edge of the water. Shadowy flecks of light dance over the shallow bed, a hint of a trout's tail in the calm behind a rock.

I never bothered to get close to Edith in the seven years she was married to my father. Somewhere deep down, I'd hoped that when Mom left him, he would at long last pay attention to me. But that never happened, so I bailed out to Louisiana. Edith came on the scene when I was busy raising two young children and didn't have the patience left over to deal with her Western brassiness. In truth I was a little jealous of her hold on Daddy, of her ability to get his attention as I never had. And before I knew it, their marriage was over.

"Come on, I've got more to show you." Edith's voice behind me makes me jump. I follow her down a faint path along the stream. Suddenly, in the bend of the creek under another steep rock bluff, there's steam rising from the water. She flashes me a smile. "Our own private hot tub. You don't mind a skinny dip, do you?"

"A hot spring?"

A man-made wall of rocks separates the hot water from the creek. Already Edith is pulling off her boots and jeans. She strips bare and wades in, drops what looks like a pinch of tobacco into the water, and takes a seat along the side of the pool. "Come on, don't just stand there."

She watches unabashedly as I take off my clothes and, sucking in my stomach, step into the water. "You do that same thing your dad did," she observes, "hunching up your shoulders like the world is out to get you. Relax, there's nobody here but us chickens."

I drop the shoulders that I hadn't even known were raised. The water is hot and smells of sulfur, with a slight swirl of current that gives the effect of a whirlpool. Goose bumps climb my torso as I lower myself onto the rock shelf beside Edith, sigh, and sink up to my neck.

"Thatta girl, let it go." As my toes explore the sandy bottom, Edith lays her head back and closes her eyes. "The best medicine there is. My grandma — she was one-quarter Blackfoot — had my grandpa rock this place up so she could take baths even in the coldest weather. She used to say it was Mother Earth giving us a gift of her own lifeblood, and she always brought a little offering of tobacco. I like putting my butt on the very same spot where she used to sit."

The water is extracting things from my skin, pulling on my muscles, forcing cells to release what they've accumulated. "Why did you ever leave here, Edith? I can't see you in an office in Denver."

She gives a harsh laugh. "Young and stupid. Had to find out what was on the other side of the mountains, I guess. I just knew the world was going by without me."

"I envy you this family history you've got to tap into."

"Well, sometimes you have to get away from something to know what you've got.

It's easy to take things for granted when you don't know any different." She cups her hands and splashes water onto her face.

"But why an accountant?"

"Why this sudden interest in my life story?"

"I was pretty shitty to you, wasn't I? I'm sorry — I like to think I've grown up some."

Edith gives me an amused nod. "I became an accountant because there was a little business school in Craig, and that was the only way I knew to get out of here. My generation didn't have the opportunities you girls did. Besides, I never would have met your dad if I'd stayed here." Shifting, I find a hot chute that bubbles up my back. "I don't have any regrets. After Frank and I split, I came back home with new eyes, a bellyful of experience — and true love." She looks straight at me, a challenge in her eyes.

"You want to know why I left your father, huh? It's nobody's business, but I'll tell you anyway." She peers off into the sky, now washed to aqua with hints of purple. "It's like this rock here —" She pats the cliff behind her head. "You see these strata, stacked one on top of another on top of another? Each layer is like a day of a life, piling up and making it what it is. Well, in your dad's case, these early layers were so hard on him that they were faulted, heavier, thicker than they were supposed to be. And none of the other layers mattered much to him. He was too busy dragging around those early ones." Her hand splays against the rock like a prehistoric plea.

"Now somebody like me comes along and wants to make him see the top layer, the one right in front of his nose, that's being made right this very instant. And I want to make it light and fun and happy for him. And for a while it worked, and it was good. But" — she splashes water up the rock, making the colors stand out — "after a while he couldn't feel my love any more than this rock feels this water. It just washed right off of him.

"So I gave more and more, thinking I could wear enough hardness away to touch him somewhere deep down." She keeps splashing water, her mouth pursed. "Until finally I had to give it up before I used myself up." Her hand sinks below the water to rest on her thigh.

A hawk flies above, landing somewhere not far off.

"I'm sorry, Edith. I never knew. . . ."

"How could you know? But listen to me, Frances" — she shakes a finger at me — "he knew what he'd lost, and he knew why. He just didn't have the means to change himself. You know what my grandmother said when she met him? She said he was haunted by the ghost of his mother and would never lose her unless she was extracted by smoke. Of course, he wasn't about to go through some Indian ceremony. He was too deep in denial."

The sun ducks below the distant line of mountains. "He was still my best friend," Edith goes on, her voice muted, "and we never let a week go by without talking on the phone. It's funny, but after all we went through, that's what I miss the most."

"Did he — did you ever suspect it might come to this?"

"I'd be lying if I said it never crossed my mind. But I didn't really want to believe it. If only he'd called me, or come out here to see me . . . maybe I could've changed his mind." She sinks deeper into the water.

I cast about for something meaningful to say. "I wanted to tell you — you were in his will."

"I figured. That piranha of a lawyer called to try to get me to come to the reading."

"Daddy left you twenty thousand dollars."

Her chin juts out, and tears glisten through the fading light. "That was good of him," she says softly. "We can sure use it around here." She stands up, her pointed nipples encased in chill bumps, her mid-sixties body still hard and lean. "I'm going back to check on my stew. Take your time, stay as long as you want." Dripping wet, she snags her clothes and heads naked up the path.

And away strides the true love my father threw away.

Edith's stew tastes as good as anything that's ever passed my lips. My contribution was a sprig of sage I was sniffing when I arrived back at the campsite. "Throw it in. That's just what it needs," she said. "Every molecule of this dish was born and raised on this ranch." And that's what it tastes like, a distillation of the blue of the afternoon sky, the red of the rocks and the sap of the willows, the sparkle of the sand and the giggle of the water.

The temperature drops as a dazzling skyful of stars emerges, enough of a show to keep us entertained all night. Occasionally a point of light streaks through the air and extinguishes itself, and I can't decide whether to feel happy or sad at that. At last I decide to let it be. The fire sizzles and pops, and to complete the tableau, a pack of coyotes sets up a yipping chorus not far off.

I think of J.P. out in his boat dropping a line to tempt a fish, or wading out into a frigid November marsh to pit his shotgun's wits against the flight of a mallard, or proudly gutting a deer he's shot with a well-aimed arrow. Like Edith, he heeds the primal instinct to fit into the natural, unsanitized order of things from which most of us have so blithely removed ourselves.

Edith has splashed whiskey into my cup from a flask stashed in her jacket pocket. The liquor stings my throat, adding satisfaction to satisfaction.

"Edith, do you know a John Yellowhorse?"

She jumps at the sound of my voice. "I don't know him, but I know who he is," she says. "Why?"

"Because apparently Daddy tried to add him to his will the week before he died. He called the lawyer's office and asked to leave him ten grand, but never went in to do the paperwork. Who is he?"

"He's a Navajo miner your dad met years ago. Lives out west near Grand Junction. Yellowhorse helped Frank find some of the richest veins of uranium in the state, which made your dad's career. But the years in the mines took their toll. He's been battling lung cancer for years now, and your dad was trying to help him get the compensation he was entitled to from the federal government." She sucks on her cup. "Last I heard, they weren't having much luck, though — too much red tape. Frank was really chapped about it."

I shrug. "I never knew the mines were so dangerous."

"The lung cancer rates among the miners are through the roof, not to mention reproductive problems and birth defects. Just another chapter in the handbook of How to Screw the Native Peoples."

"Is that why Daddy would have wanted to leave him money?"

Edith nods and tilts her head up to the stars. "I think Frank focused all the guilt he felt for his part in the whole sorry situation on Yellowhorse. But he couldn't get too involved, because Aloco's still out there exploring possible mining sites."

"Do you know how I could get in touch with him?"

"He lives somewhere out in the boonies. There's a guy in Grand Junction who would know — a good buddy of your dad's. What was his name — always reminded me of a comet. Hallett, that's it — Dave Hallett. You could call information."

"I'll do that."

The down sleeping bag hugs me like a mama. Edith and I have pulled up to the fire for warmth, lying head to head. My neck is cradled in my hands, the stars wheeling slowly through the sky. I find myself telling her about Neville's report of the radiation exposure in Kosovo, at which she's not surprised "after what she's seen in the uranium industry," and about Aida and the baby.

"I hope I get to meet Frank's great-grandchild someday" is her subdued comment.

Though I'm not keen to throw a pall over this night, I have one more question to ask. "So why do you think he did it?"

Edith heaves a sigh. "I think his time on this earth was over. I think the walls closed in on him."

"That's not an easy pill to swallow. He had children and grandchildren to think about."

"Everybody has to leave somebody — that's just the way it works." A log shifts in the fire, sending a shower of reddish-orange sparks into the inky black night. "But he's not gone, you know. I talk to him all the time."

Uncle Lex's tale of his brother jumps into my mind. And I'm annoyed to recognize a little stab of jealousy. "So what does he say?"

Edith is quiet for so long, I wonder if she's fallen asleep. Then her arm comes up to point overhead. "You see that star up there, in the Pleiades?"

"You mean the Little Dipper?"

She guffaws. "City girl. That's the Seven Sisters. Daughters of Atlas. Zeus turned them into stars to lose the attentions of good old Orion over there."

"Orion I know." Even the hare in his hand can be seen in this high country sky.

"For some reason," continues Edith in a dreamy voice, "I'm drawn to that star along the top, the one before the corner. When I watch it, it starts to glow and then to twinkle at me, and that's when I feel Frank's presence. Like right now. It's nothing direct, just a feeling that comes over me, and I know he's close by."

How about sharing him with his daughter?

The star is glowing, but I can't see much difference between it and the others in the tiny clump of stars. And the only presence I feel is a chill running down my spine.

A coyote howls. Smoke signals rise from the fire into the dark, delivering a message in code that I cannot read.

A star drops out of the sky, straight down, its fall lasting what seems like aeons.

Bacon, eggs, toast, and coffee for breakfast. I want to bottle this flavor of wood smoke to shake on all my food like Tabasco sauce. Edith takes me on a riding tour of the ranch, the sun dripping along the stems of the high grass that gives up its green as we ride through it. Missy lopes gently under me, challenging my thighs.

Now I know why all those Western movies end with riding into the sunset — because you never want to turn back. You want to keep chasing that ever-receding horizon like the finish line in an endless race.

Before leaving, I ask Edith about the mystery folder in hopes of a glimmer of enlightenment. She shrugs. "That's just like Frank to try to take his work with him to the grave. Don't drive yourself crazy trying to figure him out now."

Part Three

Metamorphic

Metamorphic rock forms from the other two main types, *igneous* and *sedimentary.* Metamorphic rock forms when heat or pressure, or both, causes changes in the "parent" rock. One of the changes is the formation of new minerals, called *recrystallization.* The new mineral grains are often larger than the old ones.

Chapter Seventeen
Zigzagging Toward Stability

The heat bears down from a flawless sky, a dry heat that bakes my lungs as I retrace my route back to Arapaho Circle. The front door stands open, beckoning me into the house o' horrors. The living room furniture stands bunched among taped boxes in the center of the room, leaving the bare walls leaking sadness.

Mitch has thankfully made the first move, broken the spell, making me realize the reason I'd done so much avoiding before. Once the first piece of furniture was moved, what was left of my childhood home would be dismantled, never again to appear in anything but memory.

"Mitch?" I call, brushing away a tear.

He appears from the hallway, gaunt and disheveled, for that instant looking like a frightened and vulnerable little boy. But just as a wave of affection and sorrow splashes over me, his face pulls on its usual sardonic mien. We quickly retreat to our usual stances.

"Looks like you've been busy, little brother. When did you get in?"

"This morning. Somebody's got to get this show on the road."

"I know. I just couldn't seem to make any progress. I did smudge it clean of bad vibes, though," I add proudly.

"Oh, great." He rolls his eyes.

"So what's the battle plan?"

"Do you want any of this stuff?" Mitch gestures to the massed living room furniture, which seems to cock an expectant ear.

I scrunch my nose and shake my head.

"Then I'll rent a truck and take it home. I've been living in a furnished apartment for too long — I want my own stuff."

"But this old stuff? You'll be inheriting some money. Why not buy something new, without all the vibes?"

He scowls at me. "I like the vibes. I don't want somebody else selling it off as so much junk."

His loyalty surprises me, especially since his childhood was so turbulent. As young children we were close, Mitch following me adoringly everywhere I went. But then there came a point when he changed, became prone to tantrums and rages. I never knew what was the matter, really; he seemed to think he'd been given a raw deal at every turn and wasn't going to forget it. I soon learned to steer as clear of him as I could, and to blow him off when I couldn't. Mom pretty much gave up on controlling him, and left it to Daddy to get out the belt when it got too bad, which wasn't exactly conducive to a rich father-son relationship.

Once he hit high school, he got involved with a druggie crowd and stumbled around glassy-eyed from then on. I'll admit we older kids did a pretty good job of paving the way for that kind of abuse, but we were convinced our search for the best high was in the name of peace, love, and transcendent reality.

Still, maybe what he's saying is that his childhood wasn't so bad after all. Or that he wants another stab at it? "Knock yourself out," I say. "I can't think of anything I want besides photographs and some of the stuff in my room. So, Sarge, tell me what to do."

"Of course Dad left everything in good order — the only biggies will be the basement and the garage. The real question is what to do about that car."

"Ah, yes, the Car." Even as I cringe, something in me refuses to admit defeat. "It's got to be aired out, at least. Did you find the keys?"

Mitch looks at me in surprise. "Are you up to that?"

I shrug. "We'll soon find out." He tosses me the keys.

Outside, the afternoon heat is already waning toward the cool evening breezes. Waving casually toward the gang of neighborhood preteens, I unlock the garage door and tug it open. The car still crouches in the shadowy garage, looking somehow less sinister, more contrite than I remembered, like a faithful servant pressed into unwilling collaboration. Filling my lungs with fresh air, I step into the sepulcher and snort back my rising panic.

Willing my mind to freeze, I pull open the car door and slip into the blue seat, into the very spot where my father took his last breath. The cloying scent is still there, worsened by the summer heat. With the turn of the key, the engine coughs to life, resurrected past its last ignoble deed. The windows whir down around me.

I grip the wheel and press on the gas, jerking backward and slamming on the brake just short of my rental car. As my breath runs out, the panic triumphs. I open the door and fall gasping onto the grass.

Mitch's shoes appear in my range of vision; then I hear the engine die and the door slam. "Get up, Frannie, for God's sake. Those kids are watching."

I shoot him a deadening look, gather what's left of my dignity, and rise to walk into the house.

I find myself standing in front of the kitchen sink looking out at the backyard. "It's so weird," I call to Mitch as he tapes up another box. "I can see Mom tying on her apron, starting dinner, whipping up one of her gastronomic experiments from *Better Homes and Gardens*."

"And look," says Mitch behind me, "there's Miss Perfect at the table, finishing her perfect homework."

I shoot him a look.

"So about the will," he goes on. "They faxed me a copy, and there's nothing in it about a John Yellowhorse."

Here we go. "No, Fowler said it was an oral request made the week before Daddy died."

"An oral request isn't binding. So that just leaves dear old Edith to fight with."

Breathe, Frannie. "Mitch, it was what he wanted. He had the right to do as he pleased."

He snorts. "*You* can run a charity if you want, but I can't afford to. I've got an appointment with a lawyer on Tuesday to see about contesting the will. I would've gone today, but he's taking a long Fourth of July weekend."

An ancient acrimony rises up the back of my throat, the taste of Mitch's eternal self-pity. With supreme effort I swallow it back down. "If you would just talk to Edith. She said Daddy was impossible to love. She described it as throwing herself against a stone wall. You of all people should know how that feels."

"She treated him like shit."

"Then why were they still good friends? They talked on the phone all the time."

"Oh, yeah? Then why didn't she warn somebody this was coming?" There's no answer for that one, and his eyebrows rise in smug triumph.

"I have the name of somebody who's supposed to know John Yellowhorse," I say. "We have to at least find out who he is."

Mitch lights a cigarette and leans his lanky frame against the wall. "You always were the sucker."

I stare at him for a long moment, then feel my mouth open and finally take the bait. "What is it with you, Mitch? I mean really. What is it that's been eating away at you your whole life long?"

He blows a cloud of smoke into my face. "Trust me, big sister. That's somewhere you don't want to go."

After a brief night at Hannah's, who's off on a meditation retreat, it's back to Dad's house. Mitch looks haggard in the morning light, as if he's had a bad night at the nearby motel, having refused to go all the way to Boulder.

I've decided to tackle Daddy's room. "Do you want the bedroom furniture?" I ask. I have visions of this dreary house being re-created in some California condo.

"Yes, I do," says Mitch with a scowl. "Don't worry. I'll give you half the fair market value."

"Oh, shut up, Mitch." Down the hall, the first thing I do is kick the suitcase. I'm sick of it yawning its what-ifs at me from the floor. And the folder may be the one Stan's looking for. Flipping once more through its coded gibberish, which seems innocuous enough, I decide maybe I'll stick it in the mail to Stan after all. One less thing to worry about. I pull it out to take with me.

The doorbell dings, a startling reminder that there still exists a world outside these walls. A UPS driver in brown walking shorts hands me a small overnight package, addressed to me from my mother. He smiles, unaware of the black hole looming behind me. Thanking him, I close the door on normalcy.

When I tear open the package, out comes a velvet ring box, pink faded to the shade of leftover bubble gum. In it lies Mom's wedding ring, a plain gold band set with a small pair of diamonds, tiny compared to the rock she got when she married Walter.

The carefully penned note on her initialed stationery says:

> *I want you to do something for me, Frannie. Take this and bury it in the backyard of your father's house. These stones were the two of us, he told me when he put it on my finger, and we would always be together. I want it to stay where we spent our married life together.*
>
> *Love,*
> *Mom*

I fling myself in a chair and throw back

my head in a silent howl. So my father left behind a pair of women who despaired of loving him. How is it that love can become such a sinkhole?

"Who was that?" Mitch appears from the garage.

I show him the ring and the note.

"Are you going to do it?"

I stare at my brother's face, trying to light on an answer. Finally I know what it is. "Not before I make a phone call."

"Walter? It's Frannie."

"Oh, how are you, dear?" says my stepfather in his sweet voice, husky from Cuban cigars. "I'm sorry to have missed the service for your father, but I didn't think it was my place."

"It's OK, Walter. Is Mom there?"

"She's resting. Shall I wake her?"

Resting? That doesn't sound like her. "Is she all right?"

Walter sends a sigh through the phone lines. "She's been rather down since your father died. It's brought up lots of old emotions, I'm afraid. I must confess, it makes me wonder. . . ."

"You just stop your wondering, Walter. You're the best thing that ever happened to Mom, and she knows it. Can I talk to her?"

After a while Mom's groggy voice comes on the line. Is she into the Valium again? "Mom, I'm not crazy about this little chore you've asked me to do, but I'll do it — on one condition."

"What's that?" Her voice sounds almost fearful.

"That you tell me what you meant by Daddy compromising his soul."

"Oh, Frances, I can't get into that right now. . . ."

"It's not an option, Mom. Mitch and I are over here bumping into hard reality every time we turn around. I want some answers, and you've got them. Now what was that all about?"

She capitulates with a deep breath. "It's so obvious. It was the uranium geology. He chose it over the petroleum end of things, even though he'd seen what the bombs did."

My brain works at following her logic.

"He fell for all that government fervor about how the science came to America first, as an act of divine retribution, so we were God's chosen people." Mom's voice has taken on a weary cynicism. "We could manipulate the forces of nature. We would light up the universe. We would be gods."

A long silence stretches over the miles.

When she speaks again, her voice is so quiet I can hardly hear. "But it was all so dangerous, giving the ultimate toys to a bunch of boys. We lived in such fear through all those years. Every time you woke up with that nightmare about the Russians coming to get you under your bed, I wouldn't speak to your father for days."

My first impulse is to defend him. After all, he didn't create the situation; it was his job. I never thought of him as having a choice. I collapse into a kitchen chair, trying for the first time to grasp my father's role in the destiny of the planet.

"He finally realized what an eternal mess had been let loose in the world," Mom goes on wearily, "but by then he had a family to support. It ate away at him from then on. Every time he'd hear a story about the dangers of nuclear weapons, or problems with power plants, he'd write it down or cut it out. He used to keep a box full of articles in the bedroom closet. But what good was that? It didn't change a thing."

"B-but couldn't he have found other work or something?"

"Not your father. Once he committed to something, he saw it through."

Yeah, even if it killed him. "I'm sorry,

Mom. I never knew."

"I didn't want you to know — you needed to be free to respect him."

"Which you didn't?"

"Of course I did — for other reasons. But the gulf between us grew so wide I couldn't cross it anymore."

"Thanks for telling me. That helps a lot."

"Does it? Or does it hurt a lot?"

"Care to join me in a burial?"

Mitch shrugs but follows me out to the backyard. My shovel bites into the dirt under the cottonwood tree that Daddy planted when the house was new. Now it towers overhead, its leaves dancing in recognition of the two kids who used to climb its branches. I dig the hole deep and set the unbroken circle in the bottom, diamonds glittering one last time before they're relegated to the dark from whence they came.

"I commend the marriage of Ann and John Franklin Aldren to its final resting place," I say. "Care to add any final words, little brother?"

"May they both get what they deserve."

I throw him a sideways look as the dirt covers the wedding ring.

* * *

I follow Mitch's descent into the dank basement, flipping on the fluorescent lights. Daddy's tool bench sits neat as a surgeon's tray, precise outlines on the pegboard wall filled with wrenches, drills, and hammers. Washer and dryer, frugal clothesline hung with a couple pairs of underwear.

Storage crates are stacked and labeled, as if he were anxious to make this day easier on us. I pull the top off one marked textbooks and thumb through *An Introduction to Uranium Geology*.

"You know," I muse, "I realize I know next to diddly-squat about what Daddy did for a living. And I never knew it bugged Mom so much."

"The Cold War was a simple impasse. We would either bully each other into submission or blow each other off the face of the earth," Mitch pronounces. "Sounds a little like our happy family."

I roll my eyes. "Yeah, but how exactly? I mean, just what is radioactivity?" I thumb through the pages toward enlightenment. " 'Uranium,' it says, 'is a silvery-white, radioactive metal, highly reactive. Named in honor of the planet Uranus, discovered around the same time, 1789. The heaviest natural element, atomic weight of 238.03. Isotopes found in nature are U-238, U-235, and U-234, with half-lives of four and a half billion, seven hundred million, and two hundred fifty thousand years, respectively. The half-life being the time it takes for half of the radioactivity to decay. Found in pitchblende and in carnotite, which in the U.S. are mined in Wyoming, New Mexico, Texas, Colorado, and Utah.' "

"Come on, Frannie, let's get going on all this shit."

"Wait, this is cool. 'The nucleus of the uranium molecule decays, releasing energy and particles in the form of alpha, beta and gamma rays.' " I read on. " 'In nature, the loss of such radiation and particles from the nucleus eventually changes uranium into a nonradioactive lead isotope. A chain reaction occurs when a nucleus is divided into fragments by an errant neutron, ergo fission, plus it releases two or more neutrons that strike others.' "

"You're wasting time. . . ."

I hold up my finger. " 'A fundamental fact of the uranium nucleus is the amount of binding energy that holds it together. An excess of positive protons in relation to uncharged neutrons creates a state of strain, of instability. An atom of uranium is therefore constantly striving to change the ratio of its nucleus, constantly zigzagging toward stability.' "

"Zigzagging toward stability." Mitch smirks. "I know how *that* feels."

There are boxes of old photographs, filed chronologically through the years of our childhoods. We sit cross-legged on the cold cement floor, dividing them into piles.

There are lots of baby pictures of me, the glorious firstborn. Then come the ones where Mitch has been added, several years' worth of the two of us when he was little, usually with my arm resting protectively across his shoulders. In these, he smiles at the camera, from a high chair, from a blanket on the lawn, from beside a snowman. But as time progresses, his smile turns to a frown, and his sullen face glares from the mouth of a tent, from astride a trail horse, from under a baseball cap. And I am no longer beside him, as if once-tangential lines have separated for good.

"Don't say it," he says as I study a snapshot of him in his Cub Scout uniform.

"What?"

"You're thinking what a pain in the ass I was. You're wondering how you ever got saddled with a brother like me."

I look up into his grown-up face. "*Au contraire,* Mitch. I'm wondering what the problem was. I mean, I always knew *how* you acted, but not why."

He snatches the picture from my hand and stares at it. "You want to know what the problem was, huh? The problem here was that stupid uniform, that stupid Scout troop Mom wanted me to join."

"Why'd you do it then?"

"Because I tried to please them. But it never worked. They always wanted something from me that I couldn't give."

I keep my hands sorting nonchalantly through the pictures. "What was that?"

He lights a cigarette and inhales deeply. "They wanted me to be a kid who *liked* the Cub Scouts, who would hit homers in Little League, and wear those little striped T-shirts and never embarrass them." He levels his gaze at me. "They wanted me to be perfect like you."

"I was never perfect."

"Huh — not according to the parental figures."

I'm staring at an elementary school picture of him, his lips forced into a smile that's nowhere in his eyes. Snatching it from my hands, he rips it in two, then in two again and finally into tiny pieces. "Forget it!"

I grab his hand. "Mitch, who did you want to be instead?"

He peers into my eyes for a naked instant. "Anybody but me," he mumbles finally. "All I ever did was disappoint people."

"Only because you were so hard to reach."

He looks at me with genuine surprise. "Gee, I didn't know you cared."

"What do you mean? Of course I care, dummy." But I must admit that, if that's true, it's been a long time since I showed it.

A thought bursts into my head. "Mitch, Bernie invited us to a class he's teaching tomorrow. It's called shamanic something-or-other. He teaches you to meet your higher guides and stuff like that. Why don't we both go?"

His grown-up mask falls back into place. "Spare me, sister mine."

That night I call Edith to thank her for the visit. But what I really want to know is if she agrees with Mom's assessment of the state of Daddy's soul.

She is blunt as always. "You mean he

signed away his soul to the devil? That sounds a bit melodramatic to me."

"But did he think the whole realm of nuclear power was a place we never should have gone?"

"Look, kiddo, it's just not that simple. When he got into the business, nuclear power was the brightest hope we'd had in a long time. And everyone was sure that, if science could perform the miracle of splitting the atom, the other relatively minor problems, like disposing of the waste, could be dealt with. Unfortunately, that just hasn't happened. We found out that, once you take it out of the ground, you can't put it back."

"And you don't think Daddy was obsessed with that failure?"

"That's too simplistic — you'll need to look farther than that for your answers. He was disappointed and disillusioned, yes, and he did follow all the issues very closely. But he also knew that every one of us participates in the problem every time we drive a car or turn on a TV or toast a piece of bread. It's our addiction to the cushy life, which has to be fueled somehow, that gets us into trouble all the way around. *And* keeps us blissfully ignorant of the long-term consequences."

Chapter Eighteen
Visitations

So here I am, diving blindly into a workshop on shamanism taught by an ex-Jewish guy from upstate New York playing the role of Indian shaman. It takes place at an urban yoga center and is peopled by a couple of dozen twenty-somethings to seventy-somethings who all look terribly calm and together. I'm not sure what brought me here for this crash course in otherworldliness, besides Bernie's powers of persuasion. Meanwhile my heart marks the cadence of an unnamable trepidation.

Following his instructions, I lie back on a blanket pilfered from Hannah's closet. Through closed eyes, I can picture Bernie, his face dark and earnest as he beats his buffalo-hide drum. It pounds in the center of me, rolling itself up to my head and back down to my groin.

He's explained that the drum is an ancient bridge to the world of the spirit, that its vibrations are those of the Mother Earth and of our own hearts. That what we're doing is a distillation of aboriginal methods the world over, available now for those of us here in America lucky enough to pay the entry fee.

As an opening number, our leader-cum-shaman has us dance around in a circle "if we were so inclined." At first I cursed Mitch for his wisdom in declining this invitation. But despite myself, I soon felt my body begin to sway from side to side in response to the throaty drumbeat, as if my middle-aged hips had just been waiting for the opportunity to make a fool of me before a dozen other people. Yet taking courage from the woman in front of me, who flapped her arms like gawky wings, I gradually gave in to the rhythm. Just as I had in New Orleans long ago.

Now Bernie intones our instructions: find an opening in the earth that draws us to it — a canyon, a body of water, even a hole in a tree trunk — and enter it. Oh, sure, simple as that. The gaping mouth of the mud glyph cave comes immediately to mind, but when I try to enter it, I get nowhere, as if an invisible force has fenced off the opening. A few more tries and I give up, forming swift visions of failure.

Still, fed by the beat of the drum, I soon find myself looking over the side of the bass boat and into a hole in the Atchafalaya mudbank. Figuring what the hell, I imagine diving out of the boat into the coffee-colored water and groping my way into the opening.

No sooner have I bridged the mouth than I am in a mud-colored tunnel, angling downward in a steep spiral. A sense of vertigo tries to pull me back but the drumbeat eggs me on. Now the tunnel opens into a wider room, the flames from a small fire in the center flickering off the soot-blackened walls. Plunked in front of the fire, I find myself seated cross-legged. There is something beyond the flames watching me. As my eyes adjust, I begin to make out a coiled shape in the shadows.

A snake. Fat and gray-brown, it is the water moccasin that eyed me that day when I looked over the side of the boat. A shiver runs through the "me" that lies on the floor of the church meeting hall.

We've been told to ask whomever we meet if they are there to teach us, but before I can form the words, the snake speaks. "I am Alma."

Fear lurks in the shadows, making my dream self rise to attempt a getaway. But the snake extends its head and touches my forearm. Not sure if I'm bitten or not, if this is indeed a poisonous snake, I sit back down.

Even as I wonder if I'm hallucinating, tears roll from my real-life eyes. I don't know why, and I can do nothing but let them flow until the prearranged signal, a *boom-boom-boom-boom-BOOM* repeated twice, pulls us back into the room, with Bernie's voice from far away admonishing us to come back up the same way we went down.

A group spill-your-guts session follows, during which the bird woman waxes euphoric about the panther she encountered, and during which I can muster no words to describe my experience. At last we break for lunch, and like a kid let out of school, I stumble out into blinding midday sun. I have no desire to think about what just happened or to speak to another living soul.

No such luck. Bernie the Shaman plunks himself on the bench beside me.

"How was it, Frannie?" His voice is soft, solicitous.

"It was fine, Bernie, just fine." I'm not about to describe my swamp tour to him, especially since I don't yet believe it myself. As a diversion, I reach into my little brown lunch bag and bite into my sandwich. "I'm just tired."

"You don't have to talk about it," he says. I can feel his eyes on me. "But treat it with respect, and don't take it lightly."

When the drum calls us back to work, I feel as if I've been run over by a steamroller. This time Bernie instructs us to look for a high place to enter what he calls the Upperworld, the realm of the Sky, as opposed to the Lowerworld of Earth.

Despite the sense of dread washing over me, I dutifully lie down and cover my eyes. This all feels too easy somehow, too simple a process for finding out the Big Stuff that every human wants to know. However, here I am, being pulled along by the insistent beat of the drum, looking for a high place to enter. A mountain seems a logical choice, but again I have no luck until the place presents itself to me: the scarred pecan tree by our barn at home.

I see myself in its upper branches, our yellow house looking small from this perspective. Then I am rising, rising through the air, breaking through a film of some kind, and into a realm of open and airy space. At first I see nothing; then I am drawn to my left toward a lush area of tall greenery. When I approach, I see that they are rosebushes covered with fat white blooms whose sweetness perfumes the air.

And there on a stone bench sits my father.

I turn and retreat. Fighting my way through something like tangled cobwebs, I finally open my eyes to the room where Bernie still beats that damned drum. His eyes are on me as I sit up, snatch my things, and flee.

The phone rings through the cool peace of Hannah's house. I let the machine answer it, but hear Bernie calling my name insistently until I finally pick up. "I was worried about you," he says. "You have to be careful how you come back. Did you follow the same way you went in? And go through the membrane?"

"Yes, Bernie, I did."

"It's no surprise that a relative would show up for you. The next step would be to ask whatever questions you have for them."

Damn, he was eavesdropping on my trip. I breathe out for a long time. "Look, Bernie, I honestly don't know what to make of all this. It feels like too much right now. I need some time."

"Of course. Just don't be scared off. I think you have a real facility for it. Not everyone gets to even one of the realms on the first try."

"Well, that's something anyway."

"That's more than something, Frannie. Don't dismiss this. I'll give you a drumming CD. That way you could continue the work as soon as you're ready."

"You can do it by CD?" What next, on the Internet? But I am suddenly too tired to hold my eyes open, and agree so he'll leave me alone. Then I sink into a sweet oblivion.

In the morning, I find a CD of shamanic drumming on the kitchen table.

In hopes of airing out the Car enough to be able to sell it, I have begun a daily ritual of backing it out of the garage in the morning and driving it back in before we call it a day. Each time I back it up a few more inches, as if every fraction of cement were a minor victory. Each time a raw place in the bottom has its scab scraped off. Each time, like a loop of film, I see Daddy's last moments — breathing in the toxic fumes and killing the life that lived inside of him, that he passed on to me, that I gave to my children, and that now sparks within my grandchild.

What was he thinking, who was he thinking of, why didn't he change his mind?

Why didn't he think of me?

"Frannie? Is that you?"

The voice sends the top of my head through the roof. It's Adelaide Stewart.

"I'm sorry, honey. I didn't mean to startle you. I just wanted to see if you kids could stop in for coffee. . . ." Her voice trails off as she steps into the garage. "Oh," she says, her hand over her mouth. "This must be dreadful for you."

I swing my legs out of the car and walk into her open arms. What solace a simple human touch can bring.

"Come on, let's get you out of here for a while," says Adelaide, leading me out into the brilliance of the afternoon. The fresh, arid air clears out my lungs. She sticks her head in the front door. "Mitch?" she calls. "I'm hijacking you two to my house for a little break. Come on now."

To my surprise, Mitch quickly appears at the door. She gives him a hug, too, bringing half a smile to his face.

We follow through her once-familiar

front door, now bedecked with a large American flag for the Fourth of July weekend. Inside the house, nothing is the same. Walls have been knocked out, skylights added, the old plaid living room set replaced by crisp cotton duck. The kitchen is twice the size it used to be, bumped out into the backyard, now devoid of its bomb shelter, and flooded with light from pairs of French doors.

Adelaide sets a plate of store-bought cookies onto the glass table and pours coffee served with red, white, and blue paper napkins. Somehow I love the old familiarity mixed with the new dimensions of this house, which makes Daddy's house next door seem like a petrified relic from the past.

I luxuriate in the catching-up prattle as long as I can. But at last the talk turns to the inevitable, and Adelaide's face puckers.

"If only I'd known. I'd meant to have your father over for dinner for ages, but life gets so hectic. . . ."

"It's not your fault." I heave a sigh. "That's what we're all left with, Adelaide — all those 'if onlys.' "

She pulls out a tissue. "He got to where he kept to himself so much, we hardly saw him. I was hoping you could tell me — I don't know — something more about what drove him to it. Just for my own peace of mind."

"That's what we're still trying to figure out. I think he was just lonely and disillusioned with the world — especially when it came to what's been done with the uranium he spent his life looking for." I pat her hand. "It's nobody's fault."

"I can't blame him for that," she says with a sniffle. "Now it's dirty bombs and terrorists and who knows what else?"

But something Mom said comes back to mind. I sit through a few more minutes, finishing my coffee, giving Mom's address to Adelaide in the pretense they might get together, all the while trying to ignore the buzz in my head.

As soon as we can politely make our getaway, I'm out the door and digging through the dark depths of Daddy's closet. Sure enough, there hides a large cardboard box marked CLIPPINGS. I drag it out into the light. Inside are arranged rows of manila file folders marked in Daddy's meticulous hand.

HIROSHIMA AND NAGASAKI says the first, in which lie folded the yellowed front pages of several newspapers from August 6 and 9, 1945, all proclaiming in bold letters variants of the heart-stopping news of the atomic bomb. Next came word of the Japanese surrender, quickly replacing scenes of horror with jubilation. Behind these are articles cut from magazines and newspapers, and neatly xeroxed and stapled papers from scholarly journals.

The next folders are marked BIKINI ATOLLS, UPSHOT-KNOTHOLE TESTS, and other odd names. The box holds a history of the uses of atomic and nuclear power, from the first bomb on. Midway through is Three Mile Island, the folder stuffed and overflowing with clippings and articles. Another fat one for Chernobyl. One on India, one each on Pakistan, North Korea, and Russia. Then one titled URANIUM MINING CLAIMS.

The last file in the box, behind a thick folder labeled GULF WAR SYNDROME, makes my stomach drop a notch. BOSNIA, it says, then added in pencil is the word KOSOVO.

Sitting on my haunches, I flip through the last magazine, newspaper, and Internet articles Daddy added to this biography of an industry: "Pentagon Poison: The Great Radioactive Ammo Cover-Up"; "Depleted Uranium: The Invisible Threat"; "U.S. Blocks U.N. Probe of Depleted Uranium Bombs in Yugoslavia"; "A Chronology of the Nuclear Waste Policy Dilemma." And the last article, titled "NATO Admits Use of Depleted Uranium in Kosovo," has a question penciled in the upper corner: NEVILLE?

These seven crisp little letters in my father's handwriting speak volumes. He knew, he knew. He knew about what Neville was trying to tell us, the danger he and the other soldiers are in, about the dirty little secret the military has been trying to keep. And here's proof in print that even when the secret gets out, none of us wants to believe it, preferring our paternalistic version of dear old Uncle Sam.

There's something more, something I'm missing. I flip back through the files to the one on the uranium mining claims. Its clippings outline the slow accretion of information on the medical problems experienced by the miners, mostly Navajo Indians, in the early boom days of the rich uranium fields of Utah, Colorado, and Wyoming. There it is. The John Yellowhorse connection.

There's no such listing in Grand Junction. I let the information operator dial the second number I've requested.

"Hello," says a man's voice, brisk but

warm, "you've reached Hallett Orchards and Produce. Please leave your name and number." *Beep!* My mouth opens but nothing comes out. It's all too complex to relay to a stranger over the phone, whoever this Dave Hallett is.

Hanging up, I turn to my resident hurdle. "Mitch, care to take a little drive?"

"Where to?"

"Grand Junction."

"That's practically in Utah. No way — you're talking an overnight trip. We've got too much to do here."

"That's where John Yellowhorse lives, and he doesn't have a phone. Before you deny Daddy's dying wishes, don't you think you'd better find out who he is?"

"Damn it, Frannie. I've only got a few days."

"Something else was going on here, Mitch, and I'm going to find out what it was."

As we join the packed lanes of Denverites heading for the holiday hills, Mitch sinks into a brooding silence beside me. I was determined to have him present at whatever I find out so he couldn't just discount my version with his usual cynicism. But I'll be in deep doo-doo if the trip isn't worth all the cajoling I had to do.

The visor fails to block the lowering sun as we rise into the mountains, and I press the SEEK button until the familiar voice of the NPR announcer gives his authoritative account of the day's news. Nothing much has changed since I've been out of the loop.

I wonder how Neville is. Kosovo has long since dropped off the media radar in favor of the more dramatic hot spots of the world. I wonder how many people even realize we still have forces there.

Interstate 70 plows straight into the Rockies, a modern-day Overland Trail, past the old boom-and-bust mining towns and hillsides dotted with yawning holes and piles of pale tailings. At Georgetown I marvel at the covey of new condos built on alluvial fans, the old path of floods and avalanches. We move from gneiss and schist into granite as we climb, past landslide tracks and fault lines that used to render Daddy euphoric.

At last we bore through the Eisenhower Tunnel, and this time I am under the Continental Divide, those raindrops splitting in two over my head. I stick my neck out the window and howl into the echo chamber of the tunnel like we always did when we were kids, but Mitch is resolutely silent.

The interstate climbs above tree line and into tundra. Now we're into the coveted cirques and moraines of the upper middle class, Arapaho and Loveland Basin, Copper Mountain, Vail, Breckenridge, where the ancestral Rockies have conveniently heaved themselves above the Denver Basin so we can slide downhill on two little sticks. Monochromatic condos and seductive outlet malls have followed the hordes into the high country, drawing environmental terrorists who burn down restaurants to try to save the dwindling domain of the Canadian lynx.

Having lost the Denver radio stations, I find a nouveau country station. Mitch glances irritably at me. "How the hell long does it take to get there?"

"We'll stop to eat in Glenwood Springs."

He glares forward, into the setting sun. "May I ask one question? Do you have any idea what you're doing?"

I'm not sure how to answer that. "I'm going to find this guy Dave Hallett, who's going to help us find John Yellowhorse. They know something about Daddy, and I want to know what it is."

"Great." He hunches himself back into the corner.

The traffic rips along as we enter steep-walled Ten Mile Canyon. The rocks change from red to gray to blotchy white, all of which would reveal volumes to the geologist. But I suddenly weary of the game of rock identification. Anyway, Daddy's not here to be impressed.

The car noses onto a Glenwood Springs exit and into the parking lot of a Mexican restaurant. Pseudo–cantina lights burn my eyes as we scoot into a sticky red booth adorned with plastic peppers.

Mitch scowls into his enchilada plate. I munch on pale lettuce swathed in greasy taco meat until I'm finally goaded into effrontery by his silence. "You're really good at punishing people — you know that?"

"Oh, please." He shovels in a mound of refried beans.

"No, really. It's this attitude you walk around with, like you're so bored and superior to the rest of the world."

"Bored, yes. Superior, no. And do you really want to go there? Because if you do, I'm going to be forced to tell you how *you* walk around capitulating to every situation that presents itself. You're like some chameleon that turns any shade anybody wants it to."

My eyes fill with furious tears.

"Oh, God, now she's going to cry." Mitch throws his napkin on the table.

"I'm just trying to figure out what happened with Daddy and why," I say through clenched teeth, "which is in our best interest in the long run."

"Frannie, it's in *your* best interest in your own mind. Dad's gone — there's no bringing him back. And you're just putting off doing the hard stuff by running all over creation being swayed by every story you hear. That's always been your highest objective, to please people." He seems to flinch. "At least those people you think worthy of your attention."

"Just what's that supposed to mean? Are we talking about you now?"

"Why would we do that? That would mean I mattered."

"How can you matter to anyone else if you don't matter to yourself?"

He stands and stalks out of the restaurant.

The perky waitress in her rickracked peasant blouse shakes her head in my peripheral vision. "Men," she says. "You done?" I leave too large a tip and walk outside into the evening chill.

Mitch leans against the hood of the car, digging in his mouth with a toothpick. "Sorry," he says.

"Me, too. Want to talk about it?"

"I thought we just did." Tossing away his toothpick, Mitch climbs in beside me.

A chubby moon rises before the headlights as the highway joins the broad sparkles of the Colorado River. The road tends downward now, out of the Rockies, with dramatic dark shapes looming north and south, hogbacks, buttes, cuestas and mesas. I'm numb with exhaustion by the time I hit the first motel off the interstate in Grand Junction. Two rooms. A mumbled good night to my brother.

It is as my weary eyes close that his sour words begin to reverberate in my head. *You're like some chameleon that turns any shade anybody wants it to. That's always been your highest objective, to please people.*

I flop onto my side. I have no idea what he's talking about. I'm just trying to do right by my father, to honor his wishes. I don't see how that's changing colors. Mitch is just too stingy to share any of Daddy's money.

But still, his remark nags at me. Maybe I'm more like the mockingbird singing in the bush that night, learning the songs of other birds just because it pleases her to do so.

With this appeasing thought, I drift into the Grand Junction of dreams.

The sounds of eager travelers wake me early. A quick shower and a sugary Continental breakfast in the lobby, and I'm back in my room looking up the number for Hallett Orchards. No one answers, so I jot down the address, then dial Hannah's number and punch in the code to retrieve messages.

There are several business and personal ones for her, then a static-filled pause and my son's voice.

"Mom? Are you there? No? Well, congratulate us — we did it! Here's the new Mrs. Broussard."

Muffled voices, then a deep, thickly accented woman's tones. " 'Allo, Mama Frannie? This is Aida. I love your son. We will be good to each other." Pause. "Goodbye."

Then Neville again. "I'll try to call again tomorrow. Don't worry about anything. It's all going to be fine. I'm still working at getting her out of here — not getting very far yet, but it takes time. I — I hate to ask, but will you tell Dad for us? I can't stand to spoil what little time we have together. And Mom? Thanks. Love you." *Click.*

The receiver is an alien thing in my hand, puzzling me for a second until I remember to replace it on the phone. Aida. Neville. I have a daughter-in-law. I'm officially to be a grandmother. Simultaneous laughter and tears. Thankfully J.P. will already have left for work, so I can revel in my secret knowledge the whole day before I have to face the music.

When Mitch answers my lively knock, even the crabby look on his face fails to dampen my spirits.

Chapter Nineteen
Junctions

It is in a wide, eroded valley that the Colorado River, formerly the Grand, meets the Gunnison — ergo Grand Junction. Retracing our tracks, we travel back east a few miles, through rich green farmlands and orchards, to the town of Fruita. There a stooped woman in a yellow scarf points me to the south edge of town.

Neat green letters on a large white sign signal the lane to Hallett Orchards. Kicking up a cloud of dust, we wind through regularly spaced fruit trees loaded with what looks to be green apricots. The sun is already hot enough to make the violet shade under the trees inviting.

Mitch doesn't move as I pull up to the office and get out to knock on the door. "Yeah!" calls a voice from within. I step into the cool air-conditioned dark, blinking at the man who's waving me into a chair, a telephone pressed to his cheek. "No, that's not what I ordered. I want the same ones I got last year."

I've taken a seat in a green plastic chair and, as my eyes adjust to the dim, begin an inventory of the man sitting at the desk. Short-cropped hair spattered generously with white to match a full but trim beard. Crisp creases in a sunburned face, forehead pale above a hat line, chapped lips. Maybe a few years older than I am, or maybe it's just the weathering. The brown eyes take me in in a fast sweep, then come back to hold my gaze. Something passes between us, like touching a doorknob on a cold winter day.

"Yeah, well, get them to me as soon as you can. It looks like a bumper crop, and I don't want to get caught short. OK. Bye." Clicking off the cellular phone, he sets it down and raises his eyes to mine again. "What can I do for you?"

"Oh, uh, are you Dave Hallett?"

He nods, but his hand moves around papers on his desk, his mind already elsewhere.

"I'm Frank Aldren's daughter."

His hand stops, his eyes lock in on me. "You — you're Frannie?" I nod. "OhmyGod." His voice is deep, dusty. He's on his feet and coming toward me, tall, trim, white T-shirt tucked into khaki pants, well-worn work boots. He takes my hand in both of his. "I still can't believe what happened. I'm so sorry. I was down in Mexico when I got the news and couldn't get back in time for the service. How was it?"

A bit taken aback by his familiarity, I nod as he goes on. "That's a stupid question. I heard you buried him back in Tennessee?"

Again I nod, but without knowing who this guy is or what he was to my dad, I don't know what ground I'm on.

"My father's ex-wife Edith said I should talk to you. Dad mentioned a John Yellowhorse to his lawyer — he wanted to include him in his will. I thought you might be able to help us track him down. But I'm sorry. I really don't know what your relationship to my father was."

"Frank taught me everything I know. We've got a lot to talk about." When the phone rings, he excuses himself to answer it. I get up and open the door, waving at Mitch to come in. Ending his conversation, Dave takes in my sidekick. "Is this Mitchell? Dave Hallett. Pleased to meet you — and again, my sympathies."

So just who are you, Dave Hallett, who

knows our names? How come I never heard of you before?

"Listen, I've got to go meet a crew that's installing some drip irrigation this morning. Why don't you guys go on up to the house, and I'll meet you as soon as I can? You happened to hit the day when my housekeeper's making her mean green chili stew."

I'm regretting not calling before showing up here — of course he's busy. "Could you tell us how to get in touch with Mr. Yellowhorse?"

"It's way out in the boonies, and no phone. I'll take you out there. You'd never find it on your own. To tell you the truth, I'm not even sure he's still alive. But it's time I found out."

"We don't want to get in your way," I tell him, wallowing around in his eyes. "You know, that motel pool was beckoning me this morning. We'll come back when it's convenient."

"Twelve o'clock then, for lunch, *mi casa.* You'll give me a good excuse for an afternoon off. I won't take no for an answer."

Mitch fumes as we retreat down the drive. "I could lose my job, and you're hanging out at the pool. Let's get back to Denver to do what we came for."

"I came to close out Daddy's business, and this is part of it."

"Great planning."

"Oh, come on, Mitch. How long has it been since you relaxed for a whole morning?"

"I can swim in California."

"Yeah, but do you?"

The pool water is unnaturally blue, agitated only by a potbellied family of mom, dad, son, and daughter, none of whose skin has seen the sunlight in a long time. My outstretched fingers enter first, slicing the water open for the rest of me. Rays of sunlight ripple along the bottom, broken by my dark, fluid shadow. A swooshing fills my ears, along with the thump of my heart — something like the sounds my nascent grandchild must be hearing right now in Aida's belly.

I keep stroking and frog-kicking underwater until my lungs cry out, then come up only long enough to gulp some air, turn, and dive down again, sluicing through the holy water until I am washed clean.

There is a different quality to the sunshine out west. Nothing gets between you and it, and it sinks into my surfaces like water into fertile soil. By the time it rides nearly overhead, I'm baked to perfection. After a second shower, and resisting the temptation to put on something that looks better than my jeans and T, I buzz the desk and book another night before ringing Mitch. He's working himself into a serious tizzy.

"Will you just give it a chance?" I plead, knowing he really has no choice since I've got the car keys.

Back at Hallett Orchards, we follow Dave's directions to a modest adobe house set back by the river under huge cottonwoods. Before I can knock, a small woman with skin the color of pecan shells opens the thickly carved wooden door. Smiling broadly, she ushers us through a spacious living room and out onto a deep covered patio. In a torrent of Spanish, she motions us to leather-bottomed barrel chairs and pours us tall glasses of iced tea.

The scene before me immediately does something to tone down the background of worry in my soul. The cottonwoods whoosh gently in a hot breeze, and beyond them, the river spreads out as if with a sigh of relief, its heavy work of carving canyons behind it now. A cropped lawn rises to the veranda, where clay jars hold yellow marigolds and red and purple verbena. My eyes fasten onto a planter whose base is a shapely woman with a narrow waist and pointed breasts, her arms raised to support the flower-filled vessel balancing on her head.

"Like it? That was my wife's favorite," says Dave at my elbow. "She insisted on hauling it back from a little mountain village in the Sierra Madres. Lupita helps me keep the flowers growing in her memory." I look up at him. He nods. "Four years ago. Ovarian cancer."

"I'm sorry." The phrase falls flat on the slate floor, but he nods anyway. He drops into a chair and takes a long pull on his tea. He's washed up and changed into a crisp khaki shirt like the ones Daddy used to wear. A geologist's uniform.

"Aloco hired me fresh out of school," he begins. "Your dad took me under his wing and, with a lot of patience, taught me everything I know. He was a crackerjack — one of the best around."

I glance at Mitch, who shrugs.

"Well, he was, and don't let anyone tell you any different. The problem was that he wasn't always willing to follow the company line, and they didn't like that. So they trumped up some supposed mistakes, or screwed up his site locations just enough to make him look bad so they could hold him back from promotion. It burned my ass to see the way they treated him, but he felt such loyalty to the company that he put up with it."

I watch the words come out of Dave Hallett's mouth, feel them go into my ears, and settle into the picture of my father that is slowly being filled in with vital details of light and shadow.

"I didn't know any of that," I say weakly. "Daddy hardly ever talked to us about his work."

Dave offers around the tea pitcher before filling his own glass and draining it again. "John Yellowhorse is a Navajo miner Frank befriended years ago, during that early scramble for uranium. Yellowhorse knew the country like he knew his wife's face. He showed Frank where all the richest veins were right from the beginning. He got screwed big-time, though. Like everybody else who worked in those mines, he got lung cancer. By some miracle he outlasted every other miner from his era, but it won't be long, if he's still around."

"The other miners died?"

Dave nods. "The company basically decided to ignore all the warning signs of radiation poisoning and wait till the miners started dying, then claim they didn't know it would happen. Frank felt personally responsible. He kept bugging the company about it, and back in the early nineties provided lots of incriminating information to the investigators who were trying to come up with a compensation plan."

The river winks at me through the trees. As the words click into place in the picture, I marvel that in all my superficial conversations with Daddy, and those rare visits, he never said anything about all this. Perhaps, as Mom contends, it was shame and guilt that kept him silent.

Lupita calls us in for lunch. We sit at a massive Mexican table with high-backed carved chairs in a dining room whose fourth wall is doors wide open to the veranda. My fork glides through thick slices of avocado and tomato, and for a moment I'm in heaven. Even Mitch has perked up, and replaced his bored expression with one almost resembling interest. He's answering Dave's questions about his job and the funeral, questions that, coming from him, feel like more than polite interest.

"So how'd you get into the orchard business, if you were so big on geology?" asks Mitch.

Dave shrugs. "I couldn't handle the politics. In that business there are always huge ups and huge downs. The peons don't win much in the up cycle, but they sure lose in the downs. It was always layoffs and transfers and cozying up to the bosses. I hated it. Plus I thought they were wrong, really wrong — corrupt, even — about all this mining stuff."

Lupita whisks away the salad plates and replaces them with bowls of fiery green chili and stacks of tortillas.

"As the tide changed," Dave goes on, "from the miracles of nuclear power to the realities of extraction and disposal, I just couldn't do it anymore. Carol, my wife, grew up in a migrant family of Mexican pickers, and she wanted to stay here. So we took on the orchard. I figure it's a kind of geology — all this soil is Mancos shale washed down from the mountains, and there are good artesian springs, and irrigation from the river. Never regretted it for a second. There are still ups and downs, but at least there's no trading on your soul. It's between you, Mother Nature, and your own fuckups."

"I bet Dad hated to see you quit the business," I offer.

"Not hardly. If anything, he was jealous.

But he loved those rocks too much. It was like they were part of him. He had the strongest attachment to the science of it of anybody I ever knew."

Sugar-encrusted flan is washed down with thick coffee that would do a Cajun proud. Finally, after dropping our car back at the motel, we pile into an old blue Jeep Cherokee.

Just as Daddy would have done, Dave narrates the dramatic landforms we pass, pointing out the wildly striated outcroppings of the Colorado National Monument to the south, the gentler inclines of the Uncompahgre Plateau around which the highway detours, and the dark cliffs towering in the northwest distance toward Utah. I'd like to paint this place. But right now, as the highway rises and falls with the landscape, Dave's resonant bass voice soothes me.

"So tell me more about the dangers to the uranium miners," I urge him.

"It started back in the late forties," Dave continues, "when the success of the Manhattan Project created a mad scramble for uranium. A lot of the deposits of 'yellow rock' were on reservation land, which meant it had to be an Indian who applied for the mining permit."

He turns south onto a dusty road that leads across open prairie.

"The conditions in the mines were atrocious. The miners spent up to twelve hours a day in them, breathing radon gas and radioactive dust, eating their lunches without washing their hands, even drinking the water that dripped off the walls."

"But was it known back then to be so dangerous?" I put up my window against the fine dust rolling in.

"They knew plenty. But the new Atomic Energy Commission billed it as a national emergency, blatantly ignoring evidence of radiation levels that were off the map. Basically they knew the cancer wouldn't show up for years, and they could get lots of yellowcake in the meantime." Dave's brown eyes meet mine briefly. "It was a clear case of profit over human life, and the Indians were expendable."

So much for the Seven Generation Rule. "Did the Indians know it was so risky?"

"Nah, they needed jobs and were glad for the pittance wages. Within about ten years they started dropping like flies. Then the Cold War ended, and the boom petered out, and the miners were left with no recourse for their health problems."

I glance back at Mitch, who seems to

have fallen asleep with his head propped on the door. I'm glad for Dave's sane and sensible presence.

The terrain has gotten considerably rougher. Striped outcroppings, sudden cliffs, and fancifully shaped rocks loom over the eroded desert. The sun burns my arm through the window glass, and dust tickles my nostrils.

"But haven't there been some payments to the miners recently?"

"The Radiation Exposure Compensation Act. 1990. Supposed to give one hundred thousand dollars to every miner or mill worker who can prove his health was damaged from working in the industry. But the Department of Justice made it nearly impossible to qualify, requiring those old guys to produce medical and employment records from all the years they worked in the mines, when a lot of them can barely speak English, let alone read and write. Frank was tormented by it. He tried to help the Yellowhorse family, but without the records, there wasn't much to be done."

My stomach has begun to feel queasy, and not just because of the road, which is now little more than a pair of deep gullies. The ocher-and-red buttes set off the fathomless blue of the sky, but I wonder if there's deadly yellow rock lurking out there. "Where are we going?"

"Not far now. Yellowhorse moved out here after the mill in Grand Junction shut down. I don't know him all that well, just came out here a couple of times with Frank."

"Stan McPhee said he'd never heard of John Yellowhorse."

Dave grunts. "He's heard of him, all right. For a little while the miners had a lawyer, a young Navajo fresh out of law school. He brought suit against Aloco, and Stan had to testify. Of course, the little guys never stood a chance."

So Stan lied. And Neil's firm probably represented the company. I chug some water and lean my head back. What more . . . what more?

At long last a rust-and-white trailer appears in the distance, crouched under a rock overhang like a giant humpbacked beetle. A blue pickup stares from four cinderblocks as we pull in, chased by a cloud of dust. The place looks deserted except for a marigold plant with a lone orange bloom on the metal step.

We emerge into a huge silence that

seems to stretch up to the edges of the sky, broken only by a grating chorus of grasshoppers, then our slamming of the car doors. Heat from the drooping sun blasts at my eyelids.

There is no sign of life from the trailer. Dave climbs the rickety steps and raps on the door. “John Yellowhorse?” he calls. “Anybody home? It’s Dave Hallett. I’ve brought Frank Aldren’s kids to see you.”

At first there’s no reply. “I think they’re gone,” I whisper. Then a creak, a step, and a moment later the door opens a crack. Light slices into a face like that of a dried-apple doll. “Mrs. Yellowhorse? I’m Dave Hallett — a friend of Frank Aldren. Is John here?”

Her faint answer comes in unrecognizable syllables. “She doesn’t speak English,” says Dave back to us. “John? Is John here?” he says to her.

“John,” she says, and opens the door to step forward. She is tiny and stooped, with a blue kerchief tied around an acorn-colored face. Waves of wrinkles rise toward the inverted V of her eyebrows, which seem to be asking a dolorous question. She gestures to our left and around the corner of the trailer, speaking vowel-filled words in a rasp of a voice.

"Around the back?" says Dave. She continues to point, speaking earnestly now. The sun catches what I'm sure is a tear in the corner of her eye. It follows a deep wrinkle toward her hairline.

"Thanks," says Dave, stepping down. He follows her gesture in long strides, Mitch and I going along with him.

We find no one behind the trailer, only sagebrush, a sagging clothesline, a water tank, and the small bluff angling toward the lowering sun. Down the dry gully that follows the bluff, a small cottonwood pulls us toward its green shadow. It sits on the damp edge of a pool of pale turquoise water. "A spring," says Dave.

And then I see it. A little ways up a hill, a wooden cross over a mound of stones: JOHN YELLOWHORSE. No dates or inscription besides the simple fact of whose bones lie in this dry grave.

My tears dry on my cheeks. I lift my face to the largeness of the land that moves off to the purpling of the sky.

The vast voice of the wind is interrupted by the hum of a motor. We turn in unison to see a small red car churning toward the trailer.

As we pick our way back, a young

woman emerges, her black hair cropped drastically short and her tall, slim form dressed in a ludicrous red-and-brown uniform. With a sullenness that matches Mitch's, she glances at Dave's Jeep before reaching into the backseat for a paper bag. When we round the corner, she passes her gaze from one to the other of us without a word.

"Hi." It's Dave who breaks the silence. "Dave Hallett." He reaches out a hand, which she ignores. "I knew your father. This is Frannie and Mitch Aldren — Frank's kids." Her expression shifts almost imperceptibly, but still she doesn't speak.

I hear a gust of wind before it hits the back of my head, blowing my hair into my face. "My dad died," I say to her. "And so did yours? I'm sorry."

"Grandfather. He was my grandfather."

Dave gives it all a moment to sink in before asking softly, "When did it happen?"

"A couple of months ago."

"So that's your grandmother inside?"

She nods. "She's trying to die, too. She won't eat. The only thing I can get down her is milk shakes and french fries from the burger joint I work at."

"I'm Frannie." I hold out my hand.

"Rose," she says with the briefest touch of our fingers.

"And this is my brother, Mitch."

Rose stares at him before nodding his way. "You may as well come in. It's a mess, though. Grandmother's blind, so it doesn't bother her."

She leads the way inside, where the darkness looks cool but sags with leaden heat. The smell of sour urine is barely mitigated by the dry breeze through the small louvered windows. The old woman lies stretched out on a built-in sofa and scarcely turns her head as we enter.

"This is my grandmother Sadie — or what's left of her." Rose goes directly to her and pulls her into a sitting position. After swabbing her face with rusty-looking water from the tap in the tiny kitchen, she opens the bag. She offers the milk shake, tearing the paper wrapper off the straw with her teeth and using it to spread the resistant lips. When she says something in the language that sounds like the rocks outside, the old woman sucks on the straw, gingerly at first, then rather greedily. Her eyeballs roll upward as if to heaven.

"Chocolate," says Rose. "She can't resist."

"You come out and feed her every day?" asks Dave.

Rose nods. "She'd starve herself to death otherwise. She refuses to come live with me in town, and I refuse to bury myself out here again."

Sadie Yellowhorse slurps on the straw. Rose pulls it from her lips and digs out the fries, feeding them to the mouth that opens now like a baby bird's.

"Are you her only relative?" I stress the empathy in my voice.

Rose goes back to the milk shake before she levels a black-eyed look at me. Sunlight glints off her cheek. "You want the whole story?"

She intimidates me, this girl. Call it racial guilt, call it a power trip, but she's sure not buying my we-have-our-grief-in-common approach.

Dave comes to my rescue. "There's a legal matter involving Frank Aldren — that's why we're here."

Her impassive gaze switches to his face.

I want her to know we're the good guys, on her side. "My father wanted to leave something to your grandfather in his will, but never finalized it." I hear a swift exhalation from Mitch behind me.

The old woman's deep voice takes us all by surprise. Her eyes are fixed on Rose's face. Rose answers her, my father's name falling in the midst of her words. The grandmother lets out a slew of down-trending words in reply.

Rose looks at me. "She says Frank Aldren was a bad man, then good, but he ended up bad."

My back goes up. "What does she mean by that?"

Rose asks the question and gets a lengthy stream of angry words in reply. I glance up at Mitch, whose scowl is fixed attentively on Sadie.

Rose waits for her grandmother to finish speaking before offering the milk shake again. Mrs. Yellowhorse sucks on it until the straw slurps emptily; then she lays her head back and closes her eyes. Rose stares out the window for a long while. The heat presses on my skin.

"She said Frank Aldren showed up on the reservation in 1957, asking about the yellow rock. Grandfather brought him samples that tested out higher than anything else they'd found. Your father" — she levels her eyes at me — "brought other men, men from the mining company, to Grandfather, wanting to know where he'd found the rocks. He liked Frank Aldren, so he showed them. They promised him two percent of the profits if he'd sign for the lease permit they needed to mine Indian land, which he did."

The old woman breaks in, intoning long phrases with her eyes closed.

"Grandmother disapproved from the beginning," Rose continues. "She says the land is not ours to own, we are only its caretakers. The mines were scarring the Earth Mother, making her mad. But the white men were insistent, promising big bonuses, and Grandfather needed to feed his family — my mother and my uncle were already born." Again Rose looks out the dingy window. "So he signed, and worked in the mine they dug about a hundred feet from their back door. But when the richest ore had been taken, the company pulled out, leaving him nothing but a permit to mine the low-grade ore that was left. It wasn't worth the trouble to get it out of the ground."

Rose's eyes fix on Mitch. "No bonus. No royalty. Only a big hole that filled up with water for their sheep to drink. My mother grew up on that meat. She died when I was two. My uncle died of kidney failure five years later. Grandmother thinks the Great Spirit kept her and Grandfather alive long enough to watch the suffering he caused. Nearly everyone else who worked in those mines is long gone."

Out back, the cottonwood waves its magic wand over the turquoise water. A pair of hawks circle lazily in the sky. When I speak, my voice sounds old and faraway. "So when did my father get good again?"

Rose translates the question to her grandmother.

"She says he got back in touch a few years ago. He tried to get them some money, but Grandfather hadn't kept any records. There was nothing to be done, but Frank Aldren kept trying."

Sadie raises herself up now and springs with surprising vigor in my direction. Before I know it, she is jabbing at the air before my chest, her milky eyes narrowed. Rose tries to press her back into the bed, but she spews angry words in my face.

"She says in the end Frank Aldren broke his promise," Rose says quietly. "They've gotten to the one place he promised they wouldn't find. He told Grandfather he hadn't told them, but Grandfather wouldn't believe him anymore." Rose's indignation seems to rise along with her grandmother's, a vindictive note ringing in her words.

"What place is that?" asks Dave.

Silence is his reply.

"When did my dad last see your grandfather?" I ask.

"Not long before he died. He came to visit Grandfather on his deathbed, but Grandfather refused to speak to him. He called him a traitor. Your father was crying when he left."

Click. The heat sucks the oxygen out of my lungs and presses at my damp forehead. I lurch toward the door, desperate for fresh air.

Behind me the grandmother lets out a sharp cry. I turn to see her hurling blistering words into the space between us. Rose nods.

"When the *Dineh* — the People — emerged into this world, they were given a choice between two yellow powders: one was pollen from the mother corn and the other dust from the rocks. The People chose the corn, and the gods were pleased. But, the gods warned, they were to leave the other, the yellow dust from the rocks, in the ground. If it was ever removed, it would bring great evil upon them."

I throw myself out into the sallow heat.

Mitch follows and hands me a bottle of tepid water from the car. "Let's get the fuck out of here," he whispers.

Dave talks with Rose at the door of the

trailer, writing in a pocket notepad. Sadie's voice calls out from the rancid dark, and Rose nods, then follows Dave toward us.

"How's the water?" she says, peering at me. "Not contaminated with heavy metals? Must be nice to have a full set of female organs."

She whirls on her heel, pulling a package of adult diapers out of her car.

Chapter Twenty
Remedial Action

"Anybody for a pit stop?" says Dave as we approach the outskirts of Grand Junction.

When I raise my hand, he pulls into the parking lot of a tiny Mexican café. Inside its cool darkness, we sit at one of a handful of scarred wooden tables while Dave, who seems to know the place, goes to talk to the owner.

"What do you know? It's happy hour," I say to my dour brother.

"Are you satisfied now?" he whispers.

I stare at his pale but flushed face. "That's hardly the word that comes to mind."

"I can't believe you told her about the will!" His fist hits the table. "The old man's dead and the old lady won't be far behind. They couldn't prove anything in court, so we don't owe them a penny."

I had hoped that seeing the Yellowhorses in person would have softened him.

"And what is it you're trying to do, anyway?" he goes on. "We didn't cause this whole situation, and no token gesture from us will make it right."

I lean away from his tirade, too shaky to take him on right now. When Dave arrives bearing thick handblown glasses of lemonade, tart and cold, I sink back into the *conjunto* music from the jukebox, which sounds a little like Cajun with its driving accordion beat.

The bartender swiftly produces a plate of steaming tamales. Corn husks. Corn meal. Yellow powder. The right choice.

"I don't understand why taking the uranium out of the ground makes it so evil," I say wearily to Dave, pretending my brother doesn't exist.

"In its natural state," he answers, "it gradually goes through a process of decay until finally — way beyond human time — it ends up a harmless isotope of lead. Left alone, it's no more evil than, say, deep water that could potentially drown you." Dave unwraps a tamale from its husk and downs it in two bites. "But its very instability is what makes it so desirable. We take it out and refine it and concentrate its explosive properties to use in our own power struggles. And we've managed to turn it into something that could destroy the whole planet."

As the weight of this day sinks in, all I want to do is sleep. Sleep away the grief, the uncertainty, and now this guilty new quandary. Dave agrees to drop us at the motel.

It is dark when something startles me from a deep sleep. As I lie there, it seems there's an echo of a voice rolling through my head. I can't make out what it's saying, but almost beyond my will, I find my legs propelling me to my bag, where I'd stuck the folder from my father's suitcase that I'd meant to mail back to Stan.

I pull it out and study its title once more: STRIATIONS OF RADIOACTIVE SHALE IN BLOCK 35, SECTION 114." It still makes no sense, but there's something like a flashing red light going off in my brain. I dial Dave's number.

"Dave, it's Frannie. I've got a file of Daddy's I'd like you to look at. I can't make any sense of it."

"Good. Gives me an excuse to see you guys again." There was the slightest hesitation before the "guys." "Pick you up as soon as I can get there — for dinner."

I knock on Mitch's door and tell him the

plan. His face darkens. "Go on, then," he mutters.

"Why don't you come, too? It would do us good to relax tonight."

"Don't be coy, Frannie. You don't want me to horn in on your party. You never have."

I'm weary of this game. "My God, Mitch, it's just a bite to eat, not a popularity contest."

"That's not it at all," he says. He glares at me for a moment, seemingly teetering on the verge of something. At last he speaks, his voice uncharacteristically low. "Since we're so obsessed with setting records straight, here's one for you. Those pictures we looked at made me remember a time, back when we were little, when it was you and me. You were there when I fell down, or got scared, or needed a buffer. With Dad so remote and hard to please, and Mom always busy with her fantasy life, I at least had you to count on."

I sit down on his bed.

"But then," he goes on, "after you started school, you left me behind. You just left. From then on, I was the annoying little brother to be gotten rid of." His voice shakes. "And then I didn't have anybody at all."

Was that when the tantrums started? Mitch would do anything to get attention, even if it was a scolding.

He looks wearily at me. "It was just nice to have someone on my side, that's all."

His raw honesty is too sharp for this time we're living, and I look longingly toward the door. Instead I put my hand on his arm.

"I'm sorry, Mitch. I didn't know. I don't think I did it on purpose. It was just part of growing up." He turns his head away. "What can I do to make it up to you?" I ask, failing to repress an impatient sigh.

He sloughs off his hangdog expression, saying, "Go on, knock yourself out with Daddy's pet. But no matter what you do, we're leaving at the crack of dawn."

Is he jealous of Daddy's relationship with Dave? "See you tomorrow then." I lamely pat his hand and make my escape.

I still have one more betrayed male to deal with. I've got to call J.P. and give him the news about Neville. He answers after the first ring.

My instinct is to neglect to mention that I'm out in Grand Junction instead of back in Denver. But honesty wins out.

"You're where? What the hell are you doing out there?"

I stare into the framed print above the bed, receding shades of mauve hills. Somehow its logical progression of tones soothes me as I run through a brief description of the situation. Then, without giving him time to respond, I add, "But that's not why I called. It's about Neville."

I give him a moment to make the leap with me. Then I say the words. "He got married yesterday. It's official, J.P. — we're going to be grandparents."

A profound silence zips through the lines. Finally he says, in a barely audible voice, "Are you happy now, Frannie?"

The pain in his voice slices through me. "J.P., I —"

But he interrupts me, saying, "I'm hanging up now. I need some time to take all this in."

And he hangs up.

I sit cradling the phone, trying to forgive him by imagining his perspective. But it's a standpoint that I can't begin to fathom.

Refreshed by a quick shower and a change of clothes, I greet Dave at the door. He's changed into jeans and a worn white shirt starched into submission by what must be Lupita's hand.

I press the folder into his hands. "This is

what I wanted to show you. Daddy had it in his suitcase when he died, and Stan McPhee asked me about it." Dave starts to thumb through the pages. "But you can look at it later," I add. "I'm starving, and I could use a break from all these trials and tribulations." He grins and leads me to the car.

Grand Junction sprawls comfortably in the crook of a southern river bend. We drive through the thick twilight to the wide avenue of the downtown, which is divvied up into hopeful craft boutiques, antique shops, and going-out-of-business sales. There's also a preponderance of art galleries, and the streets are dotted with bronze statues. The town is something of a mecca for sculptors, Dave tells me, parking behind a life-sized sculpture that makes me catch my breath.

In it a young girl swirls forward on a swing, her metal dress and hair flying behind her, the cast ropes that suspend her ending suddenly in midair. Her face wears a rapturous expression, her eyes looking skyward, and I can almost feel the flip her stomach makes as she soars.

I wish I could be her, back in that time before the darkness of real life sets in, stretching my legs to the sky.

I have no swing. But I do have this calm, solid, good-looking-in-his-own-way man who's waiting for my company. He leads me into an East Indian restaurant.

Dave orders an assortment of goodies before I get him talking about his life story — his late wife, his two grown kids, his three grandchildren, his orchard. Then I find myself talking about J.P., about Louisiana, about Neville and Maggie, happy to have impartial ears to pour it all into. *"And,"* I add joyfully, "I'm going to be a grandmother." Just hearing the words makes me happy.

"Hey, that's great," says Dave. "I highly recommend it." A better reaction than the last time I broke that news.

It's been a long time since I've dined alone with a man I wasn't related to, and I find myself relishing the experience. Dave leans toward me, listening intently as if every word I say has meaning. I feel valued, stimulated — and more than a little flattered.

The owner takes to hovering close by before we realize it's closing time. As we emerge onto the street, my friend the little girl is still swinging. I'm sure she's gone back and forth, back and forth, many times while we were inside. I wish her Godspeed.

★ ★ ★

"I want to show you something," says Dave. He drives across the river near the grand junction itself and follows a series of turns through peaceful neighborhoods. Then, out of nowhere, rises a guard house and a tall wire fence with a lace trimming of barbed wire.

"Welcome to the Grand Junction Office of the Department of Energy," says Dave. "Home to Project X, the uranium procurement program for the Manhattan Project. Opened in 1943 to oversee recovery and refining of the stuff so they could build the bomb."

I peer through the fence at the long low buildings, almost like an old school campus. "It all looks so ordinary."

"This was the center of the boom in the fifties, a happening place for a long time. They were so casual about it then that some of these buildings were even built on radioactive tailings. Now they spend most of their time trying to clean it up. *Remedial action,* they call it."

"Yikes."

"I like to imagine what it must have been like to split that first atom — when a human being first proved Einstein right, and created energy out of matter. After all, the sun's heat is a nuclear reaction." Dave stares pensively at the guardhouse. "It was just that little matter of the side effects that they chose to overlook."

The moon emerges from behind a cloud to light up the fanciful formations of the Colorado National Monument in the distance.

"We should've listened to the *Dineh* instead of sticking our heads in the sand," I offer.

We turn around and drive back down the quiet tree-lined street, alongside what I now notice are white crosses and markers lined up in neat rows on a close-cropped lawn.

A huge cemetery runs right up to the DOE's fence.

Dave swings a sideways look at me. "You don't like music, do you?"

I stare at him. "Does a fish like to swim?"

Heading back toward the downtown area, Dave veers off into a section of old brick warehouses hugging the river. Tucked between two of them is a squat stone building with a lit-up sign in pink lettering that says PETTICOAT JUNCTION.

"You're kidding, right?" I moan.

"Don't let the name throw you. It wasn't so un-PC back when this place opened."

"I'll take your word for it." The day's heat still rises from the asphalt parking lot as we head for the winking beer signs. From inside, an electric bass pounds the air. Dave ushers me into the smoke- and beer-laden den of iniquity. I love it.

He shouts an order for a local microbrew over the electric fiddle ride. A band of four middle-aged guys plays on a platform over a good-sized dance floor. Just when I've decided country rock is their specialty, they break into a Delta blues that ain't half bad either. Dave presses his way toward the only free table, to the side of a huge set of speakers whose din vibrates the tabletop. Talk being impossible, we clink our frosted mugs together and swill the slightly bitter brew in silence.

The beer is cold and the night is young, even if I'm not. When the band embarks on a lively bluegrass rendition of a Grateful Dead tune, I pull Dave to his feet and onto the floor. His hand is tough and callused, warm in my chilled fingers.

It's been so long since I've danced to anything but Cajun music that my body's forgotten what to do. I force my brain to shut down, to allow my body to move to the beat, free-form, like we used to do. Dave seems to have found the same solution, and though he looks rusty, I can tell he's got good rhythm, for which I'm grateful. Grateful to be alive.

Next they play a rockabilly tune, and we soon fall easily into a two-step. "Hey, you're good," says Dave. I grin and follow his subtle cues as he steers me in swift turns around the floor.

Another couple of dances and I feel the wind seeping out of me. Dave retrieves our beers and leads the way out a back door onto a deck over the river. Colored Christmas lights looped along the rafters sway in the cool breeze, lighting the faces of a loud party of college boys and a few couples smoking cigarettes or pressing their heads together in the shadows.

I lean over the rail to watch the dark swirl of the river. "It's hard to believe these peaceful waters are capable of carving out the Grand Canyon."

"You can wear down anything with enough time and friction," says Dave.

"Like my dad. I think that's what happened to him. Life finally wore him down. Maybe knowing John Yellowhorse was dying was the last straw."

Dave frowns into the water. "Maybe. I

just never thought this would happen."

I peer into his face. "You never saw any signs of it?"

"No, none. I mean, he was discouraged, disillusioned with his work and his relationships. I knew he felt helpless, but not hopeless."

"And yet I feel as if you knew him better than I did. In fact, I feel as if everybody knew him better. Where was I? How come he held himself back so much from his kids?"

Dave shakes his head vehemently. "It's not your fault, Frannie. It's like those apricot trees I grow. They all get basically the same amount of fertilizer, water, attention. But some of them get off to a bad start and just never recover, no matter what you do for them. They'll always be stunted and will be the ones that catch a disease or break off in a storm."

"Nah, I don't buy that there's no way to reverse the traumas of childhood. The same grain of sand that can wear a hole in a rock can build a pearl in an oyster."

Dave laughs, his teeth shining in the moonlight. "I know what you mean, though. I had to learn the hard way how easy it is to take a loved one for granted."

His wife. Now our ghosts have come to

join us, and some of the fun goes out of the evening. "I think it's time to turn in," I say, suddenly weary. "Mitch wants to leave early tomorrow."

"But that file . . . ?"

"Take a look at it when you get home — I'll call you before we leave tomorrow. I need to get Rose's address from you, too."

Dave drives me back through silent streets to the motel, cutting off the engine in front of my room. I fumble for some neutral words. "I want you to know how much I appreciate what you did for us this afternoon. It's obvious why Daddy was so fond of you."

He picks my hand off the seat and presses it to his warm chapped lips. "It was my pleasure," he says.

My other hand reaches for the door latch. "I'll talk to you tomorrow. Good night."

The path splits in front of me, and I stare frantically down one way, then the other. Each one forks again a little ways ahead, leading to an endless network of decisions, every one of which could be perilous. At last my mind is made up, and I take the left fork. A shrill bell splits the silence.

The ringing phone pulls me out of a sleep so deep that I don't know where I am. Finally I locate the intruder and give a groggy "Hello?" The clock of squared-off red numbers reads 6:30. My brain wakes just enough to run through the prime candidates for possible disasters — my children, J.P., Mitch, Mom — before the caller speaks.

"Frannie, it's Dave. I read the file. Get dressed. I'm coming to get you. If it's where I think it is, it's big, really big."

"If what's where? What are you talking about? I'm leaving this morning."

"No, you're not. I've found a ride to Denver for Mitch if he insists on going back, but tell him I hope he'll come with us."

My brain refuses to process his words. "Listen, bud, no self-respecting Southern girl makes any decisions before she's had her coffee. Call me back in a few minutes."

"I've got a thermos of Lupita's coffee, and some of her breakfast tacos, which beats anything you'll get at that motel. Now I'm not kidding. Let's get going."

"You're very persuasive. Do I have time to brush my teeth?"

"Yep, and put on long pants and hiking boots."

"I didn't bring any."

"Tennis shoes, then. And a hat. I'll be right there."

Chapter Twenty-one
Rich Veins

Before Dave pulls up, I've had time to dress and stir up Mitch with vague answers till he's mad as a fire ant. I wave Dave to my brother's room, saying, "Since I don't have a clue what we're doing, it's hard to defend myself. Care to explain?"

"This file that your dad had," says Dave, holding it out to Mitch, "is Aloco's plans for a new open-pit uranium mine. If it's where I think it is, it's a bombshell."

Mitch's response is vehement. "We're leaving for Denver, Frannie — right now." I look helplessly to Dave.

"If Frannie wants to stay," says Dave, "I've got you a ride back. My field boss will be here in half an hour to pick you up, and drop you anywhere you want to go."

"Good. *One* of us will get back to work."

As Mitch practically slams the door in our faces, I glimpse the pain behind his indignation.

"Give me a minute," I tell Dave, knocking softly on Mitch's door. To my relief, he lets me in.

"I'm not abandoning you, Mitch," I say to his stony expression. "This feels like — I don't know — like something important — for Daddy. But I have to admit, it's not just about him. It's about me doing something that is meaningful."

He throws me a nasty look as he zips his overnight bag.

I go on, undaunted. "What you said about me being a chameleon. Maybe you're right. Besides raising my kids and being a wife and teaching for my paycheck, I've let go of the things that once meant a lot to me. Maybe I do just go with the flow of whatever anyone else is doing. But that's not how I want to be."

As I speak, I can see my reflection in the mirror above the vanity. "I'm at this place in my life where I'm looking forward to a new era, and back at the old ones, too. I see where I've lost and gained, and failed and succeeded. I've done all right. But I want the second half of my life to be more deliberate, more focused. And up pops this issue that — I don't know — I feel all the way down to my gut, that's been a thread through my whole life, and that feels like it's way more important than I am. And maybe there's something I can do about it."

"Well, bully for you," says Mitch. "Meanwhile I'm hanging on to my job by the skin of my teeth. I work on commission, you know. For you, this is just like 'What I did on my summer vacation.' Who cares if old Mitch doesn't make his rent and his child support as long as Frannie finds the meaning of life?"

Defeated, I back out of the room. "I'm sorry you feel that way. I'll see you back in Denver tomorrow."

"We found him in a pod in the backyard," I tell Dave, locking my room behind me, "and my mother insisted on raising him. Now give — what are you up to?" We climb into Dave's faithful blue Jeep.

"It's what *they're* up to that burns my ass," he answers. "But we won't know till we get there."

I settle back into the seat with a foil-wrapped tortilla stuffed with eggs and chorizo in one hand and a thermos cup of sweet black coffee in the other. "One could get used to being kidnapped," I mumble. "Are you sure you're on the level?"

Dave's eyes smile into mine.

We cross the Colorado River on the same street as last night but pass up the signs to the DOE. "Aw, can't we stop, please, please?"

"Don't worry. We'll probably have to deal with them later." The sun is rising behind Dave's suddenly serious profile. He looks at me again. "I told you, this is big."

OK. This is big. Big like the immensity of the landscape ahead, like the bright aqua dome of the sky, like the sadness in my heart. But big is better than little, I think.

After following the Gunnison River for several miles, we turn west and cross it, putting the climbing sun behind us. The road plunges swiftly into a canyon called the Unaweep and, as Dave explains, directly across what's left of ye olde Uncompahgre Plateau. A faulted anticline, he says, one of two island ranges of the ancient Ancestral Rockies, which existed before today's version of the mountains. "Wait, wait, I know this," I exclaim gleefully. "The other was the Front Range."

"You got it. Most of the Uncompahgre was leveled and washed away by the surrounding sea."

"It blows my mind to think all this was once underwater."

"The earth's crust is changing all the time — it's just in geologic time, not human."

I study the strata of the rising canyon walls, like a cake with infinite layers, each a different flavor. There're chocolate, strawberry, lime, peach, and grape. It's the strawberry-lime layer, I'm told, that contains hidden plums of uranium.

"That tiny little stream in the bottom cut through all this rock?" I ask.

"Probably not — it had to have been a larger river. Maybe the Colorado, maybe the Gunnison, maybe both. But this is really neat — see, the water's flowing toward us? That's East Creek. Now right about here" — Dave points to a barely visible rise — "the water starts flowing west."

"A mini–Continental Divide," I proclaim triumphantly. But in truth it unnerves me, this precipice, this watershed, this perilous place where a choice must be made if you're not to be split in two on the razor's edge.

The walls rise higher and steeper on either side of us till at last we're through the cut of basement rock. At the tiny town of Gateway, we turn northwest again and into a relatively calm stretch along the Delores River. Who was Delores, I wonder, and how did she get a river named after her? A tough, fearless pioneer woman, or an irresistible dance hall jezebel? Did she love the man who named this flow of water after her? And what was the river called before she came along?

"See that gray hill in the distance?" Dave points to a substantial pile of finer rock than the surrounding shelves. "That's tailings from a uranium mine — probably a small, privately owned claim. They're all over the place out here."

"But what about that pond right next to it?"

"The pits fill with water and become watering holes for animals. Beware the wild game."

Mentally I hold my head. It's all too wanton, the expectations we've had of this wobbly, precarious element. Our harnessing of uranium's thirst for balance seems somehow unjust, as if we've taken advantage of someone who's handicapped. Not to mention that we have no sane solution for disposing of the glow-in-the-dark waste.

Dave turns the Jeep onto a dirt track and frowns into the distance. We jostle and jerk along for a while in silence. The huge flat top of Grand Mesa looms red in the distance. “There’s definitely been traffic around here,” says Dave, stopping the car to pull out Daddy’s file. He unfolds a map, following a minuscule line with his finger.

After covering some miles of more and more treacherous terrain, he parks and gets out, pulling on a cap and sunglasses. “We’ll have to walk the rest of the way in.”

He hands me a loaded backpack and hoists one on himself, out of which sticks the wand of what I recognize as a Geiger counter. “Leftover from my geologist days,” he says in answer to my stare.

We hike into the wilderness, nothing but the unknown ahead and the known behind. Red rocks piled in thick layers have loosened and lost pieces of themselves that we climb over and around. Our course is steadily upward, winding, wending. I brush the tops of tall sage bushes with my fingertips, releasing the crisp, pungent smell that comforts me. It is not until we are over a flat-topped rise and descending the far slope that I begin to recognize the terrain. Dry creekbed. Pale orange and purple pebbles. Red rocks, blue sky. Hawk overhead.

“I know this place,” I say quietly, and then my feet take off downhill. I can hear Dave running behind me, but am pulled along by what lies ahead.

Our feet crunch steadily on the sandy creekbed, down, around cliffs like loaves of risen bread. At last the cliffs part, and ahead is the glint of flat water. I lead the way at a lope now, and turn left toward the giant red sandstone band shell ahead.

When I stop to catch my breath, Dave comes up behind. "Where the hell are you going?"

"I've been here before — in a dream."

"Do you know what it is?"

"I know there are cliff paintings in a little cave in those ledges up there."

"Bingo!" says Dave, snapping his fingers. "This is it, then."

"What?"

"The place Sadie Yellowhorse talked about, the secret her husband made your dad promise not to tell."

Climbing the ledges in real life is harder than in my dream. But propelled by some force behind or beyond me, I scale them with no thought for danger.

There is no snake at the top, but the cave from my dream is there, a gaping, chest-high opening in the rock.

"Did you bring a flashlight?"

Dave produces a high-intensity light and

hands it to me. "Be careful," he says behind me. "It might be some critter's cozy little den." I duck through the opening. Inside it is cool and dark, safe.

Once again I find myself inside the skin of the Mother of us all, with the rusty smell and cool solidity of rock and elemental forces pulling at me. The beam startles the darkness and scrapes along the rock wall; my breath catches in my throat. There, as I knew they would be, are the paintings: herds of antelope grazing placidly, immune to the imminent danger of two frozen bow hunters.

My light sweeps to the back wall ten feet away, searching for the winged JFA figure of my dream. It is not there, but in its place is a towering white figure with large Mickey Mouse ears and bottomless circles for eyes. Its legs and arms are spread as if to say, "Come and get me." Beside it is another figure, a small dark body with no head.

Dave crawls in behind me and shines his light on the white figure. "Oh, my God."

The roof of the cave is little taller than the opening, not high enough to stand up in. So I cross my legs "Indian-fashion" on the cool stone floor. Dave folds himself behind me, one long leg bent to my left, and I lean back into his chest. His arm comes around me and his hand rests on my leg, comfortable there, demanding nothing but the thrill of this moment we share.

I cannot turn my gaze from the white figure before me, from its black stare, soothing and holy, that seems to look straight through my flesh and bones. *Listen to what the figures say,* my father told Russell. *That's where the answers come from.*

"This was your dad's special place," says Dave, his voice hushed. "He found it years ago when they were exploring a few miles west. I knew it had to be around here somewhere."

Grasshoppers rasp a crescendo outside in the sun that's an eternity from this cool, dark, secret place. We seem to be breathing from the inside of a drumhead, our exhalations rebounding off the close walls.

It's impossible to look at the figures without attempting to picture their creation. A trance it was, a revelation — a journey?

"I think I know what the white one is." My voice comes from the mundane depths of this body I inhabit.

"What?"

"I think it's the spirit of that dark figure, trying to lead it to the light."

"Hmm."

"But there's such resistance in the dark body, because he has no eyes to see his true self, no ears to listen to the wisdom, no mouth with which to ask the questions."

Aeons crawl by as we sit motionless in the eerie shadows of the flashlights' beams. If not for Dave's chest rising and falling at my back, I would spin off into the black eyes in the white head, follow the beckoning of the outstretched arms, morph through the white figure-shaped door in the stone. I lean my head back on Dave's shoulder and tell him the story of the other cave that Daddy loved, in Tennessee.

"Thank you for bringing me here," I add lamely. "I think Daddy must have felt as if he'd refound some of his childhood here."

"It's my pleasure, Frannie."

Dave's face comes closer over my shoulder until his breath mixes with mine. My chin rises and my mouth crosses the short, rocky distance to his.

His lips are weather-hardened like his hands. He cups my cheek in his palm and the kiss takes over, plunging me into a Dave-shaped space that lights little fires all through me. With a final peck, he pulls his lips away and looks into my eyes.

Our mouths smile shyly, and we turn

back to stare at the white spirit.

"Can we stay here forever?"

"I wish. But that's not a good idea," says my companion. "Here's the rest of the story." He crawls halfway out the door, bursting the iridescent bubble we've been sitting in. Backing in again with the antique Geiger counter, he places a set of headphones, warm from the sun, over my ears. Holding a metal cylinder and a boxy meter over the cave floor, he flips a switch.

My ears fill with rapid-fire clicks. The needle on the meter swings wildly.

I turn wide-eyed to him.

He nods. "According to that file, this place sits on top of one of the richest veins of uranium to be discovered in years. Aloco's getting ready to set up an open-pit mining operation here that will destroy the whole area."

The clicks stab at my brain. My eyelids clench. My lungs reject the cave air. No. No. No, no, no, no.

We maneuver back down the cliff and into the shade of the band shell. As we prepare to sit, Dave lets out a low whistle. "Look at this! There are more glyphs out here — lots more!"

Sure enough, the overhanging walls

seem to have provided ample canvas for more seekers. There are circles, lines, suns, figures, some red, some black, some white, layered over each other like beds of rock. I stare slack-jawed at them, but none has the power of the ones in the cave for me.

The arch of stone offers dwindling shade from the fierce sun. We sit among the holy to fill our bellies. Lupita has packed containers of black beans and guacamole, which we spoon into pliant tortillas. The cave mouth is barely visible from where we sit, its dark recesses tainted by the memory of the clicking in my ears.

"Should we have stayed in there so long?" I ask finally.

"Probably about like getting an X ray. If you lived or worked there day after day, it would be a different story." Dave takes a long swig of water.

The sun burns my thighs through my jeans. I lean back into the shade, like a reptile with a once-a-week meal to digest. Dave keeps stealing quick looks at me until finally I turn to face him.

"What's to be done?"

He squints up at the secret cave. "I'm not inclined to let them get away with it, myself."

"Neither am I." I stare back at the

opening high on the cliff, which visited me in my dream. My chin juts out and tears fill my eyes. "For Daddy's sake."

Dave gives me a long stare, then a high five.

As we gather up our leftovers, something catches my eye from the crook where the band shell meets the rock floor. I reach in and pull out a snakeskin, outgrown and left behind. It is pale brown, stiff but still surprisingly pliant. I wrap it in a large cloth napkin and stash it in my backpack.

Alma would like that. There are no coincidences.

It's late afternoon by the time we reach the motel. Mitch is long gone, and my message light emits a steady red blink. When I check the voice mail, it's Hannah saying I need to call J.P. about his mother.

Dave hovers uncertainly near the door.

"I've got some family matters to tend to," I tell him reluctantly. "And my head is killing me. Can I call you later?"

"Of course, Frannie," he says, making a graceful exit.

As soon as the door closes, I crawl under the bedcovers and pull the stiff bleach-scented sheet over my head. I want it all to go away.

But sleep won't come, only the looming white figure and the steady click of the Geiger counter in my head. And the meeting of lips.

After an hour or so, I give up and, donning my bathing suit, dive into the perfect blue of the swimming pool. It calms the pounding in my head, and clears my perception.

My impulse is to go hang out with Dave, to bask in his growing affection and his stolid practicality. But I have a husband whose music I already can't seem to face.

After showering and packing, I dial Dave's number. "I hate to say this, but I've got to get back to Boulder."

"Bad news?"

"No, just a lot I need to deal with. I think I'll go on back tonight."

Silence, then he says, "So I won't see you again?"

"I need to go."

"Right."

"I'll call you as soon as I know anything." Giving him Hannah's number, I make my getaway.

Chapter Twenty-two
Essential Selves

I drive like a banshee back to Boulder, possessed by a stinging urgency. I should've called J.P. before I left, but I couldn't face him with the memory of Dave's kiss still burning my lips, of his chest rising at my back.

For courage, I pull out the snakeskin from the Cave of the Holy and hang it over the rearview mirror. To remind me that we have to shed our skins in order to grow.

It's about nine when the lights from Hannah's windows appear before me. "There you are!" she says, hugging me as I burst through the kitchen door. "You need to call J.P. — he says he has urgent news." She hands me the phone.

"J.P.? I'm sorry to call so late — I just got back to Boulder. What's happened?"

He takes a deep breath. "They put Mom in the hospital — they're going to amputate her toes. Maybe more."

"Oh, no, that's awful. I'm so sorry."

"I figured you'd want to be here for her."

A pink hollyhock outside the kitchen window dances to some breezy music of its own. "J.P., I have to tell you what's happening here. We've found out that Aloco is getting ready to dig an open-pit uranium mine on some land that Daddy knew and loved. It's got a cave with some petroglyphs in it."

"So what's that got to do with you?"

"I'm not going to let that happen — for Daddy's sake."

"What the hell do you think you're going to do about it?"

"Blow the whistle on them. I'm not sure how yet. I just found out today."

"Frannie, you should be here for Mom."

I close my eyes, knowing he won't understand. Knowing too that he would never dream of not gathering with his family at crisis time to lend support and encouragement.

But it seems I've spent the last few decades of my life worrying about what everybody else wanted from me. At long last, albeit posthumously, I'm beginning to understand the workings of my own father's life, the dark places where the blind crawfish live and the hidden caves filled with import. And maybe along the way I'm starting to shine the light on my own deep recesses, and acknowledge where I've sold myself short.

"J.P., I'm so sorry, but I can't leave right now. You all can take care of it. Tell your mother I love her. I'll send her some flowers."

"What's the matter with you, Frannie? All of a sudden you go around stirring up trouble and letting everybody else deal with it? Like this business with Neville . . ."

I wish I could share with him an inkling of the urgency running through my veins, this new vision that has overtaken me. But I can't until he's ready to hear it.

"Why don't you just do what you're supposed to?" His voice is husky.

"Ah, but I am, J.P. I am."

I find Hannah in the living room, sunk into one of her overstuffed chairs. She looks at me in surprise. "You haven't been letting the moss grow since I saw you last," she says. "I couldn't help but overhear."

My insides tremble as I drop into a deep, green chair. "My mother-in-law's in the hospital. Complications from diabetes. But I can't go back now. We found this place —

I've got to connect with someone to help us fight it."

"Who is this 'we'? Mitch is back in Denver."

"A guy I met out there — Dave Hallett. Daddy's protégé." I give her a quick summary of the trip, leaving out the kiss. "I've got to figure out what to do next."

"Bernie."

"Bernie?"

"Anthropologist, remember? He'd jump on it. And he knows everybody in the field."

"Oh, Hannah, of course. That's great." We talk for a while longer until, exhausted, I say good night.

Just as I reach to turn out the light, I see Bernie's journeying CD lying conspicuously near the small stereo under the window.

My eyes and body ache with weariness, but something has begun. Something is happening alongside this life that I'm living that has gold nuggets of wisdom for me — if only I have the courage to go there. I plunk the CD on the player, lie down in the dark, and at last allow myself to descend on the insistence of the drumbeat.

As the tunnel spits me out into her cave, Alma nods her pointed head at me. "So you're back. Are you ready to work now?" she asks.

I nod, mute with terror.

"Good. Drink this," she says unceremoniously, offering a clay cup. The murky liquid smells like moldy dirt. Tipping the rough cup to my mouth with trembling hands, I sip the brew. Its taste is muddy, but it feels like lightning as it goes down my throat, giving me a charge of something that smacks of ferociousness.

I look to Alma in surprise and see that she now has a human body, an Indian woman's, dressed in a fringed white buckskin dress covered with beaded designs. Long silver braids hang down her breasts, but the top half of her face is hidden by a wooden mask. On it gleam a snake's small eyes above a fanged mouth.

She reaches out and smears a red paste over my heart. Its warmth matches the charge of the drink. "Now take a look at yourself," she commands, her voice throaty, leaving no room for argument.

And there beside her stands a version of myself that I barely recognize. She is tall and strong, larger than life, and lit from within like a Chinese lantern. Dressed in a white buckskin dress with no beading, her hair in two long dark braids, she bears her shoulders thrown back, her expression an amused challenge as she looks straight at me. I nod humbly.

"That is you in all your potential, your essential self," says Alma. "Now see yourself as you think you are."

Dingy and small, crouched beside her dazzling sister, this Frannie stares dully out of listless eyes. She looks at her companion and ducks her head shamefully. The better me reaches out to her, pulls her to her. "I will help if you let me," she says. The smaller figure curls into the illumined arms and weeps.

"There's your task," says Alma. "Become what you were meant to be." I nod. "Good. Now close your eyes and listen."

The instant I shut my eyes, a whooshing sound engulfs me, a sound that both comes from me and *is* me. My body no longer exists, but is separated into tiny bits of light that both refract and emit the sound, like color and music mixed together. I know that I have been here before, have come from here, will be here again. How could I have forgotten?

I fly or fall or climb all night long.

Magnolia calls early in the morning, her voice wavering.

"What's the matter, sweetie?"

She breaks down, sobbing, "Jay dumped me for another girl who would take him to California. All he ever wanted was a ride."

I suck in air and remember being that age, remember fresh love, remember Neil. "I'm sorry, honey. I really am. I know it hurts."

She sobs louder. "I'm such a nobody. I don't even know what my name is half the time."

"Maggie, you're only nineteen. It's just the beginning of figuring out who you are. Don't expect too much of yourself, and don't think that *any* guy is going to do it for you." But my words sound so pat, and so contrary to the example I've set for her. It occurs to me that maybe I could go deeper, beyond the prefab parental rubbish we all spew.

"Let me tell you something, honey. I've just run into a guy that I thought was the ultimate male on the planet when I was in college. We lived together for a long time, and I thought I knew him. But now he's this slimy lawyer in a silk shirt who may even have had some shady dealings with your granddad's employers."

She perks up. "Really? You never told me about him. What's his name?"

"Neil." I'm thinking how it never would have occurred to me to tell her about him. After all, it was a failed relationship, and I wouldn't have wanted her to know I had a less than perfect past. So I've let her know only a surface version of myself, just like my own father did to me, keeping to himself the things that lashed at his heart and soul.

Maggie blows her nose.

The snake scene from the night before does an instant replay in my mind. "This is what I'm learning, Maggie. It seems there's a larger version of each of us, sort of like the blueprint of who we could be. It's clear and radiant, and existed back before we began to darken our real selves with all our emotional gunk. We can ignore it and grope our way through life, without any real anchor. Or we can learn to go deep within to get back to it, to be guided by it and to try to live up to it." I feel humbled by my own words.

"But how do you do that?" She sounds like a little girl again.

My answer comes with an unaccustomed surety. "I'm just beginning to figure that out. I think you have to get quiet and listen."

Silence.

"Now let me give you some other things to think about," I go on. "Grandmère's in the hospital — it's her diabetes."

"Oh, no. Is she all right?"

"They're going to have to amputate part of her foot."

I hear Maggie crying softly. "I have to call her," she says. "What's the number?"

I hadn't thought to ask J.P. this question. "Call home and get it from Dad. But here's the other big news. Neville got married . . ."

"Cher bon Dieu!"

This Cajun invocation of God makes me smile, reminding me that my children are natives of their father's homeland. I quickly fill her in on the news — Neville and Aida and their baby, the Yellowhorse family, and the uranium mine.

"What's up with this radioactive stuff?" she asks indignantly. "Santa Fe built a special bypass on the interstate to keep all these trucks that carry the whole country's nuclear waste from driving through town. Can you imagine having a head-on with a semi full of plutonium? No one has a clue what the cleanup would be like."

"Where are the trucks going?"

"To this waste isolation pilot plant near Carlsbad. They just dump contaminated junk into these salt caves and say it won't ever cause any problems, but nobody really knows."

This makes my stomach hurt. "Neville says the military is contaminating combat areas with radioactive artillery. That's one of the reasons he's so anxious to get Aida out of the country now that she's pregnant."

"Mom, that's just awful! Can't we do something?"

Her youthful outrage is heartening. "You can help by getting on the Internet and finding out all you can about depleted uranium . . . and about what laws exist on the destruction of land sacred to the Native Americans."

"OK. I'll call you back." She hangs up, the spark of excitement in her voice making me smile. There's nothing like a good cause to make you forget your troubles.

When I get Mitch at his motel in Denver, his voice is subdued. I quickly go over the discovery that Dave and I made, hoping against hope that he'll appreciate its import.

"Huh" is all he answers.

"Mitch, what's wrong?"

"My boss is furious about how much time I'm taking off. He's threatening to take some major clients from me."

I scrunch up my eyes. "I'm sorry, Mitch. I hope . . ."

"But I'm really kind of glad," he goes on. "It gives me an excuse to quit."

"To quit? Why on earth . . . ?"

"You're going to laugh, Frannie, but last night I dreamed about Dad."

"I won't laugh, Mitch."

"He said to me, plain as day, 'Help John Yellowhorse.' He said it to me three times. It totally freaked me out."

I throw a prayerful look at the ceiling.

"He told me everything was all right, that he was sorry."

I sink to the bed, clenching the phone. "That's amazing, Mitch."

He takes a deep breath. "So I've just decided something this morning. I'm going to quit my job and move back to Denver. I want to keep the house. We'd have a hell of a time selling it anyway."

I take a moment to let this idea sink in, to try to understand.

"I don't know, Mitch. It's almost as if you'd be stepping into Daddy's shoes — like going backward."

"Hey, you're not the only one who's been taking stock. I've been crashing into one dead end after another my whole life," says Mitch. "Right now I feel like, if I come home again, I could move forward from here. Sort of take another go at my life. Besides, I think my kids would like to visit me here, and I could take them camping and skiing. They hate that little hole where I live in California."

But his turnabout still puzzles me. "Mitch, all this because of one dream?"

He is silent for a long time. "It's the first time Dad ever asked me to do anything for him."

"That's good, Mitch. That's good." I hear what's between the lines: Daddy cared enough to get in touch, and Mitch is honored. "At least that way I don't have to move any more of that damn stuff out of the house."

Mitch snickers. "Oh, yes, you do. Don't think you're leaving me with all your shit."

When our laughter subsides, I add, "Mitch?"

"What?"

"I am on your side. I'm really sorry for the times I haven't been there when you needed me. I'll try to do better."

"Thanks, Frannie," he answers softly. "Me, too."

I hang up and dial Bernie's number to see what my spiritual adviser would advise.

Chapter Twenty-three
Sacred Places

Not ten days later, our little tribe files out of the federal courthouse in Denver. As Dave Hallett holds open the door for me, our eyes lock in jubilation. Stepping out into the blinding sun of the late Denver afternoon, we are met by an expectant bevy of reporters.

Hannah was right: Bernie was the one to contact. He called in two archaeological experts on religious sites, who quickly marshaled various Native American groups fighting for the preservation of sacred sites all over the country.

Dave helped Rose Yellowhorse get in touch with the Navajo tribal council, some of whom stand with us now. They were enraged that the Bureau of Land Management, under whose aegis the mine site falls, had not consulted with them about the mining permit that Aloco had filed for.

By sheer serendipity, it was Mrs. Amoss,

Stan McPhee's secretary, who provided us a crucial bit of information. Nagged by Sadie Yellowhorse's accusations, I visited Aloco soon after my return from Grand Junction, ostensibly to return the original of the telltale file after making several copies. As usual, I had to go through her first.

When Mrs. Amoss saw the file in my hand, she pressed her hand to her chest and exclaimed, "Oh, thank goodness you found it. Mr. McPhee's been so worried about that getting out."

I sidled closer to her desk. "What's going on with that mine, anyway?"

"Why, the hearing is next week. We're all sweating it out until then."

"The hearing?"

"Federal district court — to approve the mining permit. Wouldn't your dad be proud?"

I had no answer for that.

Waved on down the hall, I plunked the file on Stan's desk. "Is this what you were looking for, Stan?"

His face went through several shades of pink before he replied, "Why, yes, Frannie. Where did you find it?"

"It was in an open suitcase in my dad's bedroom. I couldn't imagine why, so I had a geologist friend look at it. And what I want you to tell me is, did Daddy show you that site?"

Stan blubbered. "Let's see, which one is this?"

"You know which one, Stan." I leaned toward him. "Mesa County. Open-pit uranium mine."

"Ah, yes." Stan's fatherly guise began to dissolve. "It's a very rich vein, close enough to the surface, easy access. It's going to be a good producer."

I aimed my words at his eyeballs. "Did Daddy lead you to that place?"

Stan finally looked at me without guile, his fingertips meeting in front of his chest. "No, Frannie, he didn't. In fact, it was his total avoidance of the area that tipped us off. He tried to divert anybody who even thought about getting close to that place."

"Ah." I sat back in a flood of relief; this was the least I could offer to Sadie Yellowhorse. "And those petroglyphs make no difference to you?"

He shrugged. "Don't be so naive, Frannie. This is business, plain and simple. We've already spent a fortune on this project, and if we don't mine that sector, someone else will."

"You told me you'd never heard of John Yellowhorse."

"It was none of your concern." When I stood abruptly, Stan's face softened. "Be reasonable, Frannie. I've known you since you were a girl —"

I held up my hand. "Spare me, Stan. We don't know each other at all."

So today our two opposing armies lined up in the courtroom, the element of surprise in our favor. On our side were the archaeologists, the Indians, Dave, Mitch, Hannah, myself, and even sweet Magnolia, who had driven up from Santa Fe with a group of savvy young activists. They'd been keeping the sidewalk warm outside the courthouse with their no nukes placards, and tables full of petitions and information on all sorts of nuclear issues. Maggie's new specialty is depleted uranium.

In the other army were Stan and his bosses from Aloco, represented by a coven of lawyers, including none other than dear old Neil Peters. When I came face-to-face with him in the marbled halls of justice, he grabbed my elbow and hissed, "What the hell do you think you're doing, Frannie? You're in way over your head here."

I pulled my arm free. "Did Stan McPhee send you to do his dirty work?"

"Why don't you grow up, Frannie? You still think calling in a bunch of radicals is going to save the day? You know, it's not too late to change the cause of death on your father's life insurance policy."

I stared at him, dumbfounded. "Are you threatening me, Neil? I knew you'd sold yourself out, but really."

His face blanched. "I had hoped to talk some sense into you. I can see that's not going to happen."

I shrugged. "I don't think you're the one talking sense here."

He wheeled around and disappeared into the courtroom.

It is a young Navajo attorney named Luke Jackson, courtly in his gray suit, long black braid, and turquoise bolo tie, who steps up now to face the media in the slanted sunlight. He's the one who represented the miners in their earlier fight for compensation.

"The judge has granted a temporary injunction," says Luke into the prepared microphone, "to halt the granting of a permit for an open-pit uranium mine to Aloco Mining Company. Aloco tried to keep secret the fact that the location they selected to despoil was also the site of a rich collection of ancient petroglyphs sacred to the Navajo people."

His assistant holds up blowups of the rock paintings, brought out of their hiding place to deliver their message to the world. The same photographs had seemed to move the judge in the courtroom, and had moved me to grab Dave's warm hand.

"The mine would cause irreparable harm to an important cultural and religious monument," Luke goes on. "Yet Aloco would have us believe that the temporary need for nuclear fuel outweighs our right to protect the timeless and priceless art of our ancestors.

"Today we gained a minor victory," he intones, "but so far only a temporary one, in a conflict that's taking place in courtrooms all over the country. It's a fight against men with no vision in their eyes except dollar signs, who would heartlessly desecrate the sacred sites of our native peoples." He pauses to look into the television cameras. "Would they be allowed to destroy the Sistine Chapel? Nôtre Dame? St. Patrick's Cathedral? What the white man has never understood is that reverence for our Earth Mother is the soul of all native peoples. If we fail here, we fail our ancestors, and we fail the Earth."

Stan McPhee addresses his own coterie. "We will of course appeal," he says, his face flushed. "What is being ignored here is the economic impact on companies such as ours, who are simply trying to obey the law of supply and demand. We have the utmost respect for the religions of the Native Americans, but it's unjust for them to oppose the projects after significant investments have been made."

I can no longer stand to look at Stan and, behind him, Neil. As I move to leave, a reporter whose face I recognize from the local network news sticks her microphone in my face. "Aren't you the daughter of the Aloco employee who committed suicide over this?" She checks her spiral pad. "Frank Aldren?"

"Y-yes, I am."

"What do you think he would say if he were here today?"

The question hits me between the breasts. No answer comes to mind as her words tumble ponderously in my chest.

I see Maggie staring wide-eyed at my dilemma. But somehow time has stopped, along with my mind. I look at my daughter, caught there in the sparkle of the late-afternoon sun. The summer's western air has brought out the depths of her olive

Cajun skin, and some of her little-girlness has left her for good. Dressed in a striped Indian skirt, a peasant blouse, and sandals, she might have stepped out of a day twenty-five years ago.

Behind her, turned a bit to the side, stands Rose Yellowhorse in a simple black dress that sets off an elaborate silver-and-turquoise necklace. I wish I had a camera, or a sketchpad, to capture the two of them in this moment of potent young womanhood.

The reporter still aims her microphone at me, but it hangs in suspended animation. Beside her sits a cement planter full of verbena blossoms the same vivid red as the lipstick my mother used to wear. As I stare, the mass of flowers morphs into a collection of individual clusters, each in turn made up of tiny blossoms.

Together they shine their redness for all their worth, confident in their goodwill mission in this vast expanse of concrete. Something deep in my brain tries to conjure what shades of paint I could choose to do them justice.

Ah, here it is again. This is the place I used to have access to at will: the shift of vision to a dimension of unexpected clarity, where the air glistens and colors vibrate, where the process of painting is a conversation between artist and subject, where seemingly inanimate objects pose and primp and show themselves off.

Silently I welcome it back and invite it to stay.

Then I straighten my back and try to pull myself up into my own larger contours. Taking a long breath, I begin to speak.

"A few weeks ago, my father, John Franklin Aldren" — my voice wavers — "killed himself. He'd been a geologist for Aloco since the 1950s, through the boom of that industry. I believe my father's suicide was largely the result of heartbreak over the company's betrayal of his friend, a Navajo miner named John Yellowhorse, now dead of lung cancer. Mr. Yellowhorse showed my father the secret location of those sacred petroglyphs on the site that Aloco now proposes to turn into an open-pit mine, obliterating them forever.

"The unleashing of nuclear power in the world is a complex topic — one I don't fully understand. But I do know one thing," I say, my voice now steady. "If my father were here today, he would agree with the native peoples of this continent. We must take into account the repercussions of each of our actions for seven generations into the future. He himself sometimes ignored this way of thinking, for which he paid dearly with his conscience. But the best way I can honor his life, as well as his death, is to fight for that philosophy — for the sake of John Franklin Aldren's memory, and for all of us."

Hannah's restaurant supplies the food for the sunset party at her house. Riding a wave of exhilaration, we flip back and forth among local news broadcasts, two of which give the hearing top billing.

Someone hands me the phone. At the sound of Vera's voice, a spark of joy goes through me. I give her a brief rundown of what's going on.

"So you're the big celebrity now," she says. "No wonder you haven't come home."

"I'll be back before long. How's Mom Broussard doing?"

"It was rough on the old girl, losing two toes. But the doctor says she'll be all right."

"How's J.P.?"

"Not home from the hospital yet. He misses you."

"You heard about Neville?" I notice Mitch and Rose Yellowhorse deep in conversation on the front porch.

"Yeah, but I want to hear your side."

I have a sudden bolt of inspiration. "Hey, why don't y'all — you and T-Will and J.P. — fly up here and drive back with me? We could make it an adventure."

She gasps. "Ooh, I've never been to Colorado. But the guys are so busy, they could never get away."

"Then you come. We'd have a blast."

"Girlfriend, I might just do that."

Dave Hallett is standing behind me when I turn around. "You sound more Southern when you're talking to someone down there," he says with a smile.

I take his arm and lead him out to the backyard.

"So," he says, "we did good." He folds my hand in his big rough one. "We make a good team."

I smile into the crags of his face, completely at home there. "None of this would have happened without you, you know. I wish those reporters had realized that."

"You're much prettier to look at." We're holding each other's gazes for far too long. "And now you're going home?"

I nod.

"Will I see you again?"

"That's a possibility," I say flippantly, to hide the clanging of my heart. But I have to be honest with both of us. "I don't want to lead you on, Dave. I'm married to a good man, a man that I love, and that I have a long history with." I twist my glass in my hand. "The thing is, Daddy's death and then this whole business with Neville and everything else have changed things between us, changed me. It remains to be seen how that will play with J.P."

He nods. "I wish you luck. Here's a little memento for you."

He hands me a gift-wrapped box, which I open with trembling fingers. It's a framed photo of the glyph, with the towering white figure looming over the small, dark, headless body. The larger self trying to lead the blind, deaf, and dumb version out of its comatose state.

I press it to my heart. "Thank you, Dave — for this and for everything. I promise to keep you posted." Then I allow myself to touch his lips with mine.

To my everlasting surprise, Mitch is taking this house thing very seriously, with plans to knock out walls, paint inside and out, and start his life all over. I've accused him of trying to live up to the Stewarts.

After he pays off considerable debts in California, he won't have enough money left to buy out my half, so I've written him an open-ended IOU in exchange for the Suicide Car and his promise to pay the Yellowhorse family a lump sum. I also give him the name plate from Daddy's office door to attach to the tree in the backyard.

He will leave this afternoon to bid his adieus in California.

When he gets a phone call, he breaks into a smile and takes it in Daddy's — now his — bedroom. "So who's that?" I ask when he emerges.

"That's Rose, if you must know."

"Rose Yellowhorse? What did she want?"

"We were advised to try and get some members of the legislature onto this bandwagon. So she'll come to town when I get back, and we'll see what we can do."

"Oh. I see." Will wonders never cease?

Maggie and I had a blast trying on my old clothes from high school, deciding what will pass for modern hippie chic for her and what I absolutely can't get rid of. These I pack into Daddy's old leather suitcase and load, along with his box of clippings, into the trunk of his white Pontiac.

Mom calls to say that one of her friends saw me on the news, and did I really have to announce to the world that Daddy had committed suicide? Aunt Lena gives me a measured blessing, and Russell promises he and Christine will plan a vacation to see these other petroglyphs.

"See what you started by taking me to that cave?" I tease him.

"I didn't start it, and neither did you. But you sure as hell are following through."

My final gift comes in a phone call from my son, the father-to-be in Kosovo.

"Mom, did Dad tell you what he did?" There are tears in his voice, setting off alarms in my head.

"No, what?"

"It turns out one of his old cronies has a son who works for the immigration office. He called in a favor, and they managed to get a green card for Aida."

I collapse into the nearest chair, tears jumping from my eyes. "Oh, Neville. That's just great." I have to remind myself to breathe. "Thank God for that Southern Good Ole Boy System. We'll take good care of her for you."

Neville laughs. "She doesn't need much taking care of, Mom. There's still more red tape, but she should be out of here in a couple of weeks. She's going to love you — and Dad, too."

I rub my eyes. "I think we may have sold your father short, don't you?"

"Yep. I don't know how I'll ever make it up to him."

"I do," I answer, smiling. "Wait till he gets a peek at his first grandbaby."

"I hope I'm there for that."

I dial my husband. "I just talked to an ecstatic soldier. That was a good thing you did, J.P."

"He's my son, too, you know, Frannie. It might take me a while, but I come around when I have to."

"Yes, you do. I can't wait to see you."

"Well, put me on your list."

I throw a look at the ceiling and have a private laugh. "Darlin', you're at the top of my list."

The idea about the Car comes to me in the middle of the night. It occurs to me that maybe it's all in the way you look at a thing that creates the truth. That reality is relative, something with which we ourselves imbue our surroundings. If I choose not to see the car as an enemy, a willing accomplice in my father's death, perhaps it won't be one. Maybe it is as sad about Daddy as I am. Or maybe it is just hunks of metal and wiring put together into a neutral vehicle.

I can make it out to be anything I want.

So Hannah and Bernie smudge it like nobody's business and cover the steering wheel in fake leather. They even hang fuzzy red dice from the mirror, to which I add the snakeskin from the petroglyphs, a reminder to keep growing. Whatever happens next, I've got wheels, and the road leads both ways.

So I'm on my way back to the second half of my life. Back to the land of primal ooze and basic rhythms. To another generation of Broussards. And another generation of Aldrens.

Back home to see where a fresh start leads me.

Vera sits in the passenger's seat, her face sparked with sunshine. The highway in front heads south, following the watershed downhill. First we'll drop Maggie in New Mexico, where she's promised to take us to Georgia O'Keeffe's stomping grounds. There I intend to crawl inside that sharp-faced old girl's vision, where a little thing like a bone or a shell or a flower can grow so big before your eyes that it holds the whole universe in its recesses and curves and open spaces.

When I get back home, I'll do my work of going deeper and deeper into my own secret places, both sacred and profane, to find out what I'm all about. No more duck and cover. Then I'll take my brushes out of my grandmother's box and try to paint what I see.

Maybe, in the end, it's all in how you look at a thing, at a person, at your life — how you really *see* — that counts.

About the Author

After a childhood spent in the Rocky Mountains, Sharon Arms Doucet moved as a teenager to the heart of French Louisiana. There she studied and taught French for many years before realizing her lifelong dream of becoming a writer. She is the author of several books for children set in the Cajun culture, including *Alligator Sue* and *Lapin Plays Possum: Trickster Tales from the Louisiana Bayou* (Farrar, Straus and Giroux). *Back Before Dark* is her first novel for adults. She lives in Lafayette, Louisiana, with her Cajun fiddler husband, Michael, and her son, Ezra. Visit her Web site at www.sharonarmsdoucet.com.

Conversation Guide
Back Before Dark

Sharon Arms Doucet

This Conversation Guide is intended to enrich the individual reading experience, as well as encourage us to explore these topics together — because books, and life, are meant for sharing.

A Conversation with Sharon Arms Doucet

Q. Can you tell us a little about the children's books you have published and what inspired you to write your first adult novel?

A. I've written in a variety of genres for children. I've published two illustrated collections of traditional Cajun/Creole folktales, *Lapin Plays Possum* (Farrar, Straus and Giroux, 2002) and *Why Lapin's Ears Are Long* (Orchard Books, 1997). These are adaptations of the Louisiana version of the trickster better known as Br'er Rabbit. I've also written a middle-grade historical novel *Fiddle Fever* (Clarion, 2000) and a songbook to accompany a "family" album of Louisiana French music for kids, titled *Le Hoogie Boogie Songbook* (MelBay, 1995). My newest book is *Alligator Sue* (Farrar, Straus and Giroux, 2003), an original tall tale about a girl who gets blown away by a hurricane and raised by a mama alligator, then has to find out who she really is. This seems to turn out to be the theme of most of my writing, whether I'm aware of it or not.

I came back to my long-lost dream of writing after my last child, Ezra, now fourteen, was born. I quit teaching French and stayed home to begin the long process of educating myself to be a writer. I was reading a lot of picture books to my son and decided that would be fun to do. But I began dabbling in writing for adults at the same time. For me, the hard part of writing for my contemporaries was having the confidence to think that others would be interested in what I had to say. Kids are a more demanding and at the same time a more forgiving audience, I think.

Q. What was the writing process like for you for this novel? How long did it take and how many drafts were there? Did you have people guiding you along the way?

A. I started on *Back Before Dark* when I was taking graduate classes with Pulitzer Prize–winning author Robert Olen Butler. He taught for a number of years at McNeese State University in Lake Charles, Louisiana, and I would drive over there for his workshop classes. I thank him for insisting that his students write from the "white-hot place," as he calls it, where our deepest fears and feelings try to hide. I worked on it off and on for at least seven years, honing my chops through classes with Ernest Gaines and Luis Urrea here at the University of Louisiana at Lafayette. But basically I've slogged my way through it alone, except for patient advice and encouragement from the members of my writing group. As for how many drafts, writing on computer allows one to constantly make changes, so it feels to me more like one long process of revision.

Q. What do you hope to convey most strongly to readers — which themes do you consider most important? Which do you hope will generate the most discussion?

A. I think it's fairly common for us women, being the nurturers that we are, to give over our power, our potential, to someone else: to spouse and family, to a job that we don't have our hearts in, someone else's dreams, or whatever. Frannie had lost sight of her early lofty ideals and her vision, so I wanted her to come back to her own strengths and talents that she had somehow abandoned along the way. To do this, she had to go back into her own past and then begin to make more enlightened and aware choices for herself.

The theme of family influence pervades the book as well. I think it's so important in understanding ourselves to try to see how unconscious patterns we learned from our parents, siblings, and family dynamics color our emotional lives, and to really bring them to consciousness. That's the only way I know of to make mature decisions on what to keep and what to let go of.

Q. What's next for you in terms of writing projects? Now that you've had a taste of it, do you think you'll stick to women's fiction?

A. My life seems to provide me with a variety of hats, and I like both the children's writer hat and the women's fiction author hat. I think I'll be bouncing back and forth between the two of them from now on. Right now I need to bounce back to the children's world and work on some ideas I have there. After that, I'm thinking of a more historical Louisiana novel about the complex relationships between men and women, set in Storyville, the former red-light district of

New Orleans. The stories just ooze out of the ground here, and I find them irresistible.

Q. What writers have influenced you most in your career, and why? What sort of fiction do you read?

A. I fell in love with the idea of being a writer as a young girl reading Louisa May Alcott's *Little Women.* Harper Lee's *To Kill a Mockingbird* is an all-time favorite from before I ever lived in the South. Of course there's the Southern gods of fiction Flannery O'Connor and William Faulkner. I have a master's degree in French literature, and adore Flaubert and Colette and Camus. These days I juggle hats even in my reading, from Buddhism to children's fiction to contemporary literary fiction. Barbara Kingsolver, A. S. Byatt, Ernest Gaines, and Bob Butler are among my favorites. I've recently enjoyed reading Ken Wells' Louisiana trilogy to see how other writers work with the all too easy stereotypes of south Louisiana.

Q. Nuclear bombs, nuclear waste, nuclear energy and the U.S. government's use of depleted uranium on bombs become important issues in Back Before Dark. *What personal significance do these issues have for you? For readers interested in learning more about them, can you suggest some sources for further reading?*

A. This seems to be an issue that keeps finding me. Having been born in 1951, I grew up with the imminent possibility of World War III. Just like the times we're in now, there was constant fear and preparation for the worst. But even before I was born, it was a thread in my life. My mother ran away from home at age fifteen with her older sister, and they both got jobs in Oak Ridge, Tennessee. They didn't know it then, but they were actually working on splitting the atom for the bombs that were dropped on Japan. And they've both had breast cancer. My father had a brief foray into uranium geology in his petroleum geology career.

I wasn't aware of the depleted uranium issue until I started doing research for this book, and what I found was astounding. The biggest problem with using nuclear energy of any kind is that there is no safe and secure method for disposing of the radioactive waste. And lo and behold, the government finds this new use for it: just give it to the military! Now if it's not safe to dispose of radioactive waste here, it's not going to be safe to use it anywhere else, either. It was first used in the Gulf War, then in the Balkans, and now in Afghanistan and Iraq as well, without definitive studies as to the long-term consequences to health and the environment. That's why I tried to put forth the very sane philosophy of the Seven Generation Rule: we have to look that far down the road when considering each of our actions, or else we'll just keep wreaking havoc on our own environment, possibly even destroying this wonderful planet.

A simple Internet search for "depleted uranium" will bring up all kinds of compelling evidence. At this writing, one of the most up-to-date books is by the venerable Dr. Helen Caldicott titled *The New Nuclear Danger: George W. Bush's Military-Industrial Complex* (The New Press, 2002). Other fascinating books are *Metal of Dishonor: Depleted Uranium* (International Action Center, 1997) and Stewart Udall's *The Myths of August* (Rutgers University Press, 1998).

Q. You make all three settings of Back Before Dark *— the Cajun country of Louisiana, the Rocky Mountains of Colorado, and the hills of Tennessee — come vividly alive. Do you personally know these places and how did you end up* *choosing them as the settings for the novel?*

A. Oh, yes, all three of them hold very special places in my heart. Both my parents came from Appalachia and met at Berea College in Kentucky. While the characters in this book are fictional, they certainly are informed by the feelings I got from childhood visits back there.

I was born in Illinois, but spent my formative years in Casper, Wyoming, and then briefly in Denver, Colorado, so the West is part of my heart. My husband and children and I now spend our summers in the Rockies, and the rest of my family has all now ended up there as well.

We moved to Louisiana for my father's work when I was in high school. Call it love or fate or the call of my distant French ancestry, but somehow I'm still here. My husband, a Cajun musician, has been a real crusader for the Cajun renaissance of the last twenty-five years.

Q. Frannie's spiritual journey in the novel through dreams and visions is particularly fascinating. Have you experienced a similar journey in your own life? Would you encourage other women to seek out such a journey and if so, how might they go about it?

A. My own spiritual journey began in 1993 when I came down with Chronic Fatigue Syndrome. When the medical doctors could do nothing for me, I struck out on an exploration of "alternative" medicine, which led me to a recognition of the sacred and healing energies that exist everywhere just waiting for us to tap into them. One of the many things I explored was shamanic journeying, an age-old method of getting in touch with our spirit selves and guides. These early experiences were so powerful that they left me with no doubt that these ancient methods hold tremendous wisdom and potential, and it made me sort of mad that they'd ever been taken away from us. I now work mostly with Buddhist meditation practices and with the Akashic Records, a way of tapping into our wisdom sources for guidance. I'm also a member of a women's dream group, where we look for themes and symbols of how women are redreaming the world.

I think we're very fortunate to be living in a time when we're swinging back toward a deepening of our natural spirituality. There are many paths available, and each person has to find one that's right for her. The important thing is to begin the search, to remain grounded, and to trust your inner voices to lead you in the right direction.

Questions for Discussion

1. Frannie's "awakening" comes in midlife, once her children are more or less grown and on their own. Do you think this period of a woman's life offers particular opportunities for personal exploration and growth? What responsibility does a woman have for preserving her marriage when changes within herself place stresses on her relationship with her husband?

2. It takes a tragedy to lead Frannie on her path to self-discovery. Do you think it's necessary for people to suffer in order to find themselves? Why is it necessary for Frannie?

3. What do you think will happen in Frannie and J.P.'s marriage after her return home at the end of the novel? What challenges will the changes in Frannie be likely to place on her relationship with J.P., and how do you think he will react to them?

4. Frannie's father seems never to have recovered from a tragic childhood. How do you think the places and events we experience as children affect us as adults? How can we make them a healthy part of our lives?

5. Neville brings home the news that radioactive weapons were used by the U.S. in recent wars. What do you think about the military's use of depleted uranium? Do you think it's justified if it helps us defeat our enemies? If not, what should be done about it?

6. Have you visited places that you felt were sacred? Have you cultivated any such places in your own environment, life, or self? Discuss how that might be done.

The employees of Thorndike Press hope you have enjoyed this Large Print book. All our Thorndike and Wheeler Large Print titles are designed for easy reading, and all our books are made to last. Other Thorndike Press Large Print books are available at your library, through selected bookstores, or directly from us.

For information about titles, please call:

(800) 223-1244

or visit our Web site at:

www.gale.com/thorndike
www.gale.com/wheeler

To share your comments, please write:

Publisher
Thorndike Press
295 Kennedy Memorial Drive
Waterville, ME 04901